Praise for Claire Lazebnik's
Previous Novels

If You Lived Here, You'd Be Home Now

"Zany and sweet."

—*Publishers Weekly*

"A clever yet poignant gaze at a young mother navigating budding romance, living at home with mom, and the treacherous labyrinth of a typical L.A. private school."

—Gigi Levangie Grazer, author of *Queen Takes King* and *The Starter Wife*

"What a wonderful, witty story! You laugh and cry and truly identify with Rickie as she discovers who she is and finds the best out about herself."

—BestsellersWorld.com

"A sweet, surprising story about coming home, growing up, and moving on."

—Beth Kendrick, author of *Second Time Around*

"I really enjoyed it...a fun read about a woman finding herself while she finds love."

—MamaKittyReviews.com

"An affecting and entertaining novel, which I read in a weekend (from me, there is almost no higher praise). Rickie is a great heroine, flawed and funny, maybe drinks too much, but still an awesome mom. I love this book."

—Mindy Kaling

"A thoroughly charming tale about an authentically-crafted family of believable characters…with conflicts and traumas with which average readers can relate."

—Jhsiess.com

"Fierce, funny, and full of surprisingly heartbreaking twists and turns. LaZebnik roped me in with compelling characters but I stayed for her delicious storytelling."

—Annabelle Gurwitch, coauthor of
You Say Tomato, I Say Shut Up: A Love Story

"Rating: five out of five! This book reminded me of why I love reading so much!"

—StephtheBookworm.blogspot.com

"I loved this book…such a real story and clearly is something that so many young mothers go through…Claire LaZebnik is a wonderful writer."

—DebiTrentBrown.com

The Smart One and The Pretty One

"A witty romp."
—*Marie Claire* on *The Smart One and the Pretty One*

"Winning…moments of real depth combine with witty dialogue as LaZebnik deftly spins each turn convincingly to avoid easy answers."

—*Publishers Weekly*

"This sparkling novel about two sisters is both witty and stylish. You won't be able to resist LaZebnik's charming take on modern relationships. Read it!"

—Holly Peterson, *New York Times* bestselling author of
The Manny

"A funny and endearing novel that truly captures the devotion and rivalry between sisters...whether they relate to the smart one or the pretty one (or both), readers will find this book irresistible."

—*Booklist*

"Another alluring tale of two seemingly different sisters...Recommended."

—*Library Journal*

"A deliciously intimate portrait of sisters."
—W. Bruce Cameron, author of *8 Simple Rules for Marrying My Daughter*

"A fun novel...perfect for reading on a beach."

—WomansDay.com

"Claire LaZebnik explores the sister bond with warmth, wit, and honesty. I loved this novel."
—Jill Smolinski, author of *The Next Thing on My List*

"Sisters everywhere will recognize themselves in *The Smart One and the Pretty One*. Claire LaZebnik has written a touching take on love, longing, and the ties that bind."
—Heather and Rose MacDowell, authors of *Turning Tables*

"Claire LaZebnik has written a wonderfully smart and funny novel about the complexity of love and friendship between sisters. Filled with real warmth and astute observations, it made me wish I had a sister of my own. You'll enjoy every heartfelt page."
—Leslie Schnur, author of *Late Night Talking* and *The Dog Walker*

Knitting Under the Influence

"At turns hilarious, at times heartbreaking, and so, so honest about life, love, and friendship. I loved it."

—Melissa Senate

"Charming...smart, engaging characters, each of whom is complicated and real enough to be worth an entire book on her own."

—*Chicago Sun-Times*

"LaZebnik juggles periods of personal crisis while maintaining her characters' complex individuality. Social knitters, especially, will relate to the bond that strengthens over the click-clack of the girls' needles."

—*Publishers Weekly*

"[A] funny and heart-tugging story about three twenty-something Los Angeles women who drink, cry, and, of course, knit together whenever they can."

—*Arizona Republic*

"The characters and problems here are more realistically portrayed than in many chick-lit books, which makes this a nice combination of humor and heartache. Recommended."

—*Library Journal*

"Fantastic...has great, believable, and well-written characters that bring the story to life. This is a story that no one will want to miss!"

—*TCM Reviews*

"A hilarious tale, sometimes sweet and touching and sometimes out-loud laughable. But mainly it is honest and hits home about life, love, and dating."

—BookLoons.com

"*Knitting Under the Influence* is about three young women living in L.A. who meet every week to knit, share secrets, and exchange insights about the challenges of their lives. It's ultimately about how friendship helps us forge a sensible path through our frazzled lives."

—*Palisadian-Post* (CA)

Families and Other Nonreturnable Gifts

Claire LaZebnik

five
spot

Grand Central Publishing

NEW YORK   BOSTON

5 Spot
Hachette Book Group
237 Park Avenue
New York, NY 10017

www.5-spot.com

5 Spot is an imprint of Grand Central Publishing.
The 5 Spot name and logo are trademarks of Hachette Book Group, Inc.

The publisher is not responsible for websites (or their content) that are not owned by the publisher.

Printed in the United States of America

First Edition: September 2011
10 9 8 7 6 5 4 3 2 1

Library of Congress Cataloging-in-Publication Data

LaZebnik, Claire Scovell
  Families and other nonreturnable gifts / by Claire LaZebnik—1st ed.
    p. cm.
  ISBN 978-0-446-55502-9
  1. Young women—Family relationships—Fiction. 2. Life change events—Fiction. 3. College teachers—Family relationships—Fiction. 4. Families—Fiction. 5. Harvard University—Fiction. 6. Boston (Mass.)—Fiction. 7. College stories. 8. Domestic fiction. I. Title.
  PS3612.A98F36 2011
  813'6—dc22

                                    2011001850

Dedicated to the stalwart men and steadfast women of the IJC,
with a reverential obeisance to all Golden Juicer winners,
a brusque nod to the Intern,
and love forever to the President.

Families and Other Nonreturnable Gifts

Prologue

M y father always says, "It's a fine line between madness and genius," but really, how thin can the line be, given that the guy's built his home right on top of it with a lovely view of crazy on one side, sane on the other?

Wall-to-wall brilliance, though.

My mother has a different catchphrase: "Common sense is more important than genius." She should know the value of the former, having survived thirty-three years of marriage to someone who didn't have an ounce of it in his entire body. He'd leave plates of half-eaten food on the floor and then wonder why ants were invading his office. He couldn't remember where his kids went to school or when our birthdays were. The one time my mother sent him to pick up some groceries (a tale she often repeats), he returned with nothing from the list she had given him, just a box of Twinkies, a bag of apples, and a bottle of wine. He had lost the list, he told her, and was "forced to improvise." Since she needed diapers and formula for my older sister Hopkins, who was an infant at the time, Mom was forced to return to the grocery store herself—strapping the baby into the car to take with her, because a man who didn't have the common sense to call home and ask what was on the list definitely didn't have the common sense necessary to watch a baby by himself.

Mom's no slouch in the brains department herself: she graduated from Harvard, too, and went on to get an MA there,
which would have been a PhD if the professor she'd met at a
faculty tea who whisked her right off to New York for a romantic weekend hadn't soon after asked her to marry him. Which
she did, dazzled by his reputation, his distinguished-looking
gray hair, his gallantly archaic way of speaking and holding
doors for her, and of course, his blinding intellect. I doubt she
was even thinking about (and certainly wasn't using) common
sense when she let him sweep her off her feet, or about how a
twenty-year age gap might play out over time. But once the ba-
bies started coming, common sense's stock probably rose quite
a bit.

Mom's brilliant in her own way and crazy enough in her
own way, too. Not in Dad's way, of course—no, Mom sees
things clearly. Pessimism and cynicism run so deep in her that
she often uses fiction for a few minutes' respite from a reality
that can get too dark. Most of my childhood was spent standing around waiting for her to look up from a book. "Just let
me finish this chapter" was the refrain on the soundtrack of my
childhood.

But she can't ignore the real world completely, and a couple
of times a year she succumbs to a deep, dark depression that
snatches her up in the middle of whatever she's doing and
drops her down into her unmade bed in her darkened room
for several days, where she hides and ignores anyone who dares
to enter. It used to terrify me when I was little, but eventually
I learned that while those days themselves were miserable—
as we were left to the mercy of our very distant father or, in
our early years, to the overwhelmingly stifling hugs of our ma-
ternal grandmother, who couldn't remember our names but
embraced us all with indiscriminate enthusiasm—they passed
with no permanent damage to any of us. My mother would

eventually emerge from her bed and her room, be a little vague and uncertain for a day or two, then gradually return to herself: short-tempered, dictatorial, mercurial, and—admittedly—a little slovenly.

Recent pharmaceutical advances have helped. Her depressions are less frequent and much shorter now than when we were little.

Anyway, it's no surprise that my older sister's a world-renowned neurologist, no surprise that my brother's an agoraphobe—genius and madness are as much a part of my family's genetic pool as the straight brown hair and hazel eyes that my parents and siblings all share.

Me? My hair is curly and red, and my eyes are blue. Go ask Gregor Mendel how that happened.

* * *

I was fourteen when Mom decided enough was enough and told my father their marriage was over, a conversation that she reported to me and my siblings with no acknowledgment that we might not find the news as delightful as she did.

I waited anxiously for my father to pack up and leave.

No one except me seemed to notice that he didn't.

Admittedly, Dad kept a low profile after that, roaming the hallways late at night and making cups of tea at two in the morning but otherwise keeping to the top floor of the house when he wasn't at work. He created a bunker up there with his books and computer and stacks of papers, sleeping on the old daybed that was supposed to convert the attic into a guest room when needed, but really just made it easier for him to hide from his wife.

And the truth was that after making her big announcement, Mom did seem to go about her daily life for years without taking much notice of him. They lived separate lives in the same house. She dealt with Milton, my younger brother, who still lives at home and doesn't require too much in the way of daily upkeep—just the occasional snack and a reminder to shower now and then—and continued to do the least amount of work necessary to keep the big old house from falling down.

Maybe Mom needed all those years to get used to the idea of being on her own. When she told my father their marriage was over, she had made something clear to herself—that this man was not the man she would grow old with—and I guess she felt like that knowledge was enough for the moment and action could wait until later.

And now it's later.

1.

"Your father found an apartment," Eloise Sedlak—my mom—tells me on the phone. "Or rather, Jacob and I found one for him."

Jacob Corwin is my father's assistant. He was a boyish undergraduate when he first took the position seven years ago and is now a significantly less boyish perpetual graduate student with little hope of ever getting his degree since his every waking moment is taken up with running my father's life. Supposedly my father is mentoring him, advising him on his PhD thesis, but all that mentoring is going to lead Jacob right to the unemployment line if Dad ever loses his budget for an assistant or dies.

"It's in Harvard Square," Mom says. "He can walk to work. I know what you're thinking, Keats, but trust me, it'll make his life easier."

"I wasn't thinking anything," I say. "I'm just listening."

"He's moved in with a couple of suitcases, but there's tons more stuff to go through. Jacob and I are going to pack it all up this weekend, and I need your help."

"Milton's home. He can help."

"Milton's always home and he never helps. As you well know. Saturday at ten would be perfect."

"We already have plans for Saturday. Tom and I are going to—"

"You can bring Tom if you want. I need someone to carry boxes."

"But—"

"See you at ten on Saturday." She hangs up.

I say out loud, "Resistance is futile."

"Huh?" Tom looks up from the sofa, pausing what he was watching on TV. "Who was that?"

"My mother."

"What does she want?"

"My father just moved out, and she wants us to come help pack up his stuff."

"Wait," he says and turns the TV completely off. "Your father moved out? Out of the house?"

"Apparently." I come over and sit down next to him on the oatmeal-colored sectional we picked out together at Pottery Barn three years ago. I curl up against him, and his arm goes around my shoulder and pulls me snugly against his chest.

"I thought they'd always be together," Tom says, resting his cheek on the top of my head. "I mean, I know they lived in separate parts of the house, but they still seemed as much of a couple as my parents or anyone else." Tom's parents had a thirty-fifth wedding anniversary a few months ago. His mother wore pearls and his father called her "my salvation, my inspiration, my love." My parents are not a couple like his parents are a couple, but I know what he means: it felt like somehow they'd stick it out together. Until today.

He peers down at me. "You okay?"

"Yeah." I tilt my head back to look at Tom, who's steady and calm and reliable and loving and everything my father isn't, and then I look around the living room of our Waltham apartment, which is clean and neat and bright and new and everything the house I grew up in wasn't.

When Tom and I first picked this place out—it was his purchase, but we both knew I'd basically be living here, too—the two-bedroom apartment in the just-built high-rise felt almost too antiseptic. But now the house I grew up in, twenty minutes from here, in Newton, feels old and grungy by comparison, and when we leave there and drive the short distance between the two places and pull into our space in the enormous garage below our fifteen-story building, *that's* when I feel like I've come home.

"They can do what they want," I say. "I don't care. I'm an adult now. My life is separate from theirs."

"I thought we were going to go to the beach on Saturday."

"We could go on Sunday."

"I said I'd watch the game with Lou." Tom's friends all have names like Lou and Bill and Jim. I love that about him. His last name is Wells. Tom Wells. How great is that? Of course, when you grow up saddled with a name like Keats Sedlak, you admire any name you don't have to explain or spell. "But if you want, I could cancel."

"No, don't." I feel his chest move with a small breath of relief. "We can still try to make it to the beach on Saturday after we stop by the house."

"It's okay with me if it doesn't happen," he says.

I know it's okay with him. Going to the beach was my idea in the first place. I like walking on it when it's not yet summer and it's still deserted. And Tom prefers to be lazy on the weekends. He says it's his only chance to relax, which I understand—he works long hours as vice president of his dad's hospital linens laundering business—but sometimes I just want to get out and go somewhere. We don't travel much in general—not at all, really—unless you count our annual trip to Florida with his family, which is always at the same resort, with the same scheduled activities (golf for the men, lounging by the pool for the women), and meals at the same hotel restaurant. The first year it was great. The second year it was fun. The third year it was nice. Now it's just all right. Amazing how something special becomes less special with repetition.

"Yeah, no worries either way" is all I say now.

We sit there in silence for a little while, and then he picks up the remote with a questioning glance at me. I smile my reassurance—he's not being rude to me, it's fine—and he turns the TV back on. We adjust our position a bit—he raises his head, I shift my legs—but we're still comfortably curled up together. I always sit to his left.

In a month we'll be celebrating our tenth anniversary together.

We're going to combine it with my twenty-fifth birthday celebration. I turned fifteen the week before we started seeing each other.

* * *

There's a smell when you first walk in through the door of our family house, a musty fetid-sweet odor that I've never been able to trace to any specific source. Tom walks in beside me but doesn't seem to notice it. He calls out a cheerful "Anyone home?"

It's a stupid question since Milton is always home. But Milton is usually in his room, which is upstairs and at the far end of the house, so he never hears when people knock or enter. I have to call him on my cell from outside if I forget my key and need him to come down and open the door.

When there's no response, Tom tries an uncertain "Hello?"

This time we hear a man's voice faintly greeting us from upstairs, and a moment later Jacob comes rushing down the stairs. He's wearing a button-down shirt and khakis that look slightly rumpled, and he's got a smudge of dirt on his right cheek.

The whole shape of his face has changed since I first met him seven years ago. He was round faced then, with lots of light brown curly hair, but as he's gotten older and his hairline's receded, his face has grown longer and narrower, and the lids have started to droop wearily over his light gray eyes. Not so much of a cherub anymore.

I can't imagine my father is easy to work for. He's persnickety and grumpy and demanding. He's my dad so I'm stuck with him, but Jacob doesn't have that excuse.

I guess he's used to harsh treatment. He told me once he had a rough time as a teenager. He was a sensitive intellectual at a big Texas high school, which basically meant he was ostracized and bullied on a regular basis. He figured his only hope for a better future was to escape to a good college as far away as possible, so he spent his days and nights studying. He's a bright guy, Jacob: he got into Harvard, and once he went there it was like the whole world opened up. He fit in. It no longer counted against him that he was small and scrawny and would rather read than play football.

He needed to support himself, though, so he applied for a job as an assistant to a government professor. Not just *any* government professor: the most highly regarded government professor at Harvard and possibly the world, aka Lawrence Sedlak, aka my dad.

Jacob had already taken my dad's best-known course, a survey class, the popularity of which was so great it was taught not in a classroom but in a theater, and even so required a lottery to keep the number down each year to 250 students. The required reading included not one, not two, but *three* books by the professor himself, including the one used in universities throughout the world and widely considered by poli-sci geeks to be The Book on political systems, titled, with more accuracy than inspiration, *A History and Overview of Modern Political Systems.*

Jacob's interview for the assistant position was rigorous: Dad fired about a million questions at him, then made him do some research right there and then, first online—in front of him—and then in the deep recesses of one of the university libraries, "to prove you know how to read a book and won't just Google everything," the professor said. Jacob was given a time limit for finding the necessary info and had to race back to Dad's office, which is over half a mile from the library in Harvard Yard.

By the time the two-hour interview was over, Jacob was covered in sweat and his hands were shaking. Dad called him up a week later to say he had the job. Jacob says it made him prouder than getting accepted to Harvard. Since then, he's worked for Dad as a research and office assistant and, over time, more and more as a personal assistant.

He spends a lot of time with my family, showing up for most major holidays, helping out with house-related tasks, shuttling Dad back and forth from campus, and then staying for dinner more often than not. Of course, this was all before the move, which I assume will change Jacob's amount of contact with our family as much as it will Dad's.

Now Jacob greets us enthusiastically, giving me a brief hug before shaking hands with Tom, who says, "I hear the old man finally moved out."

"*He* did. His stuff didn't. You wouldn't believe how much there is to sort through. Fortunately, it's all fascinating. To me, at least. I'm trying to convince him to let me donate some of his old drafts and letters to Houghton Library."

"Are you crazy?" I say.

He takes a surprised step back. "Why not? People write dissertations on his books all the time. These materials are valuable."

"It's too weird," I say. "Strangers reading our personal stuff."

"It's your father we're talking about," Jacob says. "None of it's all that personal."

He has a point—the few times in my life I've gotten a letter from my father, it's been of the "Hope you're enjoying your stay there. I just gave a talk at Brandeis that was roughly forty minutes long and was followed by a question-and-answer period. I think it went quite well" variety. Hardly the sort of thing to make anyone blush.

Even so . . . I just don't like the idea. Expose our family to the light and who knows what hideous things might crawl out?

Tom says, "Seems like it should be your father's call, Keats."

I shrug, unreasonably annoyed at both of them. "Where's my mom?"

"Up there. She sent me down to fetch you."

We follow Jacob up the stairs to the second floor and down the hallway to the narrower stairs that continue on up to the attic. "Hey, Milton!" I yell in the direction of his bedroom door, which is closed. No response. "I'll go say hi later," I say to no one in particular, and we mount the worn and uneven wooden steps up to the third floor where my father's office, bed, and life have been for the last decade or so.

The attic apartment runs the length of the house. It's long, so you'd think it would feel big, but the angled roof and narrow, small windows make it cramped and dark. Tom—who at six foot two is at least six inches taller than anyone else in the room—ducks his head instinctively, even though he doesn't actually have to. He can stand upright in the middle of the attic and walk a few feet in each direction without stooping, but the roof is always close enough that he keeps his head warily inclined.

My mother is kneeling over a box next to the daybed, but she rises to her feet in one impressively graceful motion as we emerge from the stairway. "Good," she says. "You came."

"Did we have a choice?" I ask jovially as I come forward to kiss her on the cheek.

She ignores that and waves her hand at my boyfriend. "Tom," she says, and it's clear from the wave and the way she turns back to me immediately that she is not in any way inviting him to hug her.

My mother doesn't like Tom. It frustrates me because any other mother would love him. He's reliable and devoted and good-hearted. Handsome, too: tall and broad shouldered and muscular with a head of thick dark hair. Right now he's wearing jeans and an old blue T-shirt that matches his eyes. He came ready to help out. She should be flinging her arms around him in gratitude, but instead she just gives him that cold wave.

I understand why it bothered her when we first started going out because I was so much younger than he was—so young in general. But it's been ten years, and we've been living together happily for the past four, and I'm twenty-five now, no longer a kid. The age difference—a little over five years—has stopped being meaningful. If I had just met him, no one would think twice about it. So she can't possibly think he wants to take advantage of me, not anymore.

Maybe disliking him has just become a habit for her.

She says to me, "There's so much work to do here, you can't believe it. I feel like we'll never get through it." She's always overwhelmed by any amount of cleaning or organizing work. Her MO is to check out what needs to be done, feel hopeless about it, and abandon the project, which is why every closet and drawer in our house is bulging with stuff that should have been cleaned up and thrown out years ago.

"Is Dad coming back to help?" I survey the stacks of books and papers and boxes covering the room's furniture and floor.

Mom snorts. "It took me a decade to get him out of this house. I'm in no rush to invite him back in. I asked him to clean up before he left—apparently this is his idea of clean." She jerks her chin toward the small, slight man standing near her. "But at least he sent me Jacob, who's given me more help in the last half hour than your father has during our entire marriage, which, by the way, we're officially dissolving. I've seen a lawyer and started the divorce process."

I stare at her. "This is how you tell me?"

"The engraved announcement is in the mail," she says drily. She fidgets for a moment, her fingers tapping on the edge of Dad's enormous oak desk. Even though it's cleanup day, she's wearing some kind of multicolored, floaty bohemian skirt topped by an old pink shirt that has big round buttons down the front.

Mom always wears skirts because they flatter her figure. She's thin from the side, a board really—no breasts, no butt, nothing sticking out. But if you look at her straight on, her hips are surprisingly wide. The skirts hide that unexpected ultrafeminine width. She looks ungainly in pants, but in a skirt she's close to gorgeous with her long dark hair—threaded with gray now but not as much as you'd expect for a fifty-five-year-old woman—and her large hazel eyes, long, straight nose, and wide mouth. I got her nose, but that's it. Otherwise, I don't look much like her or much like Dad, either. "You don't even look like the mailman," my big sister Hopkins used to tease. "Poor little red-haired freak."

"Let's go downstairs," Mom says to me abruptly. "I need a cup of tea."

So much for getting down to work. But I'm not all that eager to start cleaning, either, so I'm happy to flee with her.

As we head down the steps, Tom starts to follow us. Mom halts. "Help Jacob pack up in here, will you, Tom?"

"Sure thing," says Tom and retreats back up the stairs.

* * *

I watch my mother as she whirls around the kitchen, plucking tea bags out of a canister on the counter, grabbing a couple of mugs out of the cabinet, filling them with water, and sticking them both in the microwave, which she closes with such a violent push that a stack of papers on top falls over and scatters on the floor.

"This kitchen!" she says, bending over and angrily snatching them all up. "It's a mess. I can't stand it."

I look around. She's right: it is a mess. Not only is every surface covered with old mail and dust, but the room itself hasn't been updated or repainted for decades. I'm sitting on the breakfast booth bench, which is covered with a teal and pink vinyl that was probably considered stylishly modern in 1980 but which is just plain ugly now. The faded off-white cabinets that line the wall are fussy and ornate and not like anything my mother would have picked out herself, so they must have predated my parents' purchase of the house. The floor is brown linoleum, the counters beige laminate.

The funny thing is that the house itself—a 1920s Tudor— is incredibly valuable, especially because Newton is such a desirable suburb, much more coveted than Waltham, where Tom and I live. The school system is good and the Mass Turnpike is close enough to be convenient but far enough away that you can't hear or see it.

And just as I'm thinking, *Wonder what this house is worth now?* my mother says, "I'm putting the whole thing on the market."

"Ha," I say, pleased to be ahead of her for once. "I saw that coming."

"Really?" She seems surprised. Then she shrugs. "Good. I'm glad. I was worried you'd get upset."

"It's too big for you and Milton, anyway. Now that Dad's moved out."

The microwave dings. Mom instantly wheels around, pulls the door open, and grabs at the mugs. Tea slops over the edge as she strides over to the booth and plops them down. She cooked the water with the tea bags already inside so both cups are a dark brown color now.

"Milk? Sugar?" she asks.

"Whatever you're having." I'm not a tea drinker normally. Coffee's my drug. I keep hoping it will make me feel alert, aware, brilliant, on top of my game . . . but it just makes me irritable and always needing to pee.

Mom is at the fridge in seconds. A whirl of skirts, and the milk is glugging into the mugs. Another whirl and sugar is pouring from a teaspoon. A whirl, a knock, a shove, a beat, and she's sitting across from me, her spoon clicking rhythmically against the sides of her mug, open milk carton and spilled sugar still out on the counter behind her.

No one moves faster than my mother. My main memory from childhood is of trying to keep up, pumping my little legs like crazy while I raced after her in a supermarket or department store, desperate to grab hold of a corner of the elusive skirt that was always billowing just out of my reach.

You'd think with all that energy, she would be efficient, but there's a frenzy to her restlessness. She moves a lot, just not in any particular direction. Even at the supermarket, we'd be cutting back through the store multiple times to get things she'd forgotten or missed on the first pass.

I take a sip. The tea is tepid and harsh, barely drinkable. She may have figured out how to make it quickly, but she hasn't figured out how to make it taste good. I put my mug down. "Do you know where you'll move to?"

"Definitely an apartment. Probably downtown, but maybe Cambridge or Somerville."

"What about Milton?" My brother hasn't left the house in

two years, not since he graduated from high school. "Does he know you're moving?"

Mom carefully places her own mug down on the table. There's a dark red shield on the side facing me that says *Ve-ri-tas*. Truth. "I haven't figured out what to do about him yet."

When I picture my brother, he's hunched over his computer—because he usually is—his face pale, his eyes large and expressive when they're staring at the screen, elusive and blank when they meet another person's gaze, which they rarely and reluctantly do. Even when he was little, he was a homebody, the kind of kid who never went on playdates and who would insist he was sick and had to stay home from school as often as he could get away with it—which was often, since he managed to get straight A's no matter how much school he missed. When he was sixteen, he told my mother seriously that he had thought about dropping out since he could do it legally now, but that he'd decided it made more sense to finish up.

Given that conversation, Mom should have been worried he might not make it to college, but I guess any fears she had were allayed when Milton applied to and got accepted by six Ivy League schools. We all waited to see which one he'd pick.

None, it turned out.

"I've decided I just want to live at home," he said in April of his senior year of high school. "I can go to college online."

"Why did you bother applying to real schools then?" I asked him crossly, annoyed that he had gotten into two schools—Harvard and Princeton—that had rejected *me*, and then wasn't even interested in going to either one.

"The guidance counselors would have bugged me if I hadn't," he said. "It was easier just to do it. Oh, and tell Mom I'm not going to give the valedictorian speech, will you? They wanted me to but I said no, and if *I* tell her, she'll get that tone in her voice."

My brother, folks.

He's basically been hanging out in his bedroom since then with occasional forays down to the kitchen—he doesn't even take the trash out as far as I know. When I ask my mother why she isn't doing more to get him out of the house, she throws her hands up in the air and says she's done everything she can think of, by which I guess she means that every once in a while she tells him he really should get out of the house and he ignores her.

I once suggested to her that maybe there was a real problem there, that maybe something was wrong with Milton, something that he needed professional help with. She just shook her head and said, "Milton is one of the smartest people I know. He'll be fine."

Like intelligence is all that matters.

I even e-mailed Hopkins to try to get her to back me up, but she wrote back, *If Mom decides she wants to kick him out at any point, she will and he'll be fine. He's a little spectrumy, but perfectly competent. But so long as she's happy having him at home, let them have each other.* Without any support from the actual neurologist in the family, I gave up.

The first few months after high school, Milton did at least go to movies and restaurants with us, but he's stopped doing even that. He pulled back gradually, pretending he was in the middle of doing something important and couldn't leave the house at first, but now he just shakes his head dismissively if you invite him somewhere, like you're the one who's nuts for thinking it's even a possibility.

He's more withdrawn, more reclusive, every time I see him. It scares me and I want to do something about it, but other than berating my mother and fretting to Tom, I don't know what. I'm not there that often—a couple of times a month at the most—and I'm not his mother, as Milton has reminded me often enough.

"You'll have to take him with you to the new apartment," I say now. It's weird to think of Milton anywhere but here. Maybe a change will be good for him.

"I know. I will." Mom puts down her mug a little too heavily and a few drops of tea fly out. "But I anticipate some awkwardness. Inviting a man back to my place when my adult son still lives there—"

"Whoa," I say. "Whoa. Someone's moving fast." I mop up the tea drops with a napkin.

She regards me for a moment, then says, "Keats, I'm fifty-five years old. I have been married to a man twenty years my senior for the last thirty-three years. Please tell me you're not going to be prudish about this. I don't think it's unreasonable for me to go on a date now and then, do you?"

I shake my head as I crumple up the napkin. "No. I'm sorry. It's just an idea that takes some getting used to. But maybe it's another argument for getting Milton to live on his own."

"Maybe. So far it hasn't been a problem."

It takes a moment for that to register. "Wait," I say. "So far? You mean—"

She plays with the tag on her tea bag, her face flushing. "I've gone on a few dates."

"A few dates?" I repeat. "You mean a few dates with one guy or a few dates with a few different guys?"

"Both actually."

"Are you seeing anyone special?"

"There are three men who interest me at the moment. One's an old friend, another one I met online, and the third is in my creative writing class."

"*What* creative writing class? You're taking a creative writing class?" I slump down and say accusingly, "You don't tell me anything."

Mom tilts her head to study me. "Is this upsetting you?" she asks—not apologetically, just curiously.

"Not really. I'm glad you're dating. It's just *weird*."

"Tell me about it," she says.

2.

After our conversation, Mom heads up the stairs to the third floor, and I'm about to follow her when I change my mind and knock on Milton's closed door instead.

"Mom?"

"No. It's me. Keats."

"Hold on. I'm not decent." There's the sound of rustling, and then he opens the door. "Hi," he says and pats my shoulder, which is his customary way of greeting me. "I didn't know you were here."

I hug him. His body goes rigid under my touch because he doesn't like to be hugged, and he crosses his arms protectively over his concave chest and round stomach. I'm not trying to make him uncomfortable, but when he was a baby, I carefully carried him around the house for hours, so I figure I'm entitled to a hug every now and then.

He's wearing a loose pair of sweats and a faded T-shirt. He's gained weight since I last saw him. He's been doing that a lot lately. He was a skinny teenager, but these days he's got a real belly on him.

I release him and step back, looking around. The room is a mess. There's old clothing everywhere and some dirty dishes and lots of books. You can see through the connecting bathroom into my old room, which Milton annexed for himself after I left for college. No one asked me if that was okay. It wasn't, but by the time I came home for Thanksgiving break, he had already moved a bookcase and an iPod dock in there. And a lot of empty protein bar wrappers. Fortunately, I already preferred sleeping over at Tom's by that point.

A Mac desktop with a huge monitor fills up the desk in front of us, but there are two more computers within reach: a PC on top of the dresser and a MacBook lying open on the bed.

"What are you working on?" I ask.

"This and that. I've been getting into game development."

"Oh." That means nothing to me. "How's school?" He's supposedly taking college courses online, working toward his degree, but I'm not sure anyone ever checks up on him. On the other hand, I've never known Milton to lie.

"It's okay. Stupidly easy."

"Maybe you should go to a real college. It would be more challenging." He just shrugs, and I say abruptly, "You want to go get a sandwich or something?"

"No, thanks," he says politely. "Hey, guess what? Dad's book is required reading in my gov class."

"Are you going to read it?"

"I already have," he says. "Haven't you?"

"I tried once. Not my kind of thing."

"Really? It's pretty good."

"So I've heard."

"The guy who grades us asked me if Lawrence Sedlak was my father."

"What'd you say?"

"Nothing." Milton's skin is so pale it's practically translucent except under the eyes where half-moon shapes turn the skin dark and coarse. "It was just in an e-mail, so I didn't answer. Did Tom come with you?"

"He's upstairs. So's Jacob. What about a walk? Want to go for a walk with me? It's really beautiful out."

"Maybe later," he says. "Jacob's here to help pack up Dad's stuff, right?"

I nod.

He tugs on a strand of hair. It's too long, his hair—it falls in his eyes and curls along his neck like a girl's. "It's weird not hearing him moving around upstairs," he says. "Especially in the middle of the night. It's so quiet now with just me and Mom here."

"Are you sleeping okay?"

"I don't know," he says. "Define *okay*."

"Eight hours a night?"

"I don't usually sleep in one big chunk." There's a ding from his computer. "I just have to check that," he says and darts away.

From the way he settles on his seat and peers intently at the screen, I don't get the feeling he's going to come back to the conversation any time soon, so I wander out of his room, through the bathroom—ye gods, it's filthy in there, hardened toothpaste in the sink, dirt crusted into the grout, rust stains all over the shower/bath combo—and into my old room.

There's not much of mine left in there. I know some of my old clothes are still hanging in the closet and folded in the drawers because I just left behind whatever I didn't take with me to college or Tom's. But most of the visible signs that the room once belonged to me are gone. When he claimed the space for himself, Milton took down my posters and shoved my softball trophies to the back of the dresser top where they're hidden by the flat-screen monitor he's set up there. The bed once held a pink-and-purple quilt (the height of glamour to my ten-year-old self), but now the bare mattress has a sleeping bag and a pillow on it, like someone camps out there occasionally.

But my old digital alarm clock is still on the small white night table next to the bed. I pick up the clock and turn it around in my hands. I bought it with my allowance money when I was eleven, because I was tired of being late for school. I hated the stares I got when I walked in after class had already started, but Mom was a night owl and often overslept. So I'd slouch in after everyone else, embarrassed and frustrated.

It hit me one day that my mistake was letting Mom be in charge of our mornings. So I bought this clock with my own money. From then on, the alarm would ring in my room, I'd wake up my mother and Milton (Hopkins had gone off to college at the age of sixteen, so she was already out of the picture), and by yelling, scolding, begging, cajoling, I somehow managed to get the three of us all out the door in time.

I put the alarm clock back down on the night table and leave the room.

* * *

I cross the hallway and stand for a moment outside Hopkins's room. She's not there, of course, but then she never really *was* there much, not even when she lived at home: she was always running around, taking classes outside of school or heading off to work in various labs. Even when she was home, I had orders (from her and Mom) to leave her alone and be quiet so she could concentrate on the huge amount of homework and research she was always dealing with.

It's amazing that someone I rarely see, and never really had all that much contact with, looms so large over my entire life. How do you describe the sister whose very existence makes you feel like the world's biggest loser? And proud, at the same time, because you're related to her?

Like I said, Hopkins and I didn't interact all that much, even when we lived together. I was five years younger and eons less intellectually sophisticated. Still am. We passed each other in the hallway, and Mom talked about her all the time, but meals were scattered in our house, people eating by themselves at different times, solitary figures usually hunched over a book—and without that basic contact, our relationship was limited mostly to her knocking on the bathroom door and telling me to hurry up or asking me to turn my music down because she needed to concentrate.

I can remember watching her at the kitchen table working on some project or another, her long hair falling around her face as she frowned down at the book she was reading or the paper she was writing. She barely noticed me. She barely noticed anyone. She needed my mother to drive her places and to provide a little sustenance now and then, but otherwise Hopkins was too busy thinking her own thoughts and pursuing her own interests to sit around chatting with her family. I admired her, revered her, listened to my mother talk about her achievements ad nauseam, and got used to teachers telling me they had never had a student like her before or since. But I didn't know her.

At eight, Hopkins skipped a grade. She skipped another one when she was twelve. She still got straight A's effortlessly and probably could have skipped more, but she was already so much younger and smaller than the other kids in her class that the administration felt she might suffer socially if she did. My parents argued that she wasn't being challenged enough. The school compromised by letting her take classes above her grade level for the first couple of years of high school and then at Boston College for the last two.

She was barely sixteen when she went off to college. Harvard, of course. Dad might not have been an involved parent, but that didn't mean he wasn't an influential one.

Since she already had a year's worth of college credits under her belt and was taking five courses a semester, she finished in three years, making her a college grad at nineteen. She didn't exactly take a break then, either: four years later, at the age of twenty-three, she had two degrees under her belt, a combined PhD and MD in neurology.

Note: none of this is normal. People don't do this. Only my sister.

She stayed on in Boston for a few more years, her hospital and university connections providing her with plenty of job opportunities, which she was still working her way through when she was offered her current job running a brain injury clinic in New York, where they not only see patients but also do apparently groundbreaking research. She gets asked to speak at conferences all over the world and is always being flown in to various exotic locales to consult on cases that local doctors twice her age can't handle. She doesn't have a landline in her apartment, just a cell phone number, because she's as likely to be in Stockholm or Tokyo as New York on any given day.

Not that I ever call her: we communicate by e-mail when we communicate at all, which isn't very often.

About a year ago, I went to see her give a lecture on neural plasticity and recovery after injury—of which I understood maybe forty percent—and afterward she introduced me to a woman waiting to talk to her who gripped my arm as she said, "Thank God for your sister. They said my father would probably be a vegetable, but she didn't give up on him. The work she does is nothing short of miraculous. Do you *know* how wonderful she is?"

Hopkins and I were supposed to go out for a late dinner after the talk, but there was a guy there from a big lab who was desperate to consult her about something, so she had to cancel our dinner. It was her only night in Boston.

Tom was glad: I got home in time to go to a movie with him that night.

* * *

I am, to put it succinctly, no Hopkins.

I went to school in the usual way, one grade following the other in exactly the order you'd expect: got pats on my head from my teachers for my steady, decent work, graduated at eighteen like all my friends, and went on to Smith College, where I majored in English literature and wrote papers about Jane Austen for four years.

I spent every weekend riding the bus back and forth to Boston so I could be with Tom. I lived with him during the summers, too, working as an assistant at his father's company.

I had no desire to go to graduate school, but my English degree wasn't exactly a fast track to a specific career, so after I graduated, I decided to just look for a halfway decent job not too far from where Tom and I were already living together. He offered to find me something permanent at his dad's company, but even though I was willing to settle, I wasn't willing to settle *that* hard, at least not yet.

Instead, I found a comfortable home in the English department of Waltham Community College, where I make sure there's always fresh coffee and snacks for everyone and keep things running smoothly.

I have been told the coffee I make is extraordinarily good, and when I digitalized all of our files, my boss told me I had saved her life. But she was being metaphorical, and the people who say that about Hopkins are speaking literally, so it's not exactly the same thing, is it?

* * *

By the time I make it back up to my father's office, no one's left up there except Tom, who's stolidly packing books into old printer paper boxes. He looks up when I emerge from the stairway and says, "There you are! I thought you'd abandoned me like everyone else did."

I cross the room toward him and fluff his hair a little. It's so thick I can make it stand straight up.

He leans his head against my hip and says, "It's funny being up here. I was so scared of your father I think I only came up here once in all these years. He wanted me to help him put in the Wi-Fi, remember? I was terrified."

"And now?"

"Just as terrified," he admits with a grin.

"Poor baby," I say and bend down to kiss him lightly on the lips.

He turns the kiss into a real one. I pull back because of where we are, and he rubs his face against my stomach. "Mmm," he says. He burrows his nose in deeper. I slide my fingers down to the back of his neck and then fold completely over him, torn: do I want to keep going or not? His arms slip around my waist. "We could do it," he whispers. "Right here in your father's office. That would be a first."

"There isn't a real door. Someone could walk in."

"All the more exciting."

"I never knew you were an exhibitionist."

"Me neither." His fingers slide under the waist of my jeans. It's been a while since he's been like this, all eager and coaxing, and I'm more aroused than I've felt in ages.

Ten years is a long time to be together, and sex is more comfortable than exciting these days. Same old bed, same old bodies, same time of day. That kind of thing. More and more, I find myself fantasizing during sex: a stranger has grabbed me from behind, someone who's broken into the apartment, I can't see him, I don't know who he is, but he's wild with lust, and that's turning me on even though I'm terrified.

That kind of thing.

I'd worry about it, except I read in a magazine that it's totally normal and even healthy for people in long-term relationships to fantasize like that.

Anyway, the idea of making out in my dad's old room is kind of weird and interesting, and I'm tempted to let Tom keep going but also scared of being caught, so I just hang over him, trying to decide what I want to do, feeling my body respond even while I'm weighing the options.

The body's close to winning out when there's a clatter on the steps. We spring apart so violently that Jacob, who emerges into the office, can't miss the fact he's interrupting something.

"Sorry," he says and turns red. He retreats down a step.

"No worries," Tom says genially. He's up on his feet and has recovered more quickly than I have. He points to the box of books in front of him. "Almost finished with this one. Should I carry it down when I'm done?"

"That would be great." Jacob comes all the way up into the room but avoids making eye contact with either of us. "Hold on," he says, peering into the box. "Are these supposed to be the ones we're giving away or the ones we're keeping?"

"I packed the ones that were on the floor."

"But they were sorted out," Jacob says. "There were two piles."

"Oh, sorry," Tom says. "Didn't realize we were supposed to

keep those separate. I just figured we should get them boxed up and out of here as fast as possible."

I feel my heart sink. It's not a big deal—Jacob can just sort them out again—and Tom meant well, but I feel bad anyway, like it was my fault Tom messed up.

"Can I help?" I ask Jacob, who has sunk down to his knees in front of the box and is pulling books out.

"Grab another box, will you? I'll hand you the books we don't want to keep, and you can pack them as we go. I'll keep the ones we want in here."

I look around, see the tower of boxes—Mom must have gotten this batch from the supermarket because they all have food names on them like VLASIC PICKLES and VELVEETA—and bring one back, passing by Tom who's shoved his hands in his pockets and is leaning against the angled wall as he watches Jacob fix his mistake.

"What do you want me to do?" he asks as I go by.

I glance at my watch. It's past eleven. "Why don't you run out and pick us up some lunch?"

"What should I get?"

I'm squatting on the floor, taking the books that Jacob hands me and packing them in the box, trying to figure out how they'll fit in there best. "Whatever you think."

"What about you, Jacob?"

"Don't worry about me. I can grab something later."

I say, "God knows what Mom has in the kitchen or how long she'll keep us working here. Tom might as well get lunch for everyone."

"Yeah, okay, thanks." Jacob goes back to sorting books.

"You still haven't told me what to get," Tom says to me.

"Something Milton will eat. Maybe bagels?"

"How many should I get?" Tom asks.

"Whatever you think."

"A dozen?"

"Sounds good."

"How much cream cheese? One of those bigger containers?"

"Yeah, fine."

He lingers one more moment uncertainly and then says, "Should I go now?"

I nod, and he disappears down the stairway.

For a little while, it's quiet in Dad's office. Hot, too. There's an AC unit in one of the windows, but no one's turned it on today and we're having one of those weird April heat waves. It would have been the perfect day to go to the beach.

"Look at this," Jacob says and leans over to show me a book: it's a simple cover, but the title is in a language I can't identify.

"What is it?"

"It's a translation of *Political Systems*." He moves his hand to reveal Dad's name at the bottom, the only part that's in English.

"Is that Russian?"

"Bulgarian, I think." Jacob carefully inserts the book between two others in the box in front of him. "This must be his only copy—I've never seen it before."

"I wonder how it sold in Bulgaria."

"As well as any American book about philosophies of government sells in Bulgaria, I would think." He's done sorting through the books on the floor; he stands up and starts going through the bookshelf, pushing some books to the side, pulling others out. "So," he says after a moment. "How's life treating you these days?"

"Same old, same old."

He laughs and squints at a book spine. "You sound like an old lady sometimes, Keats. You're turning twenty-five next week, right?"

"I can't believe you know that."

"Your dad likes me to keep track for him. April twenty-second?"

"You're better than those online birthday alarms."

"That's the nicest thing anyone's ever said to me."

We work for a moment, and then I say, "How's Dad dealing with the move?"

"He's okay." There's a pause. Then he says, "Only okay, though. He's never been a big fan of change. And now that he's seventy-five, it's even harder for him. Sometimes he gets confused about where he is."

That last sentence feels like a punch in the stomach. I have a vision of Dad wandering around Harvard Square, lost and alone. "You don't think it's Alzheimer's, do you?"

"To be honest, I was worried about that, but I asked Hopkins and she said it's just a combination of age and depression."

"She'd know."

"It's useful having a neurologist in the family."

"Mom should have just let him stay here," I say. "It's his house, too. I hate to think of him all alone. I bet that's why he's so depressed and out of it."

"It's not like she kicked him out because she wanted more space for herself—she wants to sell it and move. Understandably—it's way too big." His fingers fly along the book spines, tapping here and there. "I think she's actually looking out for your dad, making sure he's safely settled somewhere before all the craziness of showing the house and packing it up begins. He would have hated all that."

I think about that. Maybe he's right. Maybe Mom let Dad stay as long as it was comfortable for him here and then made sure he had a decent new home before their lives got disrupted.

"She's dating," I say and wait for his reaction. I want to see what someone else thinks of that bit of news.

But all he says is a calm "I know."

"You know? How do you know? I only just found out."

"Your mom happened to mention it to me the other day."

"She told you before she told me? What else has she told you that she hasn't told me?" I'm sort of joking, but not entirely.

He turns so he can look down at me. "Nothing, Keats. Don't make a big deal out of this. I was moving some of your dad's stuff out, and I heard a guy leaving a message on her machine, and she told me she was starting to date."

"You should have called me immediately."

"It was none of my business."

"Oh, right," I say. "It's none of your business when it's a question of letting Keats in on the whole thing. But it's completely your business to start asking questions the second you hear a strange man's voice on my mom's voice mail."

"Keats—"

"Is there anything else you're not telling me?"

"Oh, for god's sake." He goes back to studying the book titles.

I jump to my feet. "That means there is. Tell me."

"No, that means you're being annoying."

I walk over to the other box and snatch up the Bulgarian translation of my father's book. I hold it by the spine, letting the pages dangle. "Tell me or the book gets it."

"Give me a break." He makes a grab for the book, but I skip back out of his reach. "There's nothing to tell. Put the book down, Keats."

"I'm serious." I cross over to the window and stick the book halfway through the narrow opening. "Tell me or the book plunges to its death."

"That's not funny."

I cock my head at him. "I'm terrifying you by threatening to harm a *book*. It's a little bit funny."

"Give it to me."

"Wow, it's really slippery," I say. "Oops—almost dropped it!"

He runs over, but then he hesitates, too self-conscious to actually wrestle with me for the book. I think girls make him nervous: he's never brought a girlfriend over to our house, and he comes to a *lot* of holiday meals with us. So either he hasn't had a serious relationship since he started working for Dad, or he's good at keeping them secret. Given how available he always seems to be, I'm guessing the former.

He reaches toward the window, but I knock his hand away. "Don't try anything funny."

"Fine." He holds his hands up in surrender. "Put the book safely down, and I promise to tell you whatever you want, you lunatic."

"Tell me and I'll put it down," I say, just to torment him.

"At least hold the book *inside*, will you?"

I pull the book back to the safe side of the window. "So— what else have my parents told you that they haven't told me? What family secrets am I being kept out of?"

He shakes his head wearily. "Nothing that I know of."

I make a darting motion with the book, but he's anticipating that and grabs it out of my hand. I don't fight him for it. Game's over. "Is Dad dating, too?"

He inspects the book carefully, then looks up. "Do you really need me to answer that?"

"Is Mom serious about any of these guys?"

"Not that she's told me."

"Why should I believe you?"

"Because you've known me for a very long time and I've never lied to you."

"Never lied to me that I *know* of. Anyway, there's lying by omission."

"I'm not doing that, either." He slips the book back in the box. "What are you worried about, Keats? That your mother will marry someone else one day and leave your father alone forever? He's already living by himself."

"She might miss him now that he's gone."

He regards me for a moment, his light gray eyes lingering thoughtfully on my face. "I know they're your parents, Keats," he says gently, "but their marriage ended a long time ago."

3.

We all eat bagels together in the kitchen. Mom's about to bring one up to Milton, when I tell her that she's only making things worse by waiting on him, that at the very least, she should make him come down a flight of stairs to eat. So she yells up to him, and he does come down, but only long enough to put some cream cheese on a bagel and eat it in three bites.

As we finish loading the dishwasher, Mom asks Tom if he'd mind changing the sink's water filter for her, which is the kind of thing he's great at and doesn't mind doing. She doesn't have a new filter in the house, though, so he volunteers to run to the hardware store to get one.

After he leaves, Mom and I go upstairs to look through our old picture books and see if there are any I might want to take before she gives them all away to the local hospital. The bookcase is in the hallway, which is poorly lit, so we have to take the books out one at a time and tilt them toward the light to see their titles.

I'm putting aside the books I think I might want to read to my own kids one day (a couple of Dr. Seuss's, all of Maurice Sendak—whom I always secretly felt related to because our last names were so similar—and a bunch of random books I liked for one reason or another when I was little, most of which are so worn their spines are loose and their pages in danger of falling out), and after a while, Mom says, "You're awfully quiet."

"Am I?"

"I know I've thrown a lot at you today: the move, selling the house, the divorce.... You're so capable, I forget sometimes how young you are."

"I'm not that young anymore, Mom. I'll be twenty-five next week."

"That's still incredibly young."

"It's really not. And I'm fine with your selling the house. It hasn't been my home for a while. I have my own home."

Her face darkens, and she shakes her head unhappily. "I wish..."

"What?"

"You know how I feel about this. You should be living on your own at your age or with a roommate. Or even at home with me. But not with Tom. I know I've said it before, Keats, but you need to grow up before you settle down."

"You're right," I say and she looks surprised. But then I add coldly, "You've said it before. And you're wrong. I'm happy living with Tom. I feel lucky. You should be happy for me."

"I'd feel a lot better about Tom if you'd take a break from him for a while and spend some time on your own. Just so you can see what independence feels like. You were so young when you started going out with him, and you've never—"

I cut her off. "I know how old I was. But I'm not going to reject someone who's perfect for me just because I happen to have met him a little on the early side."

"I thought I was all grown-up when I met your father, but I really wasn't. I was too young to settle down and so are you."

I twitch my shoulders irritably. "Tom is nothing like Dad."

"True."

I don't like her tone. "God! You are *such* an intellectual snob!"

She considers this for a moment. "You know, Keats, I find it interesting that you leapt to that conclusion from what I said. That might reveal more about your feelings toward Tom than mine."

I grab my hair in my hands and tug hard with a moan. "Can you just leave me and my relationship alone? I'm the one here who's *fine*. I'm the one who's in a loving, long-term relationship. *You're* the one getting a divorce and dating every guy over the age of fifty in the greater Boston area and telling everyone in the whole world about it, except for me."

"Whom have I told about it?" She seems genuinely bewildered.

"You told Jacob before me," I say. "*Jacob*. He's not even a member of our family, and you told him first." I sound like a baby, but I can't help myself.

Her expression clears. "Oh, right. I forgot. We were just spending so much time together, and it sort of came up. And I knew he wouldn't care one way or the other. I guess maybe I waited to tell you because I was a little nervous about how you'd take it."

"But I'm fine with it! I'm fine with the divorce and your selling the house and even with your dating. I'm fine with all of it." It occurs to me that I've used the word *fine* a lot in the last minute with increasing hysteria.

She squints at me. "You don't *sound* fine."

"Well, I am!" It doesn't help my argument that I'm practically shouting. I take a deep breath and say more calmly, "What about the other kids? Have you told them you're dating?"

"I can't imagine Milton or Hopkins would care either way. But I did let Hopkins know that we're going through with the divorce and selling the house. I'm hoping she'll make it back in the next couple of months to go through her stuff and help us pack up."

"That would be good," I say, but I'm dubious. Hopkins is always so busy. She does try to come home each year for Christmas, but it's usually a twenty-four-hour kind of thing. We don't overlap much then because I spend most of Christmas Day with Tom's family. It's important to him to be with them, and it's important to me to be with him, and anyway, they're a lot more religious than we are, so Christmas means a lot more to them.

A few years ago, I did ask Tom if we could spend the day with my family, just for a change, and he agreed, and then I was embarrassed and horrified by how little my family did: I had forgotten what it was like at home, had spent too many years celebrating with the Wellses to remember how pathetic my family was at celebrating anything. The others were all still asleep when Tom and I arrived at nine in the morning. Eventually they woke up and stumbled downstairs, one at a time, at which point there was an unenthusiastic and sleepy gift exchange. Then we ate some French toast that my mother had burned on one side and undercooked on the other, and by eleven in the morning, everyone had retreated back to his or her computer, which is when Tom said to me, "We could still make dinner with my family." So we left.

Now we just stop by the house briefly on Christmas morning to drop off some gifts and continue on, settling down with his family for the rest of the day.

Can you blame us? Here's what Tom's mother does for Christmas: A few weeks before, she decorates their entire Brookline house with wreaths and cinnamon-scented pinecones and candles and red bows. On Christmas Eve, she arranges white-and-silver gift-wrapped presents under a white-

and-silver ornamented Christmas tree. The immediate family (which has included me for years) gathers at nine on Christmas morning to exchange gifts while enjoying fresh hot coffee and huge slices of some sweet almond coffee cake she bakes every year. People squeal and emote over their gifts, and everyone hugs everyone else at some point during the morning. The extended family arrives gradually. If the weather's decent, we all go for a walk together; if it's not, we play games by the fire until Tom's mother calls everyone together to sip eggnog and spiced cider while we exchange even more presents. After that we sit down to an enormous dinner of ham and asparagus and freshly baked biscuits, and before we move on to dessert (five different kinds of cakes and pies), we sing Christmas carols around the tree. Did I mention the baskets of fresh tangerines and whole nuts that we crack ourselves? Or the chocolate truffles? Or the—

You get the idea. His family wins, hands down. It doesn't even matter that at some point after we've all had a couple glasses of wine, Tom's mother gets maudlin and his sister gets sullen and his father gets disgusted and the cousins whisper behind everyone's back....It's still the closest thing I've ever known to the kind of Christmas you see in movies. So we end up with them, not with Mom and Dad.

Which means I hardly see Hopkins the one time of the year she comes to town—just long enough to hug and say that we both wished we could spend more time together. But it never happens.

* * *

Jacob says he's going to bring a load of books over to my dad's apartment, and I offer to go with him since I haven't seen my father in a while and I want to check out his new apartment.

Tom is back and on his knees working on the water filter when I tell him I'm heading out with Jacob. His head emerges from under the sink. "You're leaving?"

"Only for an hour or so. Jacob can bring me right back here. Or drop me off at home if you want to take off." I haven't actually checked with Jacob to see if he can take me home (it's pretty far out of his way), but he'll do it if I ask him to. "Unless you want to come with us to Dad's?"

Tom stands up, and reaches for a dish towel to wipe his grimy hands on. "No offense, but I don't really want to spend my weekend hanging out with your father. He's not the easiest guy in the world to talk to."

"Okay. I'll meet you back home then."

"We're going out with Lou and Izzy tonight," he reminds me.

"I know. I'll be back in plenty of time."

He gives me a kiss on the cheek. "Tell your dad I say hi."

* * *

Once we're inside his battered Honda Civic, Jacob tells me I can put on any radio station I like. Well, any AM/FM station—he doesn't have satellite.

I fiddle with the dial and settle on a Top 40 station.

Jacob raises an eyebrow. "You like Lady Gaga?"

"I do." I want to sound defiant, but it comes out sounding defensive instead.

He shakes his head in bemusement. "Sometimes I wonder where you came from, Keats."

"Most people in this country love Lady Gaga," I say.

"I know. I just don't expect a Sedlak to."

I shrug: guess I'm still the little red-haired freak.

Jacob's an awful driver: too slow when he's going straight,

too abrupt when switching lanes. Other drivers honk at him throughout the twenty-minute trip, but he doesn't seem to notice.

He has his own parking space in the garage underneath my father's building, which is just a block or so away from Memorial Drive. I'm impressed by the location: Dad's not only in the heart of Harvard Square, he's right on the Charles River. "How did he find this place?" I ask as we ride up to the fifth floor, the boxes stacked in a corner of the elevator.

"He didn't. Your mom did. She knew someone who knew someone who was selling and asked me to check it out." The elevator doors open, and we start unloading the boxes into the small, well-lit hallway. "At first your father wasn't exactly enthusiastic—"

"Well, of course he wasn't. He wanted to stay at home with her."

"On her advice, I didn't tell him why we were coming here, just said that he had a meeting." We finish moving boxes and let the elevator doors close behind us. "It was an ambush: I got him in the door, and then the real estate agent and I double-teamed him. Even so, I doubt he'd have gone for it if your mother hadn't shown up and made it clear that his days in her house were numbered." He takes a key out of his pocket.

I watch him as he unlocks the door. "I think I've underestimated you, Jacob. I always thought Dad ran your life. Maybe it's the other way around."

He looks over his shoulder at me. "You seriously think he runs my life?"

"You're at his beck and call, aren't you?"

"It's not like that," he says. "I'm not his errand boy or anything. I like the work I do with him and for him. I wouldn't stick around if I didn't."

I feel vaguely chastised and fall silent.

He opens the door and calls out a hello.

There's an uncertain "uh...Jacob?" from down the hallway.

We maneuver the boxes into the apartment, and I look around while Jacob closes the door behind us. There's nothing particularly special about the space. We're standing in a medium-sized living room that has a hallway leading off from one side and a small kitchen off to the other. But the windows on the far wall are large, and you can actually see some of the redbrick Harvard houses and a tiny slice of the river. "Wow," I say, moving closer. "That view."

"I know," says Jacob, joining me by the window. "Nice, isn't it?"

"Bet Dad doesn't even notice."

"We set up an office for him in the second bedroom." He leads me into the hallway. One door off of it is open and through it I can see a narrow bed, still unmade, the quilt slipping off. There's something incredibly sad about how messy and small the room is, about how my father's life has been reduced to an unkempt bed in a claustrophobic room.

Jacob doesn't seem to notice the pathos of it all—he's already knocking on the other door and then opening it with a comfortable self-assurance I envy. "Larry?" he says. "Look who I brought with me."

My father is hunched over a computer at his desk. His neck and shoulders curve forward just like Milton's. Dad's heavier than Milton and his hair is mostly gray, but give Milton another fifty years and they'll be identical. Dad's wearing reading glasses way down on his nose, and as he turns to look at us, his eyes are bleary under eyebrows that have recently grown straggly.

I haven't seen him for a couple of months, but he looks a lot older to me.

He swivels toward me in his chair, and I come over and kiss him lightly on the forehead.

"Keats," he says, and I wonder which of us is more relieved that he got my name right the first time. When we all lived together, he frequently called the three women of our household interchangeably by any of our three names. "What a lovely surprise." When he says things like that, they always sound sarcastic, but I think it's just the way he talks: he actually does seem (mildly) pleased to see me. "To what do I owe the unexpected pleasure?"

"I wanted to check out your new place."

He gestures grandly around the room. "A veritable palace, isn't it?"

"I like the view."

He shrugs and I know I'm right: he couldn't care less about it.

"We brought some boxes over from the house," Jacob says. "Mostly books and papers."

"Excellent," Dad says. "More useless detritus from a misspent life."

Jacob doesn't respond to that, just starts gathering up the dirty plates and half-empty mugs of tea that are scattered everywhere. Dad may have been living here only a few weeks, but his Sedlak slovenliness is already on full display.

There's a small sofa near the desk. It's heaped with books and stacks of papers—and more plates and cups—so I perch on the arm. "How're you doing, Dad?"

"As you see."

"Are you teaching this semester?"

"One graduate seminar."

"How's that going?"

"The way it always goes. My students began the class eager and excited to work with the iconic Professor Sedlak, and then disillusionment sets in. I am not what they expected. I am not Aristotle. I have no interest in their moral development. I teach theories of government and expect them to do the reading on time." He shrugs. "The disappointment is mutual. They're not what *I* was hoping for, either."

"Anyone want coffee?" Jacob asks brightly.

"I do," I say, jumping up a little too quickly. I follow him as he leaves the office, carefully balancing a tower of dirty dishes between his two hands.

* * *

I stand in the doorway of the kitchen and watch Jacob make coffee with the ease of someone who knows where everything is—who probably unpacked and arranged it all himself, come to think of it. "He seems kind of depressed."

"Yeah, I know." He glances over at me as he pours water in the machine. "It's good you came. He misses you guys, but he's not the type to express that out loud."

"No kidding."

"He is who he is, Keats. He's not a warm and fuzzy guy, and he never will be. But he loves you, and he's more aware of what's going on with his kids than you'd think."

"How do you know that?"

He measures out the coffee into the filter. "He asks me about you all the time. He gets worried about things like any father."

"What makes him worry about me?"

"Nothing in particular. Just the usual stuff. You know."

"I really don't. Tell me." He's still silent. "Don't make me threaten another book, Jacob."

"It's just the normal dad stuff. Like 'Is she happy with her job? Is that guy really right for her?' That kind of thing."

"Normal dad stuff," I repeat. "So . . . he also asks if Hopkins is happy with her job? And her boyfriend? Oh, wait, she doesn't have one. Does he talk about *that*? About how she hasn't had a boyfriend since college and how Milton's *never* had a girlfriend or even gone out on a date? Or am I the only one who worries him? Because I'm not as smart as they are?"

Jacob shakes his head uneasily. "This isn't a competitive thing, Keats. And I wasn't quoting him verbatim. I was just trying to convey to you—"

"Forget it." I start opening cabinet doors. Inside, they're almost entirely bare, except for a bunch of Museum of Fine Arts mugs and a brand-new set of plain white dishes (four each of plates, bowls, teacups, and saucers) and several boxes of Swee-Touch-Nee tea, which my dad drinks all day long, brewed strong with lots of milk and sugar. He taught my mom to drink it like that. I give up on the third cabinet and turn back to Jacob. "Is there anything good here? I really need something sweet right now."

"Instant oatmeal?"

"Get real, Jacob."

"You mean like cookies or something? I haven't done a big grocery run yet. Sorry. But I can go out right now and get you whatever you want."

I hesitate, then say, "It's okay. I'm fine."

"It's no problem. Coffee's all set to go, and I can be back with a doughnut or cupcake or something before it's even done brewing. Just tell me what you'd like."

"It's okay."

"How about a glazed chocolate from Dunkin' Donuts? You like those, right?"

"Yeah, but you don't have to get me one. I'll live."

"Just give me five minutes."

I watch Jacob race out of the apartment, and I feel a little guilty. It's so easy to take advantage of him.

The coffeemaker is hissing gently but it has a while to go, so I head back to my father's office.

He's typing at the computer again.

"Hi." I return to my perch on the sofa arm. "Am I interrupting?"

"Never," he says. "And always." He smiles, and I see for a second a ghost of the handsome younger man he once was, the one who my mother claims every female grad student had a crush on. He swivels his chair around so he's facing me and pats me awkwardly on the knee. "Tell me what's up with you these days." But before I can speak, he says, "Did your mother tell you she's selling the house? You were born in that house, you know. All three of you grew up in that house."

"But it kind of makes sense for her to sell it now, don't you think?"

"How unusual," he says. "Someone's actually asking me what *I* think about all this." He leans back in his desk chair. There's a small tear in the shoulder seam of his blue dress shirt. "I have to admit that I feel a bit blindsided. My plan was to be carried out of that house in a coffin. Preferably dead, of course."

"Of course." We're politely jovial with each other—it's what we do best.

"But the decision has been made and here I am." He glances around. "Where's Jacob? I don't hear the pitter-patter of little feet anywhere."

"I sent him out for dessert."

"You sent him out?" he repeats, one crazy eyebrow soaring. "Does he work for you now?"

"Well," I say, "he works for you and you're my father, so by the transitive property, he works for me, right?"

"That is a fallacy."

"Says you."

He looks mildly taken aback. "Excuse me?"

"Nothing. I was just joking. Did you know that Hopkins may come home soon to pack up her stuff? We should try to have a family dinner if she does."

"Such a complicated term, *family*," he says with a grim chuckle, and it suddenly occurs to me—really occurs to me for the first time—that my dad's heart might actually be broken. I don't know what to say to that. We're both silent for a moment, and then he says, "Do you know how long it had been since I'd last lived in an apartment? Over thirty-five years. I keep hearing people moving around me. Up above, down below, on all sides. I'm surrounded by strangers."

"You'll get used to it."

"I don't want to get used to it," he says sulkily.

"Have you tried a white noise machine?"

"No. Maybe I should."

"I can pick one up for you if you like. I'm always running errands for work anyway."

"Ah, still being challenged on the job, I see. I'm so glad you graduated magna cum laude from one of the Seven Sisters for this." His foggy hazel eyes peer at me from under those craggy eyebrows, like they're trying to pin down something that refuses to come into focus. "You're too smart for this, Keats. If you want to spend time in academia—lord knows why, but it does seem to draw us in—go back to school, a *real* school, and get a PhD."

"That's the last thing I want to do." My cell buzzes in my pocket. I fish it out and peer at the text from Tom.

U on ur way yet? Dinner's at 6:30.

I text him back. *Soon.* I lean back so I can slip the phone back in my jeans.

"Please don't let me distract you from your important communiqué," my father says icily. He hates texting, goes ballistic when he catches students glancing at their phones during class.

"I'm good."

"At what?"

Fortunately I can hear the apartment door open at that moment. I call out to Jacob, who materializes a second later, bag in hand. "Who's up for a doughnut?" he asks cheerfully.

"I'll have mine with my coffee." I stand up. "Dad?"

"Go ahead. I'll join you in a second."

But he doesn't ever emerge, so Jacob and I have our doughnuts in the kitchen without him, and then I stop by the office to say good-bye before Jacob drives me home like I knew he would.

* * *

When I get there, Tom is watching the Red Sox play the Royals on our living room flat screen. "It's going to be a long season," he says, looking up with a sigh when I let myself in. "We're already stinking up the place. Glad you're finally home. We're going to meet Lou and Iz at their place and then decide where to eat."

"I need to shower. I smell like my house."

"Okay, but make it fast. How was your dad?"

"Old." I don't mean it as a joke but Tom laughs.

"That's what happens when you have kids in your fifties." Tom's father is twenty years younger than mine and looks like an older, slightly beefier version of his son: his hair's still dark and thick, and the cragginess in his face is pretty handsome. If Tom ages the way his father did, he'll continue to be the best-looking guy in the room for the next forty years.

They're good pals, Tom and his father. They have season tickets to Fenway Park, and even though they see each other every day at work, they're still eager to go to games together or play golf on the weekends. It's sweet.

Dick, his dad, started his linens laundering business thirty years ago and gradually built it up from a small family venture to a huge industry that services most of the hospitals and hotels in the greater Boston area. Tom worked there every summer during high school and then joined full-time when he graduated from BU. He's a vice president now, but everyone there knows he's being groomed to take over the whole company. His sister Anna doesn't want anything to do with the business—although she's happy to live off its profits in New York City—but Tom says he'll welcome her into the company if she ever changes her mind.

He also says he hopes our kids will want to join him there one day. I don't say anything when he talks about that. I've always daydreamed about having a kid who becomes a famous novelist or screenwriter or something like that. But if running a laundry-washing business is good enough for the guy I plan to have kids with, it should be good enough for those kids. Right?

* * *

We see Izzy and Lou almost every weekend, probably because we like both of them, which is unusual for us. In general, I tolerate Tom's friends more than I actively like them—a lot of them acted weirdly condescending toward me when Tom and I first started dating and I was only fifteen, which maybe I shouldn't blame them for, but it didn't exactly endear them to me. I don't have all that many friends of my own, because for the last ten years Tom's taken up all of my free time. While the other girls at Smith were spending their weekends carpooling to parties on nearby coed campuses, I was riding the bus back to Boston to be with Tom, so I just didn't forge the same kind of bonds the other girls did. And the few I did get close to, like my roommates, settled in other parts of the country. But Tom and I are together pretty much every night anyway, so I don't particularly feel like I'm missing out on companionship.

And like I said, we spend a lot of time with Lou and Izzy.

Lou goes all the way back to high school with Tom, and he's a good guy, dependable and honest and basically pretty easygoing, but the one I really like is Izzy, who's halfway between my age and the guys'. She's cute and blond and sweet and kind and would pretty much do anything to keep everyone around her happy. After she graduated from high school, she continued to live at home, taking classes at a local community college, so she could help her parents care for her older brother who was born with some kind of serious brain damage and can't talk or feed himself or go to the bathroom on his own. She lived at home until she married Lou, and even now, a few years later, she still spends one day each weekend back there, driving the hour it takes for her to get to and from Salem, just to give her mother a few hours' relief from the constant drudgery of caring for Stanny.

Her desire to please occasionally tips over into mild insanity, since she hates to disagree with anyone about anything. For instance, once we were all discussing a movie we had just seen, and Lou said he hated it because it was boring, and she said, "I know! I almost fell asleep!" and then I said, "Really? I thought it was incredibly tense," and she said, "I know! I still have goose bumps!" and no one but me seemed to notice that in her rush to be agreeable she had contradicted herself in fewer than ten seconds.

You forgive Izzy for stuff like that, because it comes from such a good place, from such a genuine desire to make everyone around her feel understood. She's unlike the people I grew up with, unlike my very self-centered and argumentative family: she's proof that not *everyone* thinks being right is more important than being nice.

It takes us about fifteen minutes to get from our apartment in Waltham to their tiny house in Needham, and as we pull up I see that Izzy's strung small white lights along the latticed roof of the front porch. They twinkle cheerfully in the dusk, and I point them out to Tom, who says, "She knows it's not Christmas, right?"

"They're pretty."

"Yeah, I guess," he says, and we knock and less than a minute later Tom's on the sofa with Lou watching the game.

Izzy makes a face at me and says, "I'm starving but the game's tied."

"We'll never get them out of here now," I say.

"At least there's wine in the fridge—we can have our own party until they get hungry enough to get up off their butts." Izzy has a very slight southern accent. She's originally from Georgia, but her parents moved to Salem when she was in high school. She still dresses like a southerner, always dressier than the occasion demands. Tonight, even though it's just us and we're not going anywhere special, she's got on tight, new jeans, spike-heeled black leather strappy sandals, a silk tank top, and a small fitted jacket. I'm wearing comfy jeans and a cozy, oversized boyfriend cardigan, and I feel shabby next to her.

It's not a fair contest, though: I grew up in a household where my mother and older sister never used a blow-dryer or read a fashion magazine. What little I know about primping I've had to teach myself.

She pours the wine and asks me about my day, so I tell her my family news.

"*That's* how your mother told you she was divorcing your father? Just in the middle of a conversation about something else?" She shakes her mane of long blond hair in disbelief.

We're sitting at their small square table, glasses of wine and an open bag of chips in front of us.

I nodded. "Then when I was just a little surprised, she acted like I was overreacting."

"God, I'd be sobbing all over the place if my parents got divorced."

"I'm not actually all that sad. That marriage was over a long time ago." I realize I'm quoting Jacob, but since Izzy doesn't know him I don't bother telling her that.

"Still, they're your parents." Her big blue eyes—fanned by thickly mascaraed eyelashes—are tender with sympathy. "My parents fight all the time—I'm talking huge screaming matches—but I can't imagine they'd ever actually leave each other. They *can't*, because of Stanny."

"What's funny is I can't remember my parents ever fighting. They were actually always pretty polite to each other."

"Maybe that was the problem. Maybe they needed to scream more."

"Maybe." But I can't picture it. Ours has never been a house of raised voices. Cold, contemptuous, sarcastic, sharp voices, yes. Raised, no.

I tell Izzy I really like the lights out in front, and she says that Lou poked fun at her because they looked like Christmas lights.

"Tom said the same thing," I admit.

"Those two," she says, more fondly than irritably. "They're like peas in a pod, as my mama would say."

"Well, I love the lights."

She offers to show me some of the other little improvements she's been working on, and as we walk around the house, she points out a faux-marble finish on a cabinet, a decoupage kind of thing on a mirror frame in the powder room, and a head-board she's made for their bed by stapling fabric over layers of wood and cotton batting. It's the kind of artsy decorative work that no one in my house could even think of doing: I can't remember my mother ever even getting our windows washed or our walls painted, and she definitely wasn't standing around with a sponge full of paint faux-marbling anything.

I murmur admiringly as Izzy points it all out, feigning more enthusiasm than I'm actually feeling. It's pretty enough, but all these crafts are a little—

I stop myself before I can finish that negative thought. It's the snob in me coming out, making me want to criticize something that's perfectly lovely, just because it's the kind of thing other people do, not my cerebral, crazy family.

I tell Izzy she's amazing and the house looks fantastic, and she smiles, pleased.

We end the tour back in the living room. The guys actually notice our arrival, but only because it's between innings and there's a commercial on.

"Where have you been?" Lou says to Izzy, accusingly. "We're starving."

Izzy cuffs him on the shoulder and turns to me, laughing. "Can you believe these guys?"

"No." I reach out my hand and haul Tom to his feet. "I really can't."

We go to a restaurant where the baseball game is playing on a TV over the bar. The boys sit on the side of the table facing the TV. Izzy and I sit on the other side and share a huge salad.

4.

At work on Monday, I get an IM from Milton telling me to call Mom, which is exactly the kind of twisted, backwards way messages get delivered in my family. I call the house, and Mom answers and immediately says, "I had a great idea."

"How nice for you."

"You know how I've got to figure out what to do with all the extra furniture before we move? Well, I've decided I'm going to let you kids pick out whatever you want—tables, books, artwork, whatever—so when it's time to move, I'll know who gets what. And then I can get rid of anything I don't want with a clear conscience. I want to do it as soon as possible, so I can start taking stuff to Goodwill next week."

"Is Hopkins coming?"

"It's not sounding too likely. Not in the near future anyway. She's just got too much going on at work. But I'll ask her what she thinks she might want and pick out a few more things for her. Anyway, I thought maybe you could come over for dinner tonight and look around. Do you have plans?"

"Not that I know of, but I should check with Tom."

"By all means," she says, way too politely.

* * *

Tom groans into the phone. "We just saw them two days ago."

"Says the man who sees his father every day."

"He pays me to do that."

"I'd happily skip it, Tom, but I'm worried that if I don't tell Mom what I want right away, she'll give everything to Hopkins and Milton."

"Do your parents even own anything valuable?"

"They're not paupers, Tom."

"I know, but—" He doesn't bother to finish the thought. His parents' home is filled with bright new furniture and bright new paintings and bright new knickknacks—they both came from pretty rough backgrounds, so when their company started doing well, his mother was determined to make her house look like something she'd only seen on TV until then. She's left her past firmly in the past, and Martha Stewart has nothing on her, whereas my parents haven't bought a new piece of furniture or—let's be honest—thoroughly cleaned the whole house in decades.

Tom says, "I really don't want to go, Keats. We just saw your family. Enough's enough."

"Is it okay if I go without you?"

He doesn't like that idea, either. "I thought we were going to have a nice quiet dinner alone tonight." Of course, he did. When *don't* we have a nice quiet dinner alone together on a Monday? Or a Tuesday, Wednesday, or Thursday for that matter?

"You'll survive," I say.

"I'm sorry I actually enjoy having dinner with my girlfriend. I must really be some kind of pig, wanting to spend time with you."

"A very codependent pig, yes."

The truth is, I never know whether it's better to have Tom

with me when I see my family or not. When he's with me, I feel cushioned from their craziness, safely cocooned in my happy, normal life with him, but his presence adds some tension because they don't appreciate him.

It's pretty much a wash.

We come to an agreement: I'll go to dinner by myself and leave as early as I can.

* * *

When I pull up in front of the house, I see a couple of other cars already parked in front. One I don't recognize, but the other is Jacob's.

I let myself in and head toward the kitchen where I hear voices.

Jacob's sitting in the breakfast booth, talking to some man with a big back. The big back stands up and turns around when Jacob greets me.

The guy is probably over six feet tall with broad shoulders and hammy legs in jeans that are belted under a substantial stomach. I'd put his age at sixty, give or take a few years: his hair's gray and pulling away from the temples, but he's still got a decent head of it and the tanned and healthy looks of a guy who plays golf or goes sailing every weekend.

Maybe it's the boat shoes on his sockless feet that make me think that.

He's greeting me heartily, a little too heartily given the fact I have no idea who he is. "You must be Keats! 'Season of mists and mellow fruitfulness' and all that. You're probably sick of hearing that."

"Not really." I shake the hand he's extending toward me. It's huge, his hand—fleshy and twice the size of mine. "Not all that many people go around quoting Keats."

Jacob, who's also risen, smothers a smile at that.

"He was my favorite," Mom puts in. "Well, after Hopkins, of course. And you can't ignore Milton. The poet, I mean."

Yeah, you can't ignore the poet. Just the real kid who has his name.

Anyway, now I'm glad Tom's not with me. He hates the way my parents named us, thinks it's the biggest piece of pseudointellectual bullshit he's ever heard and tantamount to child abuse. For a couple of years, he tried to convince me to call myself Kiki, but as much as I agree with him that my given name is ridiculous, it's still my name. Plus... *Kiki?* That was the best he could come up with?

"Good thing for your kids you're not an e.e. cummings fan," the man says, releasing my hand to turn to Mom.

"I love him actually. But even I couldn't be that cruel to my own child."

They share a smile.

"And you're—?" I say because they seem to have forgotten that no one's introduced him to me.

"Paul Silvestri." The big palm extends toward me again with the apparent intention of shaking a second time. Seems like overkill, but I surrender my hand while I shoot Mom a *who the hell is this guy?* kind of look.

She just says brightly, "Dinner will be ready soon. Meanwhile, we've got wine and cheese. Keats? A glass?"

"Yeah, I'll have white. Jacob, I have a quick question for you. Come here." I grab him by the hand, pull him to his feet and into the hallway, and practically pin him against the wall. He's wearing his usual khakis and button-down shirt.

It must be easy to be Jacob and get dressed in the morning.

"Who is that guy?" I hiss at him, even though I have a pretty good guess and that's why I'm reacting like this.

But he confirms it for me. "He's your mom's date."

"What's he doing here?"

"I guess she wanted you to meet him. He seems nice."

"That's easy for you to say. She's not your mother."

"Yeah, I know," he says, and I remember that his mother's dead. So's his father. Jacob's had some bad luck in his life.

"Sorry," I say. "I just meant it's not as weird for you as it is for me. Why didn't she warn me?"

"I don't know."

"I thought she told you everything."

He sighs and gives me a look of frustration tempered by patience. I bring that look out in Jacob a lot. "Just relax. Give him a chance."

"I'll try. But it's weird."

We head back into the kitchen. "I know you've had a lot to get used to lately, Keats—"

"Yeah," I say, cutting him off. "I think everyone should feel sorry for me."

"Too bad. No one does." He walks away while I snatch a full glass of wine out of my mother's offering hand.

* * *

There's a place set for Milton at the dinner table, but when we all go to sit down, he's nowhere in sight.

"Where's the boy genius?" I ask.

"He's coming down," Mom says. "He needed to finish something up first."

"He always says that. And then he waits to eat until after we're done, so he won't have to sit and make conversation."

"That's not true," Mom says with an uncomfortable glance at Paul. "I often eat dinner with him."

"Well, I don't. Give me a sec." I get up and leave the dining room.

Upstairs, I knock loudly on Milton's door and then barge in.

He looks up from the computer with a startled expression. "What?"

"It's dinner. You have to come join us."

"I already told Mom I'd be down soon."

"Dinner's now. Save what you're doing, or I swear I'll unplug everything."

He heaves a huge, aggrieved sigh and keeps tapping.

"I mean it, Milton."

"I *know*. I'm saving it! Jesus, Keats." Another moment of tapping and then he finally gets up and follows me downstairs. He's wearing black sweatpants that are too small for him— his stomach hangs out over the waistband—and a T-shirt that says, COME TO THE DARK SIDE, WE HAVE COOKIES. I can picture my mother buying that for him, thinking it would make him laugh and giving it to him and then him tossing it in his drawer with an indifferent shrug.

But who knows? I can never tell with Milton—maybe it did make him laugh.

I introduce him to Paul who gives him the same kind of heartily enthusiastic greeting he gave me. Milton shakes his hand with a confused look in my direction. He doesn't know who Paul is or why he's here. I just shrug at him. I can't exactly explain it myself. We both look at Mom. She smiles blandly and says, "Sit down so we can eat."

Milton sits next to me and bites his fingernails while he waits for the food to be passed: he never knows what to do with his hands when they're not on a keyboard. His eyes dart around the dinner table, but the second anyone addresses him directly, he looks down at the plate in front of him and barely responds.

Paul tries to engage him in conversation, but it's hard work.

"What do you like to do in your free time?"

"Stuff."

"What kind of stuff?"

"Computer games mostly."

"Any game in particular?"

"Not really."

A few more useless attempts, and then Paul gives up and, with noticeable relief, turns his attention to me.

"So, Keats, your mother tells me you work in the English department at Waltham Community College."

I nod. Not much to add to that.

"Do you like the work?"

"It's okay," I say because it is. Okay. The work is easy, the people are pleasant, and the hours are reasonable, but the pay sucks and there's no mobility. *Okay* sums it up perfectly.

"Are you thinking of going back to school one day?"

"Why do people always ask me that?"

"Because you're young and smart," my mother says, "and you're a glorified secretary."

I scowl at her. "I know I'm a disappointment, but not everyone can be a world famous neurologist."

"No one's asking you to be a neurologist." Mom glances over at Paul, as if to gauge whether the familial argument is off-putting or not. He smiles at her reassuringly, and she adds, "Ambition isn't a bad thing, Keats."

"Excellent point, Mom. Maybe you should find some of your own."

She lifts her chin. "I raised three kids entirely by myself."

"*Very* ambitious of you. And very original—no other women your age have raised children. You really pushed that envelope, didn't you?"

"Keats," Jacob warns me in that pseudofraternal way of his that sometimes I respect and sometimes I loathe.

"No, she's right." Mom takes a sip of wine. "I probably should have been more ambitious for myself, Keats. I regret dropping out of graduate school, but at the time it felt like I didn't have any other choice."

"You're still young," Paul says to her. "There's plenty of time for you to do that now."

I raise my eyebrows skeptically.

"Thank you for the encouragement," Mom says to Paul very pointedly. "I don't always get it at home."

"I totally think you should go back to school," I say. "I'll just believe it when I see it."

"I'm already taking a class."

"Yeah, I know. Creative writing. You planning to write a novel, Mom? Like everyone else in the entire universe?"

"Hey, hey, watch it," Paul says jovially. "I'm taking that class, too! Don't be too hard on those of us with literary aspirations. They may be foolish, but they're all we've got."

"No, it's great," I say politely, because you have to be polite to strangers. "Is that how you two met?"

"Yep."

"Do you critique each other's work?"

"Sometimes."

"Do you have kids?" I ask since he seems willing to answer any question.

"Four," he says proudly. "Two boys and two girls."

"All with the same mother?"

He shifts uncomfortably. "Actually, no. My oldest son has a different mother than the younger ones."

"So how many times have you been married?"

"Only twice!" he says with a desperate gaiety.

"More wine?" Mom says. "Anyone?" Paul instantly says yes and drains his glass, then holds it out. Mom tilts the bottle to pour him a new one, but only a few drops come out. "There's another in the kitchen. Jacob, would you—?"

He's already on his feet. "Got it."

"Can you start a pot of decaf while you're in there?" I call after him. Since he's already up.

Milton says, "May I be excused?" He's eaten a couple bites of chicken and a big mound of pasta. Mom had bought the meal already cooked at an Italian restaurant, and then served it on platters like she'd made it herself. But since we'd all hung out in the kitchen before dinner, everyone saw her replate the food, including Paul, and I wonder why she didn't just serve it in the tins. No one was fooled into thinking she'd cooked: all she did was make more dishes to clean.

"I'd like you to stay down here," Mom says to Milton, "so you can pick out some furniture for yourself. And then we'll have dessert."

"What's for dessert?" Milton asks.

"Cake and strawberries."

"Do we have any ice cream?"

"I don't know," Mom says a little wearily. "I'll have to check."

"I'm in the mood for ice cream."

My mother gets up and makes her way into the kitchen, and I suddenly feel sorry for her. She invited a guy she liked to meet her kids and then...well, he met her kids.

Inspired by sympathy, I make an effort, turn to Paul, and ask him some questions about the creative writing class. He's happy to answer, and Jacob joins in our conversation.

Not Milton, though. He stares at the table and waits for Mom to come back and tell him whether there's ice cream or not.

"There isn't, just whipped cream," she says. "But no dessert until *after* the whole picking-out-furniture thing." I get the feeling she's bribing Milton into not fleeing, the way a parent might tell a toddler he'll get a cookie if he sits nicely during dinner.

"Why should I pick out anything?" Milton asks Mom after we've all gotten up from the dinner table and moved into the foyer. "I don't have my own place yet."

"I just want to make sure you get your fair share," Mom says. "We'll figure out what to do with it—put it in storage, keep it at your father's place or at mine when I get one. We just need to know what we should hold on to for you."

"I only want the stuff in my room."

"That's all yours." Mom's voice softens when she talks to Milton. I think she forgets that he's twenty now. To her, he's still the little boy who needs her. "But someday you'll have a place of your own, and you might want our old coffee table or maybe a lamp—"

"All I want is the stuff in my room. Can I go now?"

Mom raises her hands and lets them drop hopelessly at her sides. "Fine," she says. "Go. I'll pick out some things to put aside for you." He's gone before she even finishes the sentence, so she turns to me and repeats it: "I'll pick out some things to put aside for him."

"Do you honestly think he'll ever have his own place?"

"You better hope so," she says crisply. "Because Dad and I will be dead one day."

"Lovely. You know, if you just made him go outside now and then—"

"Please, don't start with that now, Keats. Here." She picks up a stack of Post-it notes in different colors, which are sitting on our old narrow marble table. "You can be green. Stick one of these on anything you like."

I unenthusiastically accept the pad of little green Post-its. "This feels weird. I shouldn't get to just mark anything as mine, not if I'm the only one doing it. It's not fair."

"I've already marked a few things for Hopkins—in yellow." She points to the little flap of yellow paper on top of the marble table. "See? I thought this would be great in her apartment."

I hadn't even thought about wanting the table, not for a moment, but now that I see it's been claimed for Hopkins, it occurs to me that it's pretty cool—and maybe even valuable—with its thick slab of dull gray-and-rust marble and spindly wire frame.

Mom didn't even ask me if I wanted it before marking it for Hopkins.

But then I think, Hopkins *should* get it. She's the one saving lives. She's the one my mother *wants* to have get it.

Mom has turned to Jacob and is fanning out a couple more pads in her hand. "Blue or pink?"

"He gets a color?" I ask. "I mean, I'm fine with it, but—" I stop, not sure how to point out that it's a little weird for Jacob to be included without sounding mean.

"I'm representing your father," Jacob explains as he—predictably—goes for the blue. "Your mother asked me to see if there's anything he could use in his new apartment."

"Oh. Right."

"But I think Jacob should pick out something special for himself, too," Mom adds. "He's been a huge help to both of us over the last few years."

"That's very nice of you, but I don't need anything."

"Nothing here is worth much," Mom assures him. "It's a sentimental value kind of thing only, so don't be noble about it."

"And even our sentiment isn't that valuable," I say. "Let's be honest."

Paul, who's standing a few feet away, a genial smile on his face, guffaws at that. I can't tell if it's sincere or not. I wonder what he makes of all this.

My mother is wearing a touch of makeup tonight and looks pretty fabulous. She's really too young and too pretty for him now that I look at them both. Also too smart and too interesting. I got the sense over dinner that she was a little bored with him, a little impatient with the conversation. And now, as he gives that overly hearty laugh, I see a very brief expression of distaste flit across her face. Or maybe it's discomfort.

It's definitely not infatuation, which is a relief. I'm not ready for my mother to start getting all starry-eyed over some stranger.

"Let the games begin!" she says. "Scatter and tag, my children. Scatter and tag."

"This family is so freakin' weird," I mutter as I walk away.

I wander alone into the living room. Mom was telling the truth when she told Jacob we didn't have anything valuable. This room has the nicest and best preserved furniture in the house, and even so, there's not much anyone would want: two matching faded sofas bought at some department store in the '80s (not old enough to be vintage or new enough to be fashionable), two plaid armchairs that I never liked, a plain wooden coffee table that's way too big for my apartment, a piano that—

Wait, the piano is interesting.

My job is so uncreative: it would be nice to come home and do something artistic, like play the piano. I'd need lessons, of course, but I bet I'd learn faster now than I did when I was young and resistant to the whole idea of practicing.

I wander over and check it out. It's an upright Kawai in decent shape, although the hinges on the bench feel a little loose when I open it to see what music books might still be inside.

I pull out my cell phone and call Tom to ask him if we want a piano.

"Why would we want a piano? Neither of us plays."

"It's free, and I took lessons for years."

"I've never once seen you play."

"I stopped when I was twelve." The truth is I gave up when

it became clear that I would never come close to being as good as Hopkins. My teacher, Mr. Chesley, thought he was motivating me by constantly talking about how my sister had been one of the greatest students he'd ever had, but it just made me want to stop trying.

I run my fingers along the shiny black wood, which is dulled now by a layer of dust. "It's pretty nice. Pianos are valuable, aren't they?"

"Are you thinking we'd sell it?" Tom asks.

"No, just saying. Maybe I could try taking lessons again."

"Well, we don't really have space for it, and I don't see the point, but it's your call. If you really want it, we'll figure something out. Are you coming home soon?"

"Not for a little while. Hey, Mom has—" I'm about to tell him about Paul Silvestri, but Jacob comes into the living room and I stop.

Jacob realizes he's interrupted a phone conversation. "Sorry," he says and moves back toward the door.

"It's fine," I say and then into the phone, "Gotta run. Bye." I turn off the phone and beckon Jacob in with it. "I'm just trying to decide if I want the piano."

"You play?"

"Not really. But I'm thinking I might like to try taking lessons again."

"The only song I could ever play was 'Heart and Soul.'"

"That's basically it for me, too." I sit down on the piano bench and pat the space next to me. "Let's see if we remember how to do it."

"This won't be pretty." He sits down next to me. "Which part do I do?"

"I'm taking the easy part." I start with the *doo, doo, doo, doos*. I have to say "doo, doo, doo, doo" as I do it to keep the rhythm steady, and Jacob laughs at me. I make a face at him, and then he starts in on the melody. We're terrible at first, both of us messing up and choppy and out of sync, but gradually we improve until it's clunky but recognizable.

We start bouncing our bodies from side to side in rhythm to the music, and Jacob sings, "Heart and soul, I fell in love with you," and then I sing, "Heart and soul, just like pink shampoo," and we keep making up nonsense lyrics and playing until I finally shout, "How do we *stop*?" and he says, "Like this," and just stops playing and so I do, too, after one last loudly sung "Doo, doo."

We both jump at the sound of applause behind us. We turn around, and my mom and Paul are standing there, laughing and clapping. We both get up and give exaggerated bows.

"That was great," Mom says. "I think the piano's a little out of tune, though."

"I think *we're* out of tune," Jacob says.

"I always was," I say. Mr. Chesley used to get excited because Milton could identify any note without looking, and apparently Hopkins learned to read music almost instantly, but to me he was always saying, "Can't you even *hear* that that's the wrong note, Keats? Listen. Can't you hear that?" I never could.

"I haven't had a tuner here in years," Mom says. "Milton won't play, no matter how much I beg him. He had such a good ear, too....Anyway, the last time a tuner came out was probably over three years ago, but back then he said the piano was in pretty good shape." She drifts closer. "Oh, look," she says. She picks up some sheet music that was on top of the piano—it's been left there for years, a remnant from the last time one of us played. "Dvořák," she says softly.

I know nothing about Dvořák. No, that's not true. I know one thing about him: he's my mother's favorite composer. And whatever that particular piece of music is, it's way beyond anything I was ever able to play.

"Hopkins always played this so beautifully," Mom says wistfully, gazing at the music. "I miss hearing her."

"Does she ever play now?" Paul asks.

"I don't know. I don't think she has a piano in her apartment...." She straightens up with sudden energy. "She should take this one! I don't know why I didn't think of this before. It may be a little difficult to get it up her stairs, but there are people in New York who move pianos—they'll figure it out. Once it's there, maybe she'll start playing again."

Jacob says tentatively, "Um, Eloise? Keats was saying she might want it."

"Really?" Mom looks at me, surprised.

"Not really." My face feels hot. I could kill Jacob. "I thought about it for like two seconds, but Hopkins should totally have it. It's basically hers, anyway."

"Are you sure?" Mom says. "I want this to be fair to everyone."

"We don't even have room for it in the apartment."

"All right then," Mom says, and quickly plops a yellow Post-it on top. "But I want you to have something special, too, Keats. Something as big as the piano." She scans the room a little desperately. "Oh—I've always loved that painting." She points to the largest piece of art in the room, an abstract painting with lines scratched into dark layers of paint.

"Really?" I say, wrinkling my nose. "Why?"

She looks hurt. "Never mind. Just...keep looking." She leaves the room.

* * *

I head next to the small, dark library off the downstairs hallway. It's crowded with overflowing and haphazardly stacked shelves of books, two worn-out, old leather armchairs, and a matching pair of tall, arching reading lamps, but the only piece of furniture that would realistically make sense in our modern, already-furnished apartment is the small round table between the two chairs. It's covered with books that have bookmarks sticking out or pages folded down to keep a place saved. Some are lying open and facedown like the reader will pick them up any minute, but a couple of those are dusty and have clearly been abandoned for a while.

My mother is a voracious but inconstant reader. She keeps different books going in different rooms of the house and is always searching for the one she wants at any given moment. But when she's really into a book—like past the three-quarters point—she won't put it down until she's done, no matter the hour or the chores or the kids waiting for her.

The table's nice, though. I pull a Post-it off my pad and stick it on top.

"Good choice." It's Jacob from right behind me. It's annoying how he's always sneaking up on people like that.

I don't respond: I'm still annoyed with him about the piano thing. What gave him the right to speak for me? To embarrass me?

"Your dad needs lamps," he says, cheerfully oblivious to my resentment. He tilts his head to study the two steel and copper floor lamps. "You think anyone would mind if I tagged those for him?"

"No. Go ahead." I move away from him and study the bookshelves. They're packed with decades' worth of books stacked every which way. I wonder how Mom's planning to deal with these: I wouldn't mind picking out a few.

Jacob says, "You play a mean 'Heart and Soul,' Keats."

"Yeah, I should enter competitions."

"Seriously, it was fun."

Again, I don't respond.

He tags the two lamps and then lingers for a moment, like he's waiting for me to say something, but I just keep walking around the edge of the room, studying the books and vases and pictures on the shelves. He's starting to say, "Hey, do you—" when my phone rings. I hold up a "wait a sec" finger and answer it. It's Tom.

"You done yet?"

I promise him I'll leave soon, and when I end the call, Jacob's gone and Mom's calling for us to come to the dining room.

Dessert is a slice of prebought and replated angel food cake with a dab of whipped cream (squirted from a canister) and a few strawberries scattered on top. Mom didn't even bother to hull the strawberries. It's pleasantly sweet, and Milton (who came back down even though there's no ice cream), Paul, and I gobble ours down and say yes when Mom asks if anyone wants seconds. Jacob eats most of his but declines more, and Mom doesn't serve herself another slice but keeps carving out little bits of cake and eating them with her fingers.

I get a text from Tom asking me if I'm coming home, so I push back from the table after my second helping and say I have to go.

"I'll walk out with you," Jacob says, jumping to his feet.

Paul follows us into the foyer at Mom's side. I leave feeling unsettled by the way he's waving good-bye to us like he's the host.

"I love my new daddy," I say as soon as the door closes behind us. "He's so big and strong—he could totally beat up Old Daddy."

"He seems like a nice guy," Jacob says. "But I don't think you have to worry about your mother's marrying him."

"I was just joking."

"I know."

The lawn is so overgrown it's more weeds than grass, and the trees that line the edge of the walkway haven't been trimmed in years, so you have to shove branches aside just to get past them and onto the sidewalk.

"I'm sure I'll see you soon," I say as we reach the point where we have to go in different directions.

"Seems likely." He leans forward and gives me a quick kiss on the cheek, then, as he shifts back, says offhandedly, "Hey, you want to go grab a drink somewhere? Or see a movie or something? It's not that late."

I shake my head. "Can't. Tom's waiting for me."

"Oh, sorry. I thought maybe he was out of town or something since he didn't come with you."

"Nah, he just hates my family."

"Really?"

"Well, hate's an exaggeration. They're just not the easiest people in the world to spend time with."

"Easy's overrated. They're good people."

"Good's overrated," I say, and we go our separate ways.

* * *

"Glad I missed it," says Tom when I recount the evening for him. "What did you decide about the piano?"

"I'm not taking it." We're on the bed where he was watching some random '80s cop movie when I got home. I immediately shoved off my shoes and joined him. Now I curl up closer and rest my head next to his on the propped-up pillow. "It seemed kind of silly once I thought about it since neither of us plays."

"Good," Tom says. "I really didn't want it."

"You should have just told me that when I asked."

When he shrugs, I can feel his shoulder rub up and down

against mine. "I didn't want to say no if it meant something to you."

"That's sweet."

Tom tilts his head toward mine and bats his eyes. "I'm a sweet guy." We watch the movie in silence for a minute, and then a commercial comes on and he says, "So your mom's in love, huh?"

"I wouldn't go that far....I wish she hadn't invited that guy—it was just weird. I couldn't tell if it bothered Milton as much as it did me."

"Milton doesn't notice anything except whether or not the Wi-Fi works."

"True enough."

He rubs his cheek against the top of my head. "How someone like you came from a family like yours is a mystery to me."

"I'm a mutant," I agree.

5.

Hopkins plans a quick trip to Boston, but the night before she's supposed to come, some Ohio congressman's son gets drunk and falls down a hill and bashes his brain against a rock. Hopkins is called in to consult, so she puts her plans to come home on indefinite hold.

I don't learn this until a couple of days later, when Mom unloads to me on the phone, complaining that Hopkins demanded she not give away anything important without making it clear what fell into that category.

"I'm terrified to get rid of anything of hers," Mom says. "But the real estate agents I've interviewed all say I have to get rid of the clutter before they can show the house." There's the sound of something rattling, and even though I have no idea what it is, I picture her in the kitchen, moving around while she's talking, pushing objects around without organizing them, moving papers from one stack to another, fiddling with the cabinet doors—in constant motion with no real purpose to it.

Me, I'm just sitting comfortably, curled up in my desk chair at work, sipping a mug of lukewarm coffee, and wondering if I should let myself have another muffin yet. I've already done most of the work I'm supposed to get done that day, even though it's still morning. Part of what I like about my job is how easy it is. Actually, that's most of what I like about my job.

"Can't you just box her stuff and stick it in the garage for now?" I ask.

"The garage is already full. And I don't want to create more boxes to sort through later—we have enough of those already. The agent I saw last week—the one I think I'll use—said it looks like we never finished moving in. Oh, that reminds me! That's why I wanted to call you. The agent has a son who was in your class at school. Cameron Evans. Do you remember him?"

"Vaguely." He had been a skinny kid with acne and blond hair who liked to talk a lot in class. "We had a couple of classes together, but we didn't hang out or anything."

"He's in business now with his father." Her voice turns a little too casual. "I got his e-mail address—maybe you guys could go out for a cup of coffee and catch up?"

I say icily, "I would think you were trying to fix me up, Mom, but of course that wouldn't make sense, given the fact that you know I live with my long-term boyfriend and we're very happy together."

"I'm not trying to fix you up. I just think it can be fun to reconnect with old friends. And you need to get out more, spend time with lots of different people, not just Tom. Even supposing he's the right guy for you in the long run"—she makes it sound only slightly more likely than hell freezing over—"how can you ever be sure of that if you have nothing to compare him to?"

"Still sounding like a setup," I say. "And I already know Tom's the right guy for me. I don't need to have coffee with a bunch of randos to figure that out."

She sniffs. "I know you think you have everything figured out. I did, too, at your age. But now that I'm dating again, I'm discovering qualities I never even knew I might expect in male companionship—"

"Yeah? Tell me about Paul Silvestri's unexpected qualities."

"Paul is a very nice man."

"So *nice* is the quality you never even knew you might want?"

"In a way, yes. *Nice* isn't the first word that comes to mind when describing your father."

"Are you saying Dad's mean?"

"No, of course not. He's just... not genial."

"Right." I examine my fingernails, wondering if I should paint them that evening. I don't always paint my fingernails, but sometimes when the mood strikes, I like to use a really freaky color on them. "Whereas Paul S. *oozed* geniality. I mean, if that's what you're going for, you've found it. A big, steaming pile of geniality."

"I'm not 'going for' anything," she snaps. "I'm just trying to enjoy myself a little."

"Me, too. And what I enjoy is coming home to Tom at the end of the day and not sitting through some miserable blind date because my mother doesn't trust my judgment."

"I am so sorry I suggested you might want to reconnect with an old school friend," she says. "What an awful, meddling mother I am."

"Oh, come now," I say. "You're not *that* bad."

There's a pause, and then she actually laughs. "Remind me again why I wanted to have kids."

"I'm sure you had your reasons."

"They escape me now.... Oh, Keats, do me a favor will you? Call Milton and just talk to him about the house. He won't even acknowledge that I'm trying to sell it. Whenever I bring it up, he acts like he can't hear me or changes the subject."

"I'm sure he hates the thought of moving."

"I'm sure he does, too. The biggest problem is that he won't let a real estate agent into his room, but once it's on the market—which I hope will be very soon—he won't have a choice. I thought maybe if you talked to him—"

"He's getting weirder and weirder by the day. Mom, you *have* to start getting him out of the house."

"Easier said than done."

"I know, but—"

She cuts me off. "I have a lot on my plate right now, Keats: the house, the move, the divorce.... Just let me take one thing at a time." Her voice worries me: there's a breathy, pressurized tone to it today. I know that sound and I don't like it. It almost always precedes a crash. "Be helpful, not judgmental, okay?"

"I'll try," I say. "But I'm a Sedlak." Maybe I'm wrong about her voice. I hope I am.

"Should I put Milton on the phone so you can talk to him about all this?"

"Nah, I'll IM him. He likes that better."

We hang up and I do a tiny bit more work—sending out some memos, calling in an order for a going-away party later that week, stuff like that—and then I figure I can take another break, so I IM Milton. *How's it going?*

The answer comes back within seconds. One thing about my brother: you can always reach him online. *Fine.*

—*Mom driving u crazy?*

—*Only when she's awake.*

—*I'm a little worried about her right now. LMK if she crashes.*

—*K*

—*she seems serious about this house-selling stuff.*

—*Why would she joke about it?*

—*u know what I mean. u going to miss ur room?*

—*No, cuz I'm not leaving.*

—*Then u better hope the buyers always wanted a son of their own.*

—*Mom won't really sell. Dad won't let her.*

—*Dad doesn't even live there anymore.*

—*It's still his house. He may want to come back.*

I shake my head even though he can't see me. I start to write something back about that and then give up and instead write, *Moving cd be great. U cd end up in a better location, somewhere u cn walk to restaurants and stuff.*

There's no immediate response, and while I'm waiting and studying my fingernails again—*purple would be cool, I think, but not a bright purple, a grayish one*—my phone rings.

It's Tom. "Hey there, baby girl."

"Someone's in a good mood."

"That's because I just made a dinner reservation for tomorrow night."

"Where?"

"It's a surprise. But it's going to be the best birthday of your life."

"You sure you're not overselling this?"

"I'm sure. Oh, and I'm going to be late coming home tonight—Dad wants me to have dinner with him and some potential client."

"Okay."

"I'll miss you. Wish I didn't have to go. I'll call you later."

When I look at the computer again, Milton still hasn't responded. I write a tentative *U there?*

Nothing. Maybe he's gone to the bathroom. Or downstairs for a bite to eat. Or maybe he's just letting me know he's done with the conversation.

* * *

"Got time to hang out?" Cathy sticks her head into my cubicle.

Cathy's a graduate student in education at UMass who's

been doing some TAing at WCC. She and I have become friendly over the last year or so—there aren't that many people in the office or even at the college who are in their twenties, so whenever she's around, she stops to chat for a few minutes.

Her timing today is perfect: since Tom's having dinner with his dad, I ask her if she wants to grab a bite to eat with me.

"So long as it's cheap. I've been living on ramen noodles, and even so, I only have about five bucks to my name until I get my next paycheck." Cathy's tall and freckled and has broad shoulders and big hands. She has red hair, but it's lighter and straighter than mine. She looks like a farm girl, but she spends her free time reading and writing poetry.

I suggest a neighborhood dive that Tom and I eat at a lot. "It's really cheap, and happy hour goes till seven. They have drinks for two bucks and a plate of grilled cheese sandwiches for three."

She thinks that sounds perfect, so we meet there at six and drink cheap wine at a high table near the bar while we compare notes about our families.

Cathy's from a small town in Missouri. She came to the East Coast for college, then stayed for graduate school. She won't ever go back to the Midwest except to visit, she says. Her siblings are all still living in the same town they were born in: her younger sister is already married and has one kid and another on the way. They talk like hicks, according to her, but she's worked hard to get rid of her accent and claims you can only hear it when she gets drunk.

She tries to be sympathetic when I complain about my family but doesn't quite get why it's so hard for me to be around them.

"It's not just that they're nuts," I say. "I could live with that. It's that they're all much more brilliant than I am and I can't keep up. I never could."

"I guess that could be rough," she says uncertainly. "But at least you can talk about interesting things with them, like literature and art. All *my* sister wants to talk about is diapers and these crazy, mean dogs she and her husband breed. Anyway, I bet you're as brilliant as they are. You're just insecure."

"No, I'm not.... Brilliant, I mean. I admit to the insecure." I drain my wineglass. "I want another. You want another?"

"I do, but I can't afford it."

"This one's on me."

"I feel bad making you pay."

"Don't. I want to. This is fun. I don't go out very often without Tom."

"How long have you guys been together?"

"Coming up on ten years."

"No—really."

"Ten years," I repeat. "Seriously."

She looks perplexed. "Wait—how old were you when you met?"

"Hold on," I say. "Let's get some more wine. And then I'll tell you our whole epic love story."

* * *

It's not really such a great story: we didn't meet cute or overcome any hardships that would make even a halfway decent movie.

It was the week of my fifteenth birthday. At that time, my one goal in life was just to fit in, but I lived in a weird, big house and had parents who didn't speak much to each other, a father who didn't speak much to his kids, a younger brother who didn't speak much to anyone, and an older sister who I barely knew because she'd gone off to college so young, but whose overshadowing brilliance was a continual reproach to my deficits even in her absence.

I escaped my family as often as I could, going out with friends on the weekends and after school, usually bumming rides from other people's parents, who tended to be more accommodating (and less nutty) than my own.

One day my friend Molly's mother dropped us off at the Chestnut Hill Cinema on her way to a silk-screening class. Molly had invited along another friend, a girl named Anna she knew from their country club. We all saw a movie together and then walked over to a bagel place to grab a bite to eat.

Anna offered to give us a ride home. "My older brother's picking me up," she said. "He doesn't mind driving people around—he doesn't have all that much else to do. He's in college, but he always comes home on the weekends."

"Why?" asked Molly.

"God, I don't know," Anna said. "He's a loser, I guess. When I go to college, I am never coming home again." We all agreed that as soon as we were able to escape our homes, we wouldn't return except to pick up our Christmas presents.

Anna's brother was a couple of minutes later than he'd said, and when he did pull up, she yelled at him and called him a moron. I was struck by how unperturbed her brother was by her show of temper: he just apologized for being late and told her he'd tried her cell but she hadn't picked up.

"I had it turned off for the movie," she snapped.

"Well, I tried," he said calmly.

She had bought a magazine with a quiz in it that she and Molly wanted to do together, so she told me to sit up front. The other girls retreated to the backseat with their magazine while I buckled myself in and snuck a few peeks at Anna's college-aged brother who was really, really cute. Big shoulders, thick hair cut short, a nicely chiseled face. His thighs were muscular inside his jeans—you could tell if you looked. I looked.

He was far too grown-up and hot for me to get up the courage to actually talk to him so I didn't say anything after my initial hi.

But after a few minutes of silence, he glanced over at me and said, "I'm Tom by the way."

"I'm Keats."

"Keith?" he said with a confused furrow of his brow. I explained my name, and then he laughed and said, "I really thought you said Keith," and then I started giggling, and we laughed for a while longer, and then it was like we could talk now, so I asked him about college, and he told me it was okay but he had a psycho roommate and so came home whenever he could, and I told him that I had a psycho family so I was very sympathetic, except I couldn't escape—yet—and I told him some stories about my dad, like how he was so crazily absent-minded that once he actually started to leave the house wearing only his boxers. I had discovered about a year earlier that the things that most embarrassed me about my parents could be turned into amusing anecdotes if told with the right sort of dry detachment, and sure enough, Anna's big brother seemed fascinated.

He assumed I was Anna's age, but she was actually a year older than me. Even if I *had* been sixteen like her, the age gap between Tom and me would still have been huge.

I left the car excited and pink cheeked from having hit it off with a guy who was that tall and mature. While the two (silly little) girls in the backseat chortled over their "Are You a Princess, a Grunge Artist, a Hippie, or a Fashion Star?" quiz, Tom and I had really talked, like peers. "See you," he said when I closed the door, and our eyes met in brief recognition that Something Had Happened.

* * *

But my buzz quickly gave way to a more realistic pessimism: I would never see Anna's brother Tom again. No college student was going to ask out a fifteen-year-old (or even a sixteen-year-old, which he thought I was). And I wasn't even friends with his sister, so it wasn't like it'd be easy to run into him.

But back at school, when I looked around at the boys my age, they seemed so stupid, so pimply faced and scrawny, so unappealing compared to Tom Wells that I knew I had to try. I *had* to.

It took me a while to get up the courage to call Molly and suggest we invite Anna to see another movie with us the following weekend. "She's really nice," I said.

"Yeah, she's okay," Molly said indifferently. "I'll conference her in." She dialed Anna, and a low male voice answered and said he'd get her. A thrill passed through my entire body at the sound of Tom's voice, and I squeezed my thighs together tightly, all curled up on the edge of my bed since I'd brought the phone in there for privacy.

While we were making plans, I said as casually as I could, "Hey, Anna, why don't you ask your brother to come see the movie with us? That way he could drive us both ways."

"Okay," said Anna. "He's such a loser he'll probably say yes."

Months later, Tom told me that he asked his sister which friends were going, and when she mentioned the redheaded girl with the weird name, he immediately said he'd drive. He was already planning to sit next to me in the movie theater. "I knew even then," he said. "You and I had a connection. And it didn't matter that you were so much younger. It just felt right."

Of course, at the time he didn't know how *much* younger. That came out later. And it did scare him off for a while, but he came back because we both knew we were meant to be together.

Our relationship grew up with us. At first, we moved slowly. Tom didn't rush me into anything I wasn't ready for. He was patient and gentle and careful. For over a year, we did things like go miniature golfing and bowling and to the movies, and he always got me home early, and we didn't do any more than kiss.

I was glad about that, but I was also scared I'd lose him because of it.

He did have a few one-night stands over the next couple of years, which he confessed to me afterward, sobbing, wracked with guilt and terrified I'd leave him because of it. I didn't like it, but I forgave him. Maybe there was some relief for me in it: I wasn't ready for sex yet, and he found a way to have it and still always come back to me.

He loved me. That was the thing that got us through all those early bumps and the awkward age difference. The moment I hopped into the passenger seat in his car, Tom Wells fell in love with me and knew I was the right girl for him forever. And if that meant he had to wait a little while for us to sleep together, he'd wait. He was in it for the long haul.

And so was I, despite my mother's frequently voiced predictions that I would lose interest in Tom as I got older and more sophisticated. I finally had someone in my life who was always there for me, who could take me away from the insane asylum I called home, who told me I was smart and beautiful, who truly *believed* I was smart and beautiful, not just some disappointing post-Hopkins letdown. He was kind, adoring, handsome, loyal, constant, a safe haven whenever I needed it, a home that I could curl up on.

Most girls don't find their Prince Charming when they're only fifteen. I guess what I lack in brilliance, I make up for in luck.

6.

When I finish telling Cathy the story, she says, "That's in-credible." She's scarfed down two entire plates of grilled cheeses: six small sandwiches altogether. I guess it's a nice break from those ramen noodles. "Were your parents okay with the age difference?"

"They didn't love it, but they're not the kind of parents to tell me I couldn't see him or anything. I do remember my father working the words *statutory rape* into a conversation with Tom years ago as a joke, which gives you some insight into his sense of humor. But they let me do what I wanted."

"I don't know why it surprises me so much: my parents were like eighteen when they got married. But here on the East Coast it feels different—people are just so much older when they settle down. You two live together, right?"

"Yeah, ever since I graduated. But even before then, I used to spend all my weekends with him. His first apartment was kind of gross, but after I graduated, we got a nicer place. I mean, legally it's *his* place, but we picked it out together."

Cathy shakes her head. Wisps of reddish hair fly around her forehead. She cut it recently, and it's a little short for someone her height, makes her head look too small for her body. She has beautiful eyes, though, big, green, and thoughtful. "The lon-gest relationship *I've* had was with my college boyfriend, and that didn't even last two years." She munches on a crust of grilled cheese. "I haven't had a date in ages. I just don't meet anyone new."

"I've only ever had one boyfriend, though. I've never even dated anyone else."

"Have you wanted to?"

"Not really. Dating seems so awkward to me—having to make conversation with a stranger, trying to figure out what you have in common—" I interrupt myself, leaning forward abruptly. "You know what's really weird?"

"What?"

"My *mother* is dating now."

"Your mother? Wait, what do you mean? I thought she was still married to your father."

"She is technically. But they're getting divorced and he's moved out." Mentioning my dad's apartment makes me think of Jacob—and all of a sudden I have a brilliant idea.

I stop in the middle of a sentence and think for a moment.

Yeah, it's brilliant.

"You okay?" Cathy says.

"I'm great. Just wondering... How would you feel about being fixed up with a guy?"

"Depends on the fixer-upper. If it's my grandmother, I would run in the opposite direction. But if it's you... Do you have someone in mind?"

"Yeah, this great guy who works for my dad and—" I'm interrupted by the bartender who's come over with two more glasses of wine. "We didn't order these," I say.

The bartender nods down toward the other end of the bar. "They're from those two guys. They said to tell you that they've never seen two beautiful redheads out together before and the least they could do is buy you both a drink."

Cathy's mouth opens up wide in a combination of surprise

and amusement. "Where? Those guys? At the end?" She peeks. They're watching us. She quickly ducks her head, her pale skin reddening. "Tell them we say thank you."

The bartender nods and walks away. He's a real Bostonian, big and tough, with a raspy voice and a nails-on-chalkboard accent. We watch surreptitiously as he gives them the message, and then the guys smile right at us and move in our direction. "Oh god," Cathy says. "I think they're going to come over! Did you know they'd do that?"

I shake my head. I don't have any experience with flirting in bars since I've never been single. Cathy clearly hasn't had much, either. "Maybe by sending a message back through the bartender, you kind of invited them to come over?" I say.

"We can talk for a minute, right?" she whispers just before they reach us. "It would be rude not to?"

But then she goes all flushed and silent when they start chatting us up, so I'm forced to make all the small talk—yeah, it is funny we're both redheads, but we're not related; we're just friends, and they're pretty different shades anyway, and no, that wasn't what brought us together; actually we sort of work together at the community college, and what do they do?

They work at a big insurance company, running analyses and crunching numbers, which they cheerfully admit is boring, but hey, it's a steady job in this economy so they're not complaining, not a bit.

There's some talk about where we're all from originally, and the taller one expresses a lot of interest in the fact that Cathy's from the Midwest and kind of moves over to talk to her more about that, because even though he grew up in Stoughton, just thirty minutes away, he visited his relatives in Michigan a lot when he was growing up, so that makes him an honorary midwesterner, right?

The shorter guy inserts his body between me and Cathy,

smoothly turning the general conversation into two separate, private ones. He's reasonably cute, and while we chat about good neighborhood bars, I wonder what it would be like to go out with someone who isn't almost a foot taller than me. I've always liked Tom's size. When we hug, my head presses against his chest, and it feels safe and cozy there, but it does mean I have to put my head back to look him in the eyes, and during sex, we're not exactly face-to-face. It's a silly thing to complain about, and I'm not actually complaining. But that's the thing about only ever being with one guy: you wonder what it would be like if things were different, not because you *want* them to be different, but because you're a little curious.

For a while, I politely make conversation with Shorter Guy while Cathy blushes and stammers at Taller Guy (the girl's *got* to get out more), but after a few minutes of this, I'm done. I mean, I want to help Cathy out, and maybe she and T.G. have a future together, but this particular game's boring when you're not actually on the prowl. I lean sideways so I can signal to Cathy around S.G.'s torso.

"I really should head home soon," I tell her. "I'm sorry. But you should stay."

"Wait," Shorter Guy says. "You're leaving? Why? You have to go wash that red hair of yours or something?" He winks jovially.

"Yeah," I say, sliding off the stool. "That's exactly what I have to do."

"I better go, too," Cathy says, also standing up.

"Aw, come on," Taller Guy says to her. "Don't let her drag you out of here. Let me get you another drink."

Cathy looks vaguely terrified. She's a smart girl and a well-respected teacher at the school, and one day she'll probably be a high school principal, but right now she looks like a five-year-old who doesn't know where her mommy is. "I think I should go," she says nervously.

"At least give us your phone numbers," says T.G.

"You give us yours," I say, and I think that's when they know they've wasted their ten bucks on our drinks. Their voices are curt as they rattle off their phone numbers. I only pretend to enter them in my phone.

Once we're outside, Cathy says, "That was kind of fun, wasn't it? No one's ever sent me a drink before. But I don't go out to bars much."

"That could definitely be a contributing factor. You know, you could text that guy and see how he responds. If he seems nice, you could—"

But she's already shaking her head. "Too weird."

We say good night, and it isn't until I'm back in my car that I realize we never finished our conversation about fixing her up with Jacob. It still feels like a good idea to me. They're both graduate students. They're smart and academically inclined. Neither of them is originally from the East Coast. They're both mildly attractive in a nerdy way. Neither seems to go on many dates.

There is, admittedly, a less than ideal height difference—she'd probably tower over him—but I know couples like that and it's no big deal. It's kind of endearing actually. I do wish Cathy had a little more...spirit I guess is the best word—she's so self-effacing sometimes—but it's not like Jacob is Mr. Dynamism. He's funnier than she is and maybe a little quicker and more interesting to talk to...but overall, it's a good fit.

The only thing is, I feel funny telling Jacob I'm fixing him up with someone. He's never mentioned his love life to me or to anyone else in my hearing, so it feels weird to suddenly just say, "Here's the number of a girl I think you'd like." But it seems even more awkward to have Cathy cold-call him and say, "Hey, there! I'm a friend of Keats!"

I'm parking in our building's large, well-lit garage when the solution hits me: I'll have them both over for dinner and invite a couple of other people so that the fix-up will feel a little less obvious.

I like this idea and not just because it gets those two together. Making dinner sounds like fun. Tom and I don't entertain that often: it always feels easier to just go out with friends than to have them over. And neither of us is a particularly good cook. But I've always wanted to be the kind of person who throws casual dinner parties, and this is a good excuse for one.

I'm walking toward the elevator, thinking about what I'll serve my guests, when I hear someone calling my name. I turn. Tom waves at me as he pulls his car into the space next to mine. He joins me just as the elevator arrives. "Where were you?" he asks as we step inside. "I assumed you were home hours ago."

"I grabbed a bite to eat with one of the grad students from school—Cathy Miller."

He leans over and sniffs at my mouth. "You smell like alcohol."

"We had a couple of glasses of wine."

He frowns. "You're too small to drink that much and then drive."

"I'm fine. They were spread out. Hey, I just had a really fun thought."

"What's that?"

"I'm going to fix up Cathy and Jacob."

"Your father's Jacob?"

"Yeah."

"Why? Is Cathy short?"

I laugh as the elevator doors open and we head down the hallway to our apartment. "Not at all. She's kind of huge actually. Tall, I mean—she's thin. Well, pretty thin." I shake my head to get myself back on track. "It's just that they're really similar—their interests and all that. I was thinking we could invite them both over for dinner. And some other people, too, just to make it more fun. Maybe Lou and Izzy?" I reach the door first but wait for him to get out his key.

He unlocks it, then gestures for me to go inside first. He's gentlemanly that way. "Sounds like a lot of work. Why not just tell them to call each other?"

"They're both really shy. I don't think they'd ever do it."

He lets the door swing shut behind us. "Will we also have to help them have sex if they hit it off? I'm not sure I'm prepared to go that far. Although it could be interesting. . . ."

"Oh, oh!" I interrupt him as another idea comes to me. "We can do it this weekend and say it's for my birthday!"

"But you and I will still celebrate it tomorrow, right? I made a reservation."

"Of course. That'll be my real celebration. This will just be an excuse to invite them over. But it means they'll say yes, because you have to when it's for someone's birthday!"

"Does that mean I have to do whatever you say tomorrow?"

"Yeah." I move right up close to him. "You'll basically be my slave."

"Interesting." He grins down at me, but when I start to put my arms around him, he pulls back. "Oops, watch out for my arm."

"Why? What's wrong?"

"Nothing—I just pulled a muscle at work."

"Poor baby. Want me to rub it?" I reach up, but he holds me off.

"Nah. That sounds painful. I may try putting some ice on it later."

"Okay." I head over toward my computer. "I'm going to go send out an e-mail about dinner before I forget."

* * *

This is what I write in the e-mail, which I send to Jacob, Cathy, and Izzy:

> *I totally forgot about my birthday up until right now, so I know it's kind of late notice, but can you come over on Sunday for dinner and cake?*

I blind copy them all. I don't want either Cathy or Jacob wondering why they're on such a short list when we're not birthday dinner close.

Izzy e-mails me back immediately to say they're going to the Sox game that night and can't come. I'm bummed they can't make it. I can't think of anyone else to invite: Lou and Izzy are kind of our go-to friends for last-minute stuff.

"Would it be weird if it's just the four of us?" I ask Tom a little while later. He's watching TV in the bedroom. "You and me and Jacob and Cathy?"

"They left," he says, staring at the screen.

"Who?"

"The people who care about this conversation."

"Very funny."

"I get you with that every time," he gloats.

I stick my tongue out at him, but he doesn't notice.

I decide to hold off on a decision until Jacob and Cathy respond. Later that night, I get back a *Sounds great* from the former and a *Thanks for thinking of me! I'd love to. What can I bring?* from the latter.

I decide not to invite anyone else. The worst that could happen is that they'll sense they're being fixed up. They'll be fine with that if they like each other and maybe resent it if they don't.

But I think they will.

* * *

The next morning, Tom gets up early and runs out to Dunkin' Donuts to bring me back breakfast in bed. It's not much of a surprise since he always does that on my birthday, but it's a tradition I love.

He snuggles up to me in bed—carefully because he says his arm still hurts—and asks me if I'm happy, and I am, blissfully happy, lying there lazily popping little bits of crunchy-soft doughnut into my mouth in between sips of hot, milky coffee.

Mom calls me at work and tells me she remembers every detail of That Day twenty-five years ago, and assures me that even though I tore out of her too quickly for her to get an epidural so it was her most painful delivery, she forgave me the second she looked into my big blue eyes. "And saw that crazy red fluff on top of your head," she adds. "That was a shock. But a good one." She tells me the same thing pretty much every year.

Around noon I get a big vase of flowers delivered to my desk. They're ostensibly from Dad, although I suspect that Jacob was the one who actually ordered them, especially because the card says, "Happy birthday, Kesha. I love you. Dad." My father has never said the words "I love you" to me in his life. I picture Jacob dictating the note to the florist over the phone and it makes me laugh: he probably made sure he was out of Dad's hearing. And probably also spelled my name letter by letter in the vain hope that the florist might actually get it right.

No one gets my name right.

Hopkins e-mails me and Milton IM's me, both to say happy birthday.

I'm hoping to get there soon, Hopkins writes. *We'll celebrate your birthday and say good-bye to the house all at once.* Given how long it's taken her to actually make it to Boston, I figure we'll probably be able to squeeze a Fourth of July celebration into the mix. Maybe even Labor Day.

Milton's IM starts with:

—*Hey, happy bday and all that stuff.*

—*Tanks,* I write back.

—*What are u doing to celebrate?*

—*T's taking me out tonight.*

—*Cool. Have a good one. Bye.*

At least he remembered.

At four in the afternoon, I hear the first wobbly strains of "Happy Birthday to You." My boss Rochelle, chairman of the English department, enters holding a cake with seven lit candles, followed by whoever's in the office that afternoon. I ask Rochelle what the significance of the number seven is, and she says, "That's how many candles were left in the box. You need to buy more, sweetie." I'm touched she remembered my birthday: I'm in charge of every other celebration around here, so she had to make a real effort to organize all this.

When Rochelle finds out that Tom's taking me out to dinner that night, she insists that I leave early and go home and make myself pretty for him.

So by the time Tom comes home at six thirty, I've showered and pinned my hair up and am wearing a dress I've never worn before, very '50s looking with a tight bodice and a full skirt. When he walks in, I arrange myself on the sofa like some kind of odalisque, lying on my side with my arm stretched languorously along my torso and my back arched. "Just let me jump in the shower," he says, walking past me without noticing. "I'll be right out."

I'm slightly annoyed, but all is forgiven when he comes back out fifteen minutes later freshly showered and breathtakingly handsome in a tie and jacket. He gathers me up in his arms, tells me I look beautiful, and gives me a deep, long kiss. "I've been thinking about you all day," he says. "About this moment. When I have you all to myself for the rest of the night." I kiss him back and wonder if he'll be inspired to just carry me into the bedroom, but when he releases me, he checks his watch, says that our reservation is at eight and we'd better get going or we'll lose it.

He won't tell me where we're going, but I recognize the restaurant and squeal as we pull up in front: it's one that I've been wanting to go to forever and have clipped reviews and articles about. I hadn't even thought he was paying attention.

Inside we're led to a really nice corner table near a window, and Tom informs me proudly that when he made the reservation, he let them know that it was both my birthday and our anniversary and that tonight needed to be extra special.

"Let's take our time," he says. "No rushing through the meal, no talking about work, or complaining about our families. Let's just enjoy being here together."

We sit there grinning at each other happily, but it does occur to me to wonder what we'll talk about if we can't discuss work or families.

Food, as it turns out. The waiter brings our menus, and after Tom orders a bottle of wine, we spend some time discussing the various options and agree that I should get the lobster and he should get the steak, both of which are wildly expensive, but Tom says that it's our night to splurge.

He's in a funny mood, kind of overexcited, which is sweet but weird. He startles when the waiter shows up at his elbow to pour the wine, which Tom tastes and—to my embarrassment—proclaims "delightful." He gets nervous around waiters in fancy restaurants, tries too hard to impress them, and ends up sounding pretentious.

He gets up at some point "to use the restroom," but I know he's arranging some kind of birthday/anniversary surprise, and sure enough, after we've finished our entrees but before we've ordered any dessert, the waiter brings over a slice of chocolate cake with "Happy Birthday and Anniversary!" squeezed in around the edge of the plate in raspberry sauce letters.

"You like chocolate cake, right?" Tom says. "I picked it for you because you usually get something chocolatey. But if you'd rather have something else—"

"It's perfect. Share it with me."

"I will. But first I want to give you your presents."

"Yay!" I put down my fork and push the plate away.

He slips his hand inside his jacket and pulls a box out of the inside chest pocket. He hands it to me and watches eagerly as I open it.

There's a necklace inside. I scoop it up to examine it. An extremely large oval purple stone dangles from a thick gold chain. "That's so pretty," I say.

"Do you like it? My mom helped pick it out."

I'm not surprised. It looks like something his mom would pick out. She doesn't have bad taste—she's an attractive woman who dresses well—but she's over fifty and likes the kinds of things you'd expect a woman her age to like. Which aren't necessarily the kinds of things a twenty-five-year-old would like.

"If you're not crazy about it, we can exchange it for another color or something completely different," Tom says.

I once returned a gift he gave me. He had told me I could, but when he found out, he looked so hurt I resolved never to do it again. Not unless it was something so awful and so expensive it would be crazy not to. This necklace doesn't qualify as either, so I say firmly, "It's great. I love it. Tell your mom I say thanks."

His face lights up, and I'm glad I went with the pretend-you-like-it approach. It's a perfectly nice necklace, and I'll find times I can wear it—mostly to his parents' house, I'm guessing. Anyway, the point is he took the time to go shopping with his mom to find me a gift. I'm lucky I have a boyfriend who cares enough to do that, who doesn't just grab something at the drugstore or hand me a twenty and tell me I should go buy myself a nice present. He cares.

I put it back in the box, then reach for my fork.

"Hold on," Tom says. "That was just your birthday present. I still have to give you your anniversary present." He starts to slip his arms out of the jacket.

"Um, Tom?" I say as the jacket comes off. "If this present involves your going full monty, maybe it should wait until we get back to the apartment. Not that I don't love the idea—"

"No, that's your *third* present," he says with a laugh. The jacket's off, and he's unbuttoning his left sleeve at the wrist and rolling it up.

"Then why are you getting undressed?"

"Hold on. You'll see." He keeps rolling up his shirtsleeve.

"You got a flu shot? For me? Aw, honey!"

He shakes his head, preoccupied: he's rolled the fabric so tight it won't budge, and he swears and struggles with it and has to pull the shirtsleeve down again. He's more careful this time to keep the folds smooth, and he's able to pull it up almost to his shoulder. He extends his arm out to me, twisting it a little from the shoulder so I can see the exposed area above his elbow.

It's a little pink and a little inflamed, but even so, I can clearly make out the letters of my name written in dark black ink.

No, not written.

Tattooed.

Tom's had my name tattooed on his arm.

Keats

Like that.

* * *

And I had thought it was hard to pretend to be happy about the *necklace*.

He's waiting for my reaction, his excited eyes flickering up to mine and then back down to his arm like a little kid who's painted a picture on a wall and isn't sure whether his mom is going to praise him or punish him.

"Wow!" I say after I've opened and closed my mouth a couple of times without saying anything. "This is. Incredible. I can't. Believe it." I sound like I'm talking in Morse code. I clear my throat and get out an entire "When did you do it?"

"Yesterday." He beams. "Remember how I said my arm hurt? This was the real reason I didn't want you to touch it and why I came to bed after you and was wearing that long-sleeved shirt all night. I had the bandage on underneath. It really hurt. I had to take a painkiller to get to sleep."

I hadn't even noticed. I think I was asleep by the time he came to bed.

"I wasn't really having dinner with my dad," he adds. "That was all a setup so I could sneak out and do this. But Dad knew he was supposed to cover for me."

"Your parents knew you were getting a tattoo?" I'm surprised. The Wellses are fairly conservative people. Politically and every other way. It's one of the reasons I've avoided getting them together with my parents, who are as liberal as they come. Another reason is that my parents aren't at all interested in getting to know them.

Tom smiles sheepishly. "Not exactly. I only told them I

was getting you a surprise present and didn't want you to know."

"So they don't know you got a tattoo?"

"Not yet." He wiggles his arm a little. "But they won't mind. Dad got one when he was in the army, so he can't really have a problem with it. Anyway, forget about them—what do *you* think?"

His face is so hopeful, so excited, so eager for assurance that he's done something wonderful.

I feel sick.

I don't want my name tattooed on Tom's arm. He should have asked me first. It's *my* name. If he had, I would have told him not to do it. But he went ahead and did it without asking, and now it can't be undone.

"It's such a surprise," I say. The waiter comes by to fill our water glasses, and I see him look at Tom's arm and his eyebrows soar. He grins at me and briefly touches his hand to his heart as he moves away again. I guess he finds the gesture touching. Which probably means *I* should. I reach across the table and squeeze Tom's extended hand. "I can't believe you did that for me."

"Ten years, Keats," he says and finally lets go of his sleeve. It shifts down so it covers the tattoo, although the fabric is still all bunched up around his elbow. "I wanted to do something really special. I mean, once you make it an entire decade, you know it's forever. I had to do something to honor that."

Most of the girls I know have gotten tattoos. Izzy once told me she has one—"but it's private, just for Lou," she said coyly and never did say exactly where on her body it was or what it looked like. I've thought about getting one myself—maybe a little rose or snake on the back of my shoulder.

But I've never thought for a second about getting Tom's name tattooed on my body. Now, as he gazes at me hopefully,

I realize that he wants me to do what he did. He wants me to get his name engraved permanently on my skin. In my flesh. He's too nice to put me on the spot about it—and it's probably worth more to him if I come to it on my own anyway. But he wants me to. I can see it in his eyes.

I think of all the celebrities who've fallen in love and gotten tattoos and later tried to get them removed. WINO FOREVER and all that. I always thought they were idiots.

I still do.

But it's different for us, right? Tom and I—we really are forever. He's right: you make it ten years, and that's all the proof you need that you're a couple who'll never break up.

It would make him so happy if I showed him the kind of faith he's showed me. I'm not scared of the pain. I'm not worried about how it will look.

I just don't want Tom's name in permanent ink on my body.

And I don't want mine on his.

I take a really big sip of wine. "Did it hurt a lot?"

"Yeah. But I survived." You can tell he's proud of himself. He survived a painful ordeal. For me.

"You used someone reputable, right? And made sure everything was clean and sterilized?"

"No, I went to the sleaziest guy I could find and had him spit in the open wound. Come on, Keats, give me a little credit."

"Sorry."

He pulls the fabric up again and surveys his arm proudly. "I think I picked the best place to put it, don't you? On weekends, when I'm wearing a T-shirt, everyone will see it. But when I'm dressed for work, it's covered. Smart, right?"

"Very smart." I feel like I need to praise him more. "I like the font you chose."

"Oh, good. Me too." He lets go of his shirt and picks up a fork. As he digs into the cake, he says offhandedly, "So how do you think your family would react if you got a tattoo with my name on it?"

I give a short laugh. "You've met them, right?"

"Meaning?"

"My father has this whole speech about tattooing. You've never heard it? He equates it with branding cattle and docking dogs' ears. My mom just thinks it's low class. And Hopkins—" I stop. "Actually, I don't know what Hopkins would think about it."

"My sister already has one."

"Oh, yeah." I'd forgotten that. We don't hang out with Anna that much because she's kind of hard on Tom, just like she was the first day I met them both. She's fine with me, but for some reason, Tom seems to drive her crazy and she's always finding fault with him. But she does have a little tattoo above her wrist that says PEACE, which is ironic given her personality.

"Anyway," Tom says, pretending to be focused on the cake but surreptitiously sneaking a peek at me, "it's not like I expect you to do this too, or anything. It was just something that felt right for me."

"It was really, really sweet," I say.

"You like it?"

"No, I *love* it," I lie.

7.

We've already made three separate trips to the market on Sunday to grab things I didn't know we didn't have until I couldn't find them, when I realize fifteen minutes before the guests are due to arrive that I don't have any French bread for the artichoke dip, so I ask Tom to race out one more time.

He wonders out loud—with some justification—why we didn't just order in. "It's only Jacob and that girl, right? They'd probably be happy with anything we put in front of them. For graduate students, a free meal is a free meal."

Since I've spent the last three hours slaving away in the kitchen, and my feet hurt, and I'm sweaty, and I still have to shower, dry my hair, and get dressed before they come, I'm not in the mood to figure out what would have been a better plan than the one we're committed to. "It's my birthday dinner and I wanted to make a friggin' home-cooked meal. Do you really have a problem with that?"

He holds up his hands in surrender, tells me he'll get a baguette, and flees.

I spoon the thick artichoke mixture into a little pan and put it in the oven to get hot and bubbly (as per the directions on my laptop—all the recipes I'm using are online, and I have to keep tabbing back and forth between them) before I race to the bathroom and stand in the shower just long enough to wet my hair and condition it (with my curly hair, actual shampooing is like a once-a-week thing) and run a razor up my legs. I'm wrapped in a towel and combing my hair when the phone rings the special intercom ring that means someone's downstairs and needs to be let in.

I race to the phone, hit the buzzer, call down that we're on the eighth floor and to turn right out of the elevator, then race back across the apartment to our bedroom, where I throw on some underwear, a pair of jeans (because I said it would be casual), and a glittery tank top (because I want to look nice). I'm still trying to decide what shoes to wear when the apartment doorbell rings.

I run on bare feet across the living room, prop a smile on my face, fling the door open—and gasp audibly.

Jacob's standing there.

My dad's at his side.

* * *

I gape at them while they both wish me a happy birthday.

"I know we're a little early," Jacob says, apparently misinterpreting my stunned silence. "I thought it would take longer to get here than it did. No traffic."

He's holding my father by the elbow, and as they move into the apartment, I see why. My father's gait is unsteady. He lifts each foot tentatively and sets it down gingerly, like he's not sure it will land on something solid.

I come around to his other side. I don't actually hold his elbow, which I feel would embarrass us both, but I do keep my hand poised an inch or two below it. It's not particularly helpful, but it's there if he stumbles, which seems way too possible.

A shard of guilt slices into my heart at seeing him so slowed down. I should have called him this week. I should have invited him tonight in the first place. I should be paying more attention to how old he's getting.

"Where's Tom?" Jacob asks as we settle my father into one of the armchairs.

"Um…" I'm so thrown by my father's appearance at my doorstep and by his overall appearance that it takes me a moment to remember. "Tom? He ran to the store for something."

"You should have called us," Jacob says. "We could have stopped on the way."

"He'll be back in a sec. Do you mind if I go dry my hair really fast?"

My father waves his hand regally, dismissing me. "I was wondering if that was the new hair fashion," he says to Jacob jovially as I move away.

In the bathroom, I set the blow-dryer to the maximum heat and power, bend over at the waist, and shoot the hot air at my roots. My hair will end up frizzy, but since my guests are here, I don't have time to use the diffuser.

As I stand back up and flip my hair over my shoulders, I try to remember what I wrote in my original e-mail to Jacob that might have made him think the invitation included my father. Nothing. I had said almost nothing in my e-mail. Maybe that was my mistake.

Tom finds me in the bathroom just as I'm dabbing some stain onto my cheeks and lips. "You didn't tell me you were inviting your father" is how he greets me as he enters, still holding the bag with the baguette poking out of the top.

"I didn't invite him! I invited Jacob, and I guess he just assumed I meant he should come with Dad."

Tom grins. "Maybe Cathy will fall in love with your dad. I mean, he's available now, right? We're giving her two bachelors for the price of one. She should be thrilled."

"Very funny. This is going to be so weird. The four of us and...Dad."

"Yup," he says cheerfully. "Happy birthday, babe."

* * *

The plus side is that Cathy really *is* thrilled to meet my father.

"I read your book in college," she tells him. "It was amazing."

I watch Dad with just a touch of anxiety. He could go either way with a statement like that: raise his eyebrows derisively and say something cutting or accept it as a compliment. To my relief, he chooses to be gracious and thanks her in a pleasantly condescending way before turning to me and asking when my mother will be arriving.

"She's not." I pretend not to notice the disappointment that crosses his face. "This is the party! Who wants a glass of wine?"

While Tom takes care of the drink orders, I try to get a conversation going between Jacob and Cathy about their studies, but my father interrupts almost immediately to ask why my mother isn't there. "Did she have other plans?"

"No. I mean, I don't know. I didn't invite her, Dad."

"Keats didn't actually invite you, either," Tom says, coming in with the wine bottle and glasses. "I mean, we're happy as always to see you, Larry, but it's totally a surprise." He jerks his chin in Jacob's direction. "We didn't realize Jacob would be bringing a date." And he laughs.

I picture myself bashing the wine bottle on the edge of the coffee table and twisting its jagged edge into Tom's eye. I have to remind myself that he's the man of my dreams and I love him a lot because right now I. Just. Want. To. Kill. Him.

Jacob is staring at Tom, a half-eaten oval of French bread halted halfway to his mouth. "I thought..." He slowly turns his head to look at me. "I just assumed you meant both of us. Since it was your birthday."

"I did! I mean, maybe I didn't at first, but this is great." I awkwardly pat my father's knee. "I'm so glad you're here, Dad. I feel honored." I force a smile as I look around our little group. "This is perfect. The five of us here. I'm so happy." Could I sound any more idiotic?

Tom's pouring wine, unconcerned, oblivious to how he just made things much more uncomfortable for everyone there— except him, apparently. He hands each of us a glass and holds his own up, saluting me. "To Keats. Happy birthday to the love of my life."

I wonder if there's anything more annoying than being called something like that by a guy whose death you're still fantasizing about. "Thanks," I say through clenched teeth as everyone raises a glass to me and we all drink, some of us more desperately than others.

I try again to get Cathy and Jacob to talk directly to each other by doing the hostessy prompting thing—"So, would you guys say that teaching freshmen is easier than seniors or vice versa?"—and they both respond, but the conversation is awkward and stilted, and eventually my dad steps in. He's not a good listener. If he has to spend time away from his computer and in company, he wants to be the one everyone's listening to. So he starts talking.

Once he gets going, he won't stop unless someone or something makes him, and after half an hour of Dad's explaining to us that the problems in the Middle East are based more on ancient and conflicting ideas of government than on the more obvious schisms of religion and ethnicity, Tom starts noticeably fidgeting and glancing at the TV, which I insisted we keep off for the dinner party. He's missing a baseball game—the one Lou and Izzy are at. I know he'd much rather have gone with them, but he hasn't complained about it since this is for my birthday.

It occurs to me that the sooner I get dinner on the table, the sooner this mistake of an evening will come to an end, so I excuse myself and head toward the kitchen.

When I get there, I realize that Jacob has followed me in.

"Can I help?"

"You know how to toss a salad?"

"Gee," he says, "I'm not sure. Maybe you could draw a diagram for me?"

I'm not in the mood to joke around. "The dressing's in that bowl. Just whisk it a little more before pouring it on, will you?" I bend down to take the lasagna out of the oven where it's been staying warm for the last half hour. I put it on top of the stove and peel back the tinfoil. The cheese is bubbling and it looks pretty good. *At least I didn't ruin the food*, I think.

Jacob says in a low voice, "I'm sorry I misinterpreted your invitation, Keats. I guess I just assumed that since it was your birthday party, you wanted your dad here."

"It's no big deal." I go to the refrigerator to get out the bowl of Parmesan cheese I grated by hand earlier that day out of some crazy Suzy Homemaker belief that I shouldn't buy it pre-grated. Ninety percent of the time I eat takeout Chinese food and pizza for dinner, so why I insisted that everything be homemade and top quality tonight is beyond me. It made sense earlier. But not now, not when I'm thinking I just want these people out of my house. Including Tom. Especially Tom.

Why did he have to point out Jacob's mistake? He's supposed to be the host, for god's sake, and make people feel welcome in our home, not make them feel bad about a minor misunderstanding. Especially not when it was going to make an already awkward evening even more awkward.

"I'm actually really happy to have my dad here," I say. "The only reason I didn't invite him in the first place is because I know he doesn't like to go out much."

"He really wanted to come tonight," Jacob says. He's poured the dressing on the salad and now he's tossing it carefully, gingerly. When Tom tosses a salad, lettuce flies everywhere, and if I complain, he grins and says, "I can't control my own strength," but Jacob just gently scoops and tumbles the leaves with the servers. "He's been kind of—" He searches for the right word. "Kind of nostalgic, I guess. Wistful. I think he misses being with his family."

"He didn't spend any more time with me when he was still in the house."

"I know. It's not logical. But something about moving out has shaken him up."

"Then I'm especially glad you brought him tonight." I glance up in time to see the relief on Jacob's face, so maybe I've fixed the damage Tom has done.

"So how do you know Cathy?" he asks. "I've never heard you mention her."

"Through work. She's so nice, I wanted us to become better friends." *Man, I'm smooth. A born matchmaker.*

"Cool. Salad's all tossed. What else can I do for you?"

"Carry it into the dining room, by which I mean the table in the living room."

"Got it." He picks the salad up. As he moves past me, he leans his head in toward mine and whispers, "If you'd just told me it was a setup in the first place, Keats, I'd have known not to bring your father."

I whisper back, "But would you have come?"

"Yeah," he says, a little sadly. "I can use all the help I can get." He leaves the kitchen.

* * *

"So," Tom says when all our guests have gone, "think they hit it off?"

I'm looking around the kitchen. How did five people make so many dishes? I wish I hadn't used separate plates for the salad. "They barely said two words to each other."

"That's because your father never stopped talking."

He has a point. Dad orated at dinner. That's the only way to put it. If people were bored, he was oblivious to it, although both Cathy and Jacob looked convincingly interested in whatever he was saying. Not Tom, though. He's never found my father particularly fascinating—and I kind of love him for that because most of the time I don't, either.

It worried me that my father said he was tired and needed to get home when it was still pretty early. We had just finished eating the lasagna, so I rushed out the flourless chocolate cake—it had taken me twenty minutes that afternoon to whip and fold in the egg whites—and everyone sang a quick and tuneless "Happy Birthday to You."

Dad handed me an envelope with an iTunes gift card inside. I thanked him but the gift had to be Jacob's idea. No way Dad even knows what iTunes is.

Cathy gave me a small knit beanie in dark green. There was no tag on it, so I asked her if she had knit it herself, and she said with horror, "God, no! Why? Does it look homemade?" I assured her it was great and put it on. It was itchy, but I was worried it would hurt her feelings if I took the beanie off, so I left it on, reaching up surreptitiously to scratch underneath it when she wasn't looking.

Jacob and Dad left as soon as they'd eaten their cake, but Cathy stayed for a while longer. Too long really. It wasn't late, it was just that both Tom and I were ready for the evening to be over. But she had finally found her voice (now that the guy I wanted her to make an impression on was gone) and chatted away happily about the class she was student teaching and how at least five of the kids didn't speak any English and how she had invented some sign language to communicate with them. And by "invented," she seemed to mean that she used the same universal gestures for writing and walking and listening that anyone would use.

Tom and I did our best to smile and look interested, and when she finally sighed and said, "This was so lovely, but I probably should go grade papers," we did our best not to look *too* relieved.

I pulled the beanie off and tossed it on the table the second Tom closed the door behind her.

"So what do you think I should do now?" I ask Tom as we stand there in the kitchen surveying the damage. I feel discouraged.

"Let's get a load of dishes going and leave the rest for tomorrow."

"No, I mean about Jacob and Cathy. Do I wait to see if one of them asks me for the other's phone number? Or should I try to talk to them, push them a little bit?"

"Keats," he says wearily, "you put them in the same room for an entire evening. If they want to see each other again, that's up to them. Your work is done."

"I know, but they're both so clueless."

"They're adults. They can figure it out. Anyway, why do you care so much?"

"I don't. But they both seem kind of lonely."

"Jacob chooses to spend all his free time with an old man. You can't do that and expect to have a social life."

"But it's my father he's spending time with. If he didn't, I might have to. So that means I owe him some help."

"Which is what you gave him tonight. You're done." He puts his arms around me. "If you really want to take pity on someone, I could use that massage you offered me a few nights ago."

"But it's my birthday. *I* should get the massage."

"It's not your birthday. That was four days ago."

"It's my birthday dinner night." He looks skeptical. "Fine. We'll compromise. You give me a massage."

"How is that a compromise?"

"Yeah, about that...I'll figure out an answer while you're rubbing my back."

"You always win," he says amiably.

"When I win, you win," I say, coaxing him along toward the bedroom, abandoning the dishes until the morning.

"How do you figure?"

"Shh," I say and throw myself facedown on the bed. "Don't talk. Rub."

8.

When I check my e-mail the next morning, I have one from Milton. He's CC'ed Hopkins on it. It's short.

Mom was in bed all day. Still there.

That's all, but that's all he needs to say.

I e-mail them both back. *Should we do anything?*

A minute later, Hopkins's response comes: *I'll take care of it. I'll call her shrink and see if he thinks we should play around with her meds. I think we can cut this one off quickly.*

It's a relief to leave it in Hopkins's hands, but I can't shake the worried, sick feeling—too many childhood memories of anxious days spent waiting for Mom to emerge and be herself again.

Tom comes into the living room where I'm still staring unhappily at the computer and says, "Everything all right?"

"Yeah, fine," I say and get up and go into the bathroom to get ready for work. What's the point of talking about it? His mother goes to a resort in Arizona once a year when she feels like she needs a break. It's not that he wouldn't understand or be sympathetic, it's just that I'm sick of being the one with the messed-up family. Anyway, maybe Hopkins is right and this one won't be bad. She should know, right?

* * *

Sure enough, Milton e-mails us late on Tuesday afternoon. *She's up. Quiet. But up.*

And when Mom calls me at work two days after that, she sounds like herself. Her speech is back to its normal rhythm— well, maybe just a little slower than usual—as she informs me that she found a box filled with some old letters of mine. "Can I toss them?"

"I don't know. I'm not sure what they are."

"You want me to look through them while I've got you on the phone?"

"No, don't." I was a counselor in training for a couple of the years Tom and I were dating, and I didn't have e-mail or phone privileges, so he wrote me long letters. I don't know if those letters are in there, and I don't even remember if there was anything that racy in them—I think he mostly talked about his job working for his dad that summer and what movies he'd seen— but they're private, and I don't want my mother reading them. "I'll go through them next time I'm home."

"I can't just leave everything lying around for you all to go through at some unspecified later date," she says irritably. "I'm trying to get this house in showing condition and I can't sit around waiting for you and Hopkins to take time out of your busy lives to help out for once."

Normally I'd snap back, but given her current fragility, I keep my temper. "I'm sorry you're overwhelmed, Mom, and I know Hopkins hasn't made it home yet, but I really have been doing my best to help." It's frustrating because I *know* her. She's not actually working that hard. She's seeing a big job in front of her and panicking about it rather than just working through it. That's the reason our house is and always has been a mess: instead of attacking the problem slowly and steadily, she looks around, flips out at how much there is to do, flings her hands up, and complains to anyone who'll listen that it's an impossible task. That panic may even have triggered this last depressive episode. "I'll come pick up the box, if that's what you want."

"That would be— Oh, wait, I just remembered. I'm going out to dinner near your place tomorrow night. I could drop it off. And maybe a few other things, too."

"Why do I have a feeling I'm about to have something dumped on me that no one else wants?" I say. "Like the dining room table? Or Grandma's old dresser? Or Milton?"

"Now that you mention it…" At the sound of her laugh, I release the breath I've been holding through this whole con- versation—if she can laugh, she's okay. "He's very easy to take care of, just feed and water him once a week."

"Nice try."

"So did you have a good time on Sunday?"

I'm confused by the abrupt change of topic. "On Sunday?"

"Your birthday dinner."

Shit. Who told her about that? "It wasn't really my birthday dinner. It was just dinner."

"Your father said it was a birthday celebration. I think it's great that you invited him. He needs to get out more. I just wanted to know how it was, that's all."

And to let me know that you know you were excluded, that I in- vited Dad and not you. "It was totally last minute," I say hastily. "And my real birthday celebration was with Tom, on my actual birthday."

"Did he get you anything exciting?"

He carved my name into his flesh. Does that count? "A neck- lace," I say.

* * *

When she drops off the box at our house, she's not alone. I answer our door and she's standing next to some guy I've never seen before, a guy with thick gray hair and a hand-somely craggy face. They're both holding boxes. "Hi," Mom says brightly. "Keats, meet Michael Goodman. Michael, meet Keats."

Michael raises his box slightly. "I'd shake hands, but..."

"Come in," I say, "and you can put it down."

He does—they both do—and then we shake.

Tom enters from the bedroom, where he was watching TV. "Oh, look who's here," he says with a questioning glance at me. I had forgotten to tell him Mom was dropping by, and he's wearing sagging sweats and a stained, worn-out T-shirt.

Michael introduces himself, and it's their turn to shake hands.

"So where are you two kids off to this evening?" I ask.

"Kurosawa retrospective in Coolidge Corner," Michael says.

"A little *Throne of Blood* action?"

"*Rashomon* actually, but I'm impressed. Most kids your age don't know Kurosawa."

"I learn just enough about stuff like this to make it sound like I'm more sophisticated than I actually am."

"Have you ever seen a Kurosawa movie?"

"A couple, but only because she made me." I nod in Mom's direction.

"You?" Michael asks Tom, who shakes his head. "What kind of movies do you like?"

"I'm an action junkie," Tom says. "James Bond, Jason Bourne—that kind of thing."

"Kurosawa's a great action director," Michael says seriously. "*Seven Samurai* was the inspiration for a lot of Westerns that came after it."

"Yeah?" Tom says. "Cool. I didn't know that."

I can't stand the expression on my mother's face—the po-litely bland mask that suggests she can't let her actual feelings show when Tom's talking—so I say abruptly, "You guys should probably get going if you're having dinner before the movie."

"Right," Michael says, glancing at his watch.

I wave my finger at him. "Just make sure you get her home by ten."

He raises his eyebrows. "That might be difficult. The movie starts at nine."

"I don't know why I bother to set a curfew," I say with a sigh.

He grins. "Moms always push back when you try to set rules, don't they?"

Okay, I'm kind of liking this guy. He's a lot more engaging than Paul. Better looking, too. I try to telegraph my approval to Mom, but she's tugging him toward the door. "Let's go," she says. "Uh, Tom? There's one more box in the car...."

"No problem." Tom goes down with them, and when he returns with the box, I say, "What did you think?"

"About what?"

"Mom's date."

"That was a date?"

"Of course. What else?"

"I don't know." He heads toward the bedroom. "I hadn't really thought about it much. I guess I just assumed he was a friend or something." He disappears into the bedroom.

Sometimes I wish I lived with another girl.

* * *

A couple of hours later, I'm reading the *New Yorker* on our bed, trying to block out the loud noise of the ESPN highlights show that Tom's watching, when the phone rings. Tom picks up the handset, glances at it, says, "Your dad," and tosses it to me.

Only it's not Dad. "Keats? It's Jacob. I wanted you to know there's an ambulance on its way in case you wanted to meet us at the hospital. I can't reach your mother and—"

"Wait," I say. "What's going on? Is Dad okay?"

Tom looks up, concerned. "What?" he whispers. "What's happening?"

I put my hand up to keep him quiet so I can hear Jacob.

"I think it's his heart," he says. "I have to go. Can you meet us at St. Christopher's?"

I'm already on my feet.

* * *

Tom insists on going with me. He drops me off in front of the hospital and goes to park. I race into the emergency room and tell the nurse who I'm looking for. She lets me through, into a web of hallways and examining rooms in the back, where I immediately spot Jacob pacing in front of a closed door. I run over and we hug briefly.

"They're examining him," he says. "I don't know anything yet except that it's his heart. The EMTs gave him oxygen and some kind of blood thinner, I think."

"What happened? Did he pass out? Was he in a lot of pain?"

"I don't know all that much. I wasn't around. I'd been teaching all afternoon and called him just to check in, and he sounded awful, so I asked him if he'd eaten anything all day and he said no, so I picked up some food, and when I got there, he was on the floor, but conscious. He couldn't get up, said it felt like something huge was pressing down on his chest, and he wasn't strong enough to get to the phone."

"If you hadn't gone over—"

"I wish I hadn't stopped to get food."

"Yeah," I said. "If he dies, it'll be all your fault."

He manages a bleak smile. "Thanks, Keats. You really know how to cheer a guy up."

I touch his arm. "You're the only one who's been checking up on him. I feel awful. Grateful to you, but awful. Did they say how serious it was?"

"The EMTs seemed pretty calm, for what that's worth."

"So you came in the ambulance with him?"

"I didn't want him to be alone. I left a voice mail for your mom by the way."

"She's at a movie—her phone's probably turned off." I'll have to track her down somehow. I need her here with me. "Can I go in and see him?"

"I don't know. They shoved me out. But I'm not a relative."

"I'll go ask a nurse. If you see Tom before I do, tell him to wait here with you."

He nods and sags against the wall, his hands in his pockets, his head bowed.

* * *

The nurse is useless, just says I should sit tight and wait for the doctor.

I feel pretty stupid for having left to go talk to her when I come back to find the doctor already deep in conversation with Jacob and Tom. I rush over in time to catch the word *stable*.

"Is he going to be okay?" I ask.

"This is his daughter," Tom tells the doctor.

The doctor shakes my hand. "Aman Malik."

I mutter something about how it's nice to meet him even though it's an absurd thing to say under the circumstances. "How is he?"

"We need to insert a stent as soon as possible. The meds we've given him aren't doing the trick."

Everyone's looking at me. I realize I'm supposed to say something. "Yeah?" is my brilliant response. God, I wish my mother were here.

Dr. Malik tries to explain. I hear, "The heart, as you know, is a muscle" and then after that, he sounds pretty much like the adults in a Charlie Brown cartoon. He's waaa-waaa-waaaing, but the words don't coalesce into anything meaningful. Jacob and Tom are nodding like they understand what he's saying, so the problem's clearly in my head, not with the doctor.

I feel more and more desperate. When he pauses and looks at me, I can think of only one thing to say, which is *I want my mommy*, only I try to make it sound more grown-up than that. "I'd like to have my mother in on the decision making."

"Will she be here soon?"

"I think so."

"We'll get started with the paperwork. It always takes longer than you think. Tell the nurses to page me once your mother gets here." He starts to move away.

"Wait," I say. "Can I see him?"

"Of course." He seems vaguely surprised I'm asking. "He's right in there." He nods toward the door.

I start to go, stop, look at Jacob. "Come with me." I can't go in alone. I'm scared of what Dad might look like. Jacob nods, and we move toward the door together. "Tom, will you try to get hold of my mother? Call the theater if you have to."

"Which theater?"

"Coolidge Corner." He was standing right there when Michael told us that's where they were going. "Don't you remember? The Kurosawa movie?"

"Oh, yeah. Right." He pulls out his phone and Jacob and I go into the exam room.

My dad's lying on the bed with his eyes closed, covered by a thin blanket, his hair rumpled, his face pale and sunken.

There's an oxygen line in his nose and an IV in his arm. "Hey," I say.

At the sound of my voice, his eyes flicker open. He manages a smile. "How can it not be indigestion?" he says in a voice that's not much louder than a whisper. He has to take a breath between every couple of words. "It's always indigestion. You think you're having a heart attack, and you go to the emergency room, and they tell you it's just indigestion and to go home and relax. I've been waiting for them to say that."

"Sounds like you're going to be waiting awhile longer." He seems too fragile to kiss, so I just pat his arm. He nods briefly, but his eyes close again like he doesn't have the energy to keep them open.

"It's a good thing Jacob came by the apartment," he murmurs.

"I just wish they'd made that sandwich faster," Jacob says. "The guy at the counter was taking forever. If I'd known—"

"You'd have skipped the mayo?" I say.

"Yeah. Stupid mayo."

"I told you I wasn't hungry," Dad whispers. "Why does no one ever listen to me?"

"You might have mentioned that you were having a heart attack," I say. "He would have listened to *that*."

"It must have slipped my mind," my father gasps out.

* * *

Tom appears at the door a few minutes later and beckons to me. When I join him in the hallway, he tells me proudly that it was hard work, but he finally got a message to my mother and now she's on the phone. He hands me his cell so I can talk to her.

"I'm on my way," she says. "Sorry you had trouble reaching me. How's he doing?"

"You mean aside from the near-fatal heart attack?"

She ignores that. "Have you called Hopkins yet?"

"No."

"That should have been the first call you made. She's the only one of us who knows anything."

"She's not a cardiologist."

"She probably remembers more from her cardiology rotation than most cardiologists ever know. I'd like her to talk directly to the doctors there. Actually, what I'd really like is for her to come right away, but I don't know how likely that is."

How ironic. All this time I've been wanting my mommy, and she just wants my big sister.

Mom is going on. "I'm also going to call our internist and see if he can meet me at the hospital." Maybe she notices I'm being quiet. "Don't worry, Keats. People have heart attacks and recover all the time. Your father will be fine. Maybe he'll even start taking better care of himself—sometimes a scare like this is the best wake-up call."

Her calm tone irritates me. "We're lucky Jacob stopped by when he did," I say. "Otherwise, we'd never have even known Dad was lying there unconscious."

"Yes, we owe Jacob a lot," she says evenly. "And I promise you that I'll still be able to sleep at night despite any attempt on your part to make me feel guilty."

"Wow," I say. "Really?"

She sighs. "Just call Hopkins for me, will you?"

I hang up, hand Tom his phone, then pull out mine and start dialing.

"Who you calling now?" Tom asks.

"My sister. Mom wants her to talk to the doctor because apparently she's the only person in our family who knows anything about anything."

The call goes directly to Hopkins's voice mail.

I leave a terse message explaining the situation and telling her to call either me or Mom. I don't have to worry about scaring her. Hopkins doesn't get scared by stuff like this.

My mother arrives twenty minutes later. I'm relieved to see her but slightly weirded out that Michael Goodman is accompanying her.

"This is a fun date," I say to her when he excuses himself to go to the men's room.

"Don't start," she says. "He had to drive me here, and he was nice enough to say he'd come in and see if there was anything he could do to help."

"He doesn't find the whole thing a little awkward? *You* don't?"

"We're grown-ups, Keats. He understands the situation."

"Which is what exactly?"

"That I needed to come to the hospital immediately because my ex-husband was having a heart attack. Oh, thank god, you're here." That last isn't addressed to me, it's to a middle-aged man who, despite his off-hours slacks and patterned sweater, still channels *doctor* with his distinguished white hair and little black bag. They greet each other warmly, and then she introduces him to me as Dad's internist Dr. Hanson.

He informs us that he's already spoken to Dr. Malik and feels confident that he's making all the right decisions. He and Mom go to see Dad together, and Tom asks me if we can leave now that my mother's here.

"I feel better staying. But you go ahead."

He hugs me tightly, kisses me, says, "He'll be okay. Everything's going to be fine."

"I know," I say, and he heads toward the exit.

I'm getting a little paper cone cup of water at the bubbler when Michael reappears.

"She went in to see my dad," I tell him. "I'm sure she'll be out soon."

"It's fine," he says. "No rush."

I wonder how long he plans to hang around. "Did you get to see much of the movie?" I ask as we sit on a bench in the hall outside Dad's room. I feel like I'm at a cocktail party and have to make polite conversation with a stranger. A really bad, stressful cocktail party.

"Enough," he says. "Especially since I've seen it several times before." He downshifts suddenly. "I'm really sorry about your father, Keats."

"Thanks. No one seems too worried."

"I'm sure he'll be fine. But it's never fun to spend time in a hospital—as a patient or a visitor."

Before I can respond, Jacob emerges from Dad's room and joins us. "You going to go back in there, Keats? They're discussing the operation."

"What's the point? I'm no Hopkins."

"They're not checking degrees at the door."

I shrug and don't move.

Mom comes out of the room a moment later, her cell phone to her ear. I can't hear what she's saying, but she's listening intently, and I'm guessing it's Hopkins on the other end. Eventually she ends the call and comes over to us. "She's going to talk to Malik now, thank goodness. Michael, you don't have to wait around."

"Are you sure?" Michael stands up. "If I can help in any way..."

"You've been a huge help already," she says. "Come on, I'll walk you out."

Michael shakes my hand and says good-bye to Jacob, and then he and Mom walk down the hallway, so close that their arms brush against each other. Neither of them moves any farther apart.

"Wow," I say, watching as they turn the corner. "There's

nothing like your husband's having a heart attack to make you feel all young and flirty again."

Jacob just sighs, which annoys me.

"I can't believe her," I say. "It's sick."

"She was on a date, Keats. And she's divorcing your dad. Some women wouldn't have shown up at all under those circumstances."

"Maybe that would have been better than her showing up and being all over that guy."

"She wasn't exactly all over him," Jacob says. "Come on, give her a break." Then more gently, "I know this is all really hard on you—"

"Oh, just be quiet," I snap, so he stops talking, and we sit there in silence.

After Mom rejoins us, Dr. Hanson invites her and me into the room, where he informs us that he's already talked to Hopkins and she's in favor of the stent procedure, so of course, Mom immediately signs the necessary paperwork.

Dad mostly seems to be listening to the conversation, but sometimes he closes his eyes, maybe dozing, maybe not, it's hard to tell. When they're open, his gaze follows Mom around the room. She's kind to him, pats his hand, asks the doctor lots of concerned questions about the operation and his prognosis, but she's very calm and seems more like a fond sister than a wife of thirty years.

Dad's eyes are hungry for her under his crazy eyebrows, devouring her features whenever he can keep them open. When she touches his arm, his hand reaches for hers, but he's too weak to hold on for more than a moment or two, and when his grasp slips, she moves her hand away.

After the consultation, there's a bustle of activity as the nurses come in to prep my dad for the surgery. Dr. Hanson wishes us well, promises to follow up with the attending doctor, claps Dad on the shoulder without actually making any eye contact with him, and leaves.

Mom and I go sit with Jacob again. I wait for her to tell him he should go home, but she doesn't. He offers to find some coffee for us. She says that would be lovely and orders me to go with him.

"A walk will do you good," she says. "There's nothing more enervating than sitting around waiting for news. And it's going to be a long wait now."

Jacob spots a nurse and asks her where we can get coffee. "There's a machine in the main hospital lobby, but the coffee in it is pretty disgusting," she says. "The cafeteria's closed for the night, but if you're willing to leave the building, there's a McDonald's about two blocks away that's open until midnight."

"Let's do that," Jacob says to me. "I could use one of their hot fudge sundaes. Or three. I never ate dinner."

"Really?" I say. "Why's that? Something come up?"

As we walk away from the hospital, I say, "Do you think Mom's right, that he'll be fine?"

"I do," Jacob says. "I think it will be a tough few weeks, and then he'll be back to normal."

"*Normal,* meaning old and frail." I remember how Dad had needed Jacob's support to walk into my apartment the other night. His heart was probably already failing then, and we just didn't know it.

"They can't make him younger," Jacob says. "But maybe they can make him healthier."

"Or turn him into a cyborg."

"That would be good. Especially if they gave him X-ray vision."

"It would be wasted on Dad. It would never even occur to him to look under girls' clothes."

"Which is, of course, the whole point of X-ray vision."

We go into the restaurant and order a couple of sundaes and three coffees.

"Let's sit down for a few minutes," I say. "The sundaes will melt if we don't eat them right away. Mom can wait for her coffee."

"I'm not convinced this stuff can melt," he says, eyeing the plastic container dubiously. But we sit down at a table anyway and dig in.

It doesn't seem like a night for light conversation, so at first we're silent while we eat, and then I say, "You've never told me exactly what happened with your parents, Jacob—how they died. Is it rude of me to ask? Do you hate talking about it?"

"I don't mind." He plunges his spoon in and out of his sundae, gazing down at the holes he's creating. "Basically they—we—just had really bad luck. Mom had some kind of disease when she was a kid—I don't even know exactly what it was, and she always said it might not have been correctly diagnosed in the first place. Anyway, she got better, that wasn't the problem, but when she was still sick, the doctors gave her a million X-rays, and I guess it was a podunk little hospital in the middle of nowhere, and they weren't particularly good at giving X-rays. So she died of leukemia when I was like five. Then when I was twelve, my dad had this pain in his stomach and he ignored it for too long—just kept popping painkillers; he was like that, always Mr. Stoic—and his appendix burst, which would have been bad but not fatal, except he picked up a staph infection in the operating room, which got into his blood and killed him." He smiles bleakly. "Like I said, really bad luck."

"God, Jacob, that's awful. Who took care of you after your father died?"

"I moved in with my mother's brother's family. It wasn't a happy experience. I was"—he gestures at himself—"like this.

Unathletic, small, nerdy...a little intellectual kid from New Jersey, and suddenly I'm living with these huge, sports-crazy Texans. Football was a religion to them. They're not mean or anything—they meant well, and my aunt would have done anything to make me feel at home—but I wasn't like them and we all knew it. And the school situation was really tough."

"I'm sorry." I push away my sundae. I feel weighed down by the sadness of the world, by an old man with a tube in his nose and a teenage boy, smart and sensitive, but stranded all alone in the world. "I can't believe you can even bear to walk into a hospital, given your history."

"I don't love it. This is my first time in years."

"Trust my family to drag you back down into something unpleasant."

Jacob looks up at me. There's a tiny smear of hot fudge at the corner of his mouth. "Your family? Your family is what *saved* me. Your family is—"

"Crazy?"

"Yeah," he says. "In the best ways. Seriously, Keats, screw the hospital—I'd crawl to hell and back for your parents." He wipes at his mouth with a napkin, which is a big relief. I was ready to spring at him and get that fudge sauce off myself. He balls it up and drops it in the sundae dish. "Come on. Let's bring your mother her coffee. And Keats—"

I'm already standing up and slinging my bag over my shoulder. I stop and say, "What?"

"Go easy on her, okay? She's in a tough position right now."

It's annoying and I'm on the verge of snapping at him that he has no right to tell me how to deal with my own mother, but because I was just picturing the lonely teenage boy he once was, I stop myself and just say, "I know," and leave it at that.

* * *

An eternity later, the doctor comes and tells us the operation went smoothly.

We don't exactly pop a champagne cork or anything, but Mom and I hug and Jacob looks relieved. I immediately call Tom and tell him. I've clearly woken him up but he's happy to hear the good news and says he'll come pick us up whenever we want to go home.

A little while later, they let us see Dad, who's been transferred to a real hospital room now, but he's out cold and we don't wake him up.

When Tom comes to pick up me and Mom, Jacob says he's going to stay at the hospital. "No one's waiting for me at home, so I might as well make myself useful," he says. "I'm good at sleeping in a chair—I do it at the library all the time."

Once again he's a better child to my father than I am. I wish I could just be grateful and not feel like he's showing me up.

9.

Dad stays in the hospital for a few more days. He gets stronger by the hour and pretty soon he's demanding his laptop, which Jacob fetches from the apartment along with some journals and mail and Jacob's own car, which he left there when he rode in the ambulance. He pretty much camps out in the hospital room, working on *his* laptop when Dad's asleep, leaving only when Mom and I ask him to run an errand or when someone wants time alone with the patient.

I spend most of the weekend at the hospital, and when I go back to work on Monday, Rochelle lets me leave early. Her own parents have had a lot of health problems recently, so she's pretty sympathetic.

Tom goes with me that night to see my dad. He tries to be jovial and hearty—"Sounds like you're going to be just fine, Larry!" But my father responds with his usual dryness— "Such a meaningful word, *fine*, especially in this context"—and I think they're both relieved when the visit's up.

Hopkins checks in regularly by phone and says she'll fly out in a few days. "I don't need to see him while he's still in the hospital," she says to me during a quick phone conversation. "There are enough doctors there already. I assume that he'll move back in with Mom when he leaves?"

I assume so, too.

"He'll go home when he leaves the hospital, right?" I say to my mother when we meet with the cardiologist on Tuesday during my lunch break.

"Yes, of course," Mom says brightly. "Back to his apartment."

"I meant *home*, home."

She just turns to the doctor. "So when do you think he'll be released?"

"I think he'll be ready tomorrow, barring some unforeseen blip."

Then he bids us a cheerful good-bye, clearly pleased with the whole situation: *Look, Ma, I saved another life!*

Once he's gone, I start to say, "Dad needs to be—" but Mom cuts me off before I can finish the sentence.

"Forget it, Keats. He's not moving back to the house. For one thing, it's not his home anymore, and for another, I'm in the middle of trying to sell it. The last thing I need is an old man in pajamas wandering around, looking like death warmed over. People will run screaming out of there."

"Gee," I say. "Some people might call that attitude heartless."

"Thanks for being so understanding." She shakes her head slowly. "I'm not trying to win an ex-wife of the year award, Keats, but I don't think I'm being cruel, either. I'm willing to help take care of your father, but I don't want him back in my house. It took me ten years to get him out the first time. If I let him slip back in, I'll never get him out again. Especially now that he's ill. Of course, if you want to take him in, be my guest. Don't you and Tom have an extra room?"

"You mean Tom's office?"

"Your father needs care, and you're saving space for file cabinets? Some might call that heartless."

I hate the way she always twists things around on me.

"Come on, Mom—the guy was your husband for, like, thirty years. And you're not willing to give him a place to recover?"

"He's your blood relative, not mine." She prowls restlessly around the small conference room. I have a feeling a lot of people have been given bad news in here. There are boxes of tissues everywhere you look. Mom straightens one of them now so it aligns with the edge of the large square table, then wheels around suddenly, her skirt twirling. "As I said, I'll do anything else. I'll check in on him, do his grocery shopping, pick up his meds, keep him company—but I won't live with him again. Once he's back in his apartment, you and I can take shifts caring for him—"

"What about at night? He shouldn't be alone at night, the doctor said. Not at first."

"Hopkins is coming in a couple of days. She can stay with him while she's in town."

"And until then?"

Mom folds her arms and looks at me expectantly.

"I don't want to sleep over there," I say. The very thought makes me want to cry. I love my apartment. I love sleeping with Tom. I don't want to have to stay at my dad's.

"But you will," Mom says.

* * *

I bring my overnight bag to work the next day. Rochelle comes to talk to me in my little cubicle and notices it immediately. She's like that: eyes like a hawk. Nothing slips by her.

I explain my plan for that evening, and she asks me about my dad. She knows who he is, of course. When she first interviewed me two years ago, the first thing she said was, "I assume you're related to Professor Sedlak over at that other school?" When I admitted I was his daughter, she peered at me with her unnervingly large and glittering brown eyes and said, "He could probably get you a job upriver from here. Harvard Square's a much more exciting place to spend your days. You sure you don't want that?"

"I want this job," I said. "If you'll take me."

She studied me thoughtfully for a moment, then got very businesslike, asking me how many words I typed a minute and that sort of thing. She hired me as her assistant and in less than a year had promoted me to office manager.

After I fill her in on how my dad's doing, she changes subject abruptly. "Did you get a chance to read Mark's newsletter draft?"

"I tried. It wasn't easy to get through."

"I know, right? I love the guy, but you'd think he never took an English class in his life." Mark Connelly, who maintains our website, is a tech whiz, but every time he has to write any text at all, it's an ungrammatical and incoherent mess. "Look, Keats, I know it's not in your job description—"

She doesn't have to finish. We've had this conversation so many times we now do it in shorthand. "It's okay," I say. "I don't mind."

She stands up and a beautiful smell of musk and patchouli wafts off of her. I love the way Rochelle smells. I love the way she looks, too, with her huge silver hoops, silk tank tops, and severely tailored pants: businesslike and gorgeous at the same time. Not many women can pull that off. Rochelle's not young, either—I've heard both fifty-three and forty-seven, from different people—but I guess style is ageless.

She thanks me, then shakes her head. "You're too good for this job, Keats. If I were a better person, I'd tell you to go do something more with your life. But I don't want to lose you. Do you remember Lois? The woman who trained you? She always ran around like a chicken with its head cut off, frazzled, like she couldn't keep up. And she couldn't. Nothing was ever done on time. You—you're always relaxed, chatting with people—but you get everything done and done well. You're a force of nature, Keats."

"Hey, could you tell my boss how great I am?" I say jovially. "Maybe she'll give me a raise."

"In this economy?" She gives a gentle hoot. "Sweetheart, be glad you've got a job. I know I am. The pay's shit and the hours are long, but I'm telling you there are a hundred people who would kill to be in our shoes."

"In yours, at least," I say, glancing down at her gray suede pumps.

"They are pretty, aren't they?" She surveys them with a sigh of satisfaction, then moves to the doorway. "Can you have the newsletter rewritten by this afternoon?"

"Yup," I say, because it will take me less than half an hour to rewrite Mark's draft. The sad thing is it probably took him an entire day of wrestling with the words to screw it up so badly in the first place. But I'll figure out what he was trying to say and rephrase it all, and Rochelle will tell him I did a "light edit" on it, and that's all he'll think it was, because it will say what he meant to say in the first place—what he thought he had succeeded in saying but hadn't. Only Rochelle and I will know that I've rewritten every single word.

I'm barely into it when I get another visitor. Cathy peeks in the opening that's not a doorway because there's no actual door. "Got a second?"

"Sure."

She enters and leans her hip against the edge of my desk. "Is it true that your dad's sick? Someone just told me he was in the hospital."

People at the office are very interested in my dad's heart attack. I'm the only person who works there who isn't over forty, and everyone else already has a sick parent or two. I feel like I've just become a member of a club I hadn't known existed until now.

"He was. He should be home now." I look at my watch. "As of about an hour ago, if all went well." Mom and Jacob were going to drive him to his apartment and get him settled there.

"Oh, good. I was really shocked to hear he was sick. He seemed so vibrant and healthy at your birthday party."

Is she serious? He seemed like a physical wreck to me that night. "Well, the good news is he's really doing great now." I switch gears. "Hey, Cathy, speaking of that dinner...After everyone left, I started thinking about how you and Jacob are around the same age and in the same field, and it occurred to me that maybe, you know..." I let my sentence trail off.

Cathy cocks her head at me. "Is he the guy you wanted to fix me up with? I was wondering about that."

I nod. "He's a really good guy. Seriously, he's like my brother. Except he's better than my real brother. Less crazy. I mean, I love my brother, but he's nuts."

"How long have you known him?"

"Jacob?" I lean way back in my seat so I can prop my feet up on the desk. "Feels like forever. Maybe six years?"

"Wow. So what kind of girls does he usually date?"

"I have no idea. He's never brought anyone to meet us."

She twists her mouth. "He didn't seem all that into me."

"That's only because my father sucks all the attention toward himself. It makes it hard for anyone else to connect. And Jacob's a little shy."

"So am I."

"See? A perfect fit."

"Yeah, maybe. Let me just think about it first." She pulls a book out of her backpack. "I wanted to show you this: I found my old school copy of your dad's book and I'm rereading it. It's amazing. That whole section about Russia over the centuries—it's like a disaster movie, where you want to yell at the characters to stop what they're doing, but you can't. Don't you think?"

"I've never actually read it."

She stares at me, openmouthed. "You're kidding."

"I tried once and couldn't get through it. It's not really my kind of thing."

"God, if he were my father—"

You'd be a lot crazier than you are, I think. But I just smile and shrug and hope she doesn't feel the need to launch into what's so great about the Russian section of Dad's book.

But she does.

* * *

My mom's ready to walk out the door when I arrive at Dad's apartment, but I stop her because I need some information about his medication and emergency contacts and all that. She's mislaid the paperwork, but I find it eventually on the kitchen counter, under a half-empty cup of tea.

"Don't leave him alone tonight," she says as we huddle in the kitchen together, speaking in low voices so he won't overhear. "Once he's been safe at home for twenty-four hours, we can stop being so vigilant, but stick close for now."

"You sure you don't want to stay?" I ask hopefully. I had tried to get Tom to come meet me here, but he'd opted to spend the evening with Lou and Izzy instead. "We could get Chinese food, have a little wine, turn it into a pajama party?"

"Doesn't that sound lovely," she says sarcastically, pouring herself a glass of water. Then she turns the water off and looks at me, laughing. "Actually, it *does* sound lovely. I don't know why I said it like that. A Chinese food pajama party with you would be fun. But I already have plans for tonight."

"Michael? Or Paul?"

"Would you believe contestant number three?" She says it lightly, but her cheeks turn pink.

"God, Mom, you're such a player."

"Hardly." She leans against the counter and gently tilts her glass from side to side, staring at the water like she's conducting an experiment in molecular cohesion.

"I thought women your age were supposed to have trouble finding guys to date."

"Maybe it's different in a university town—lots of old guys around that no one wants."

"Michael was kind of dreamy."

That tinge of pink on her cheeks deepens. "I know. Charming, too."

"So do you like him better than Paul? Or this third guy I haven't met yet?"

"Actually, you have. It's Irv Hackner."

"Wait—Mr. Hackner? As in Mrs. Hackner's husband?" They were old friends of my parents, usually included in the very few parties my parents ever threw.

"Ellie died three years ago."

"Oh." I feel like I should have an emotional reaction to the news, but I can't really remember much about Ellie Hackner. She was petite, I think, and blondish. The name is far more familiar than the actual person. "Doesn't it feel weird for you to date him?"

"A little. It just sort of happened. We started e-mailing, just as friends. Then we got together for coffee. We've only been out on a couple of what you'd call real dates."

"Define *real*."

She puts the glass down and smooths her skirt. The woman can't be still for five seconds. "He pays for dinner, and I give him a kiss on the cheek at the end of the evening."

"You're a wild woman."

She smiles without meeting my eyes. I get the feeling she's enjoying some private joke. One I'm just as happy not to be in on.

"If you keep this up, Mom, you're going to break some hearts."

"I hope so," she says, and when she looks up, there's an avaricious gleam in her large green-brown eyes that I've never seen before. It makes her look decades younger. "I would really like to break a heart or two. I never have."

"You sure about that?" I jerk my chin in the direction of my father's bedroom.

The light fades from her eyes. "I didn't mean like that."

"It's all fun and games until it's not."

She puts down her glass and says a dispirited good night.

After she leaves, I pick up the glass and mug she used and put them both in the dishwasher, along with a bunch of other dirty dishes I find in the kitchen. I wander slowly out into the living room, trying to get up the energy to go in and see my dad.

The living room is filled with the flower arrangements people have sent, and I amuse myself for a while wandering from one to another, reading the notes tucked into the stems or dangling from the vases. There are some work-related ones (the dean of faculty, a couple of colleagues, his graduate seminar students) and a few from friends.

The biggest, most dramatic bouquet is from Tom's parents. They're a little over the top, the flowers a little too colorful, the arrangement a little too big, and the note—"You're in our prayers"—is exactly the kind of thing that would drive Dad nuts, so I slip it out and toss it in the wastebasket. They meant well.

On the coffee table is a small flowering plant from an unexpected source. "Hope you get well soon," the card reads. "All my best, Michael Goodman."

Mom's date sent Dad some get-well flowers? Is that what people do under these circumstances? Not that these circumstances are common or anything, but still…

"That's just weird," I say out loud to the empty room.

There's no response. I take that as agreement and head into Dad's room.

* * *

It's not easy coming up with things to talk about. We've seen each other a lot recently, so we've used up any news, and he's not the kind of father who wants to chat about TV shows or restaurants or how my old high school friends are doing.

Instead, he asks me whether I'm ready yet to get serious about my future, a conversation that holds no hope of being enjoyable for me.

It's not just the topic that makes talking to him a drag. He also deliberately uses arcane words, then asks me if I know what they mean. If I say I don't, he tells me I need to be reading better books and educating myself, but if I say I do, he presses me for a definition, and even if I have a vague sense of what the word means, my attempt to articulate it always fails, and I end up stammering and feeling stupid.

He's done this to me my whole life.

When he finally moves on from the topic of Keats's Wasted Life, it's to give me a lecture about the heart, both as muscle and as literary trope. It's clearly something he's put a lot of thought into, but none of his observations seem all that original to me, and after a while, I can't restrain a yawn, which sends him into a long rant about the deterioration of the American attention span—which makes me so bored I could scream, which I guess proves his point.

"First it was books, then it was articles, then it was blog

posts, now it's those Twitter things," he says. "People are no longer capable of processing information that takes more than a sentence or two to be conveyed. In another generation, we'll be communicating entirely in emoticons, and elegance of language will be as dead as the ancient Mayans."

He's a fun guy to spend time with, my dad, especially when you add in how morbid he's become since his heart attack.

"I suppose I'm luckier than most," he says a little while later. "I have three children and a few books that will live on after I die. Even so, who'll remember my name in a century or two? No one. Not that it will matter to me then, of course. Dead is dead. It's only in the here and now that the thought stings."

He wants me to reassure him that his books will always be read and his descendants will always revere his memory, so I do. But I feel like a kid being forced to set the dinner table: I chafe at the chore and do a sloppy, half-assed job of it.

"We should have some dinner," I say when even this miserable conversation sputters to a stop. "What do you feel like eating?"

"I'm not hungry," he says. "I'm never hungry anymore."

He has gotten noticeably thinner over the last week. His cheeks have caved in, and his pajamas hang on him. He looks a decade older than he did at my birthday party—and he didn't look so great back then.

"You have to eat something, Dad."

"Why do people always say that? It's not like healthy human beings will let themselves starve to death. It's only the old and the dying who turn away from sustenance, and it's in everyone's best interest to let them go gentle into that good night."

Self-pity much? I'm not going to indulge him. "Dad, I promise you that the second I locate an ice floe in the greater Boston area, you're on it."

"That's my girl," he says proudly. Odd what wins approval

from this guy. "You get your lack of sentimentality from your mother. You're both pragmatists."

I think of my mother, smiling coyly to herself at the thought of breaking hearts, and wonder if she's as pragmatic as Dad thinks. She does seem to be practical and unsentimental about anything concerning *him* these days, but maybe that's because sentimentality would only complicate things at this point.

I slide to my feet. "And now I'm going to order in some dinner, and you vill eat it and you vill like it."

"I do so enjoy hearing a Nazi accent come out of my daughter's mouth," he says. "Brings back so many fond World War II memories."

"How *was* life in the Third Reich?" I shoot back as I leave the room.

I cross through the living room and let out a startled yelp when something moves inside the kitchen.

It's just Jacob.

I lean against the doorway to let my heart rate go back to normal.

"I thought you were a burglar," I say. "You almost had your second 911 call of the week. Was there something you neglected to tell us about the heart attack? Did you surprise Dad the way you just did me?"

He smiles good-naturedly. "You know, at the time, it seemed like good fun to hide in the closet and jump out at him wearing a gorilla mask. But in retrospect—" He looks a little different today, and I'm trying to figure out why. I realize he's wearing jeans instead of his usual khakis and a T-shirt instead of a buttoned-down oxford. I guess this is rugged Jacob, which isn't very rugged. The T-shirt is a soft blue, and his arms are more skinny than buff. Still, he looks infinitesimally less nerdy than usual. "Sorry I didn't call ahead," he adds. "My phone battery died a sudden, inexplicable death."

I come the rest of the way into the kitchen. "I'm sure it had a good life."

"You think? Shoved in pockets, left behind in coffee shops, accidentally dropped in the toilet more than once...."

"I take it back. It probably committed suicide. And by the way...*more than once?*"

"You don't want to know. Anyway, I just came by to drop off some food and see how your dad was doing. Oh, also—" He picks something up off the counter and shows it to me. It's a big square envelope with "Professor Sedlak" written in large, loopy letters on the front. "A get-well card from his graduate students."

"I hope it's a cartoon picture of a guy in a hospital bed," I say. "With a pun. Oh, please, let there be a pun. 'Best wishes for a *hearty* recovery.' Something like that."

"One can hope." He leaves the kitchen, which I figure gives me permission to poke through the contents of the bag he left on the counter: a couple of turkey sandwiches, an apple, an orange, and a small bag of pretzels.

When he comes back a couple of minutes later, I point to the groceries. "We're being very healthy, aren't we?"

"Trying to. The doctor said your dad should be careful what he eats."

"That explains one turkey sandwich. Who's the other sandwich for?"

"You."

I give him a look. "Liar. You didn't even know I was here. You'd give away your own dinner just like that, wouldn't you?"

He shrugs. "There's more where that came from. How long are you staying?"

"All night. Mom thinks someone needs to be around full-time for a day or so."

"I can stay tonight if you want to go home."

"It's okay. I cleared my calendar." I wonder if he can tell how tempted I am to say yes. I don't think so. I'm working hard to hide it. The only thing keeping me from saying, *Yes! You stay! I go! Good-bye!* is some sense that because it's my father and not his, I should be the one camping out on a sofa tonight.

"Oh. Okay." A pause. "Do you want me to leave you alone?"

"God, no! I'm desperate for company. And I want to order in a pizza, but Dad probably shouldn't have that, and I don't want to eat an entire pizza by myself." I reconsider. "No, actually, I do, which is why you have to stay and throw yourself on the bomb."

"You sure you don't want some time alone with him?"

"Are you kidding me? I've been here less than an hour, and already he's driving me nuts."

"He hates being so helpless. That's what makes him irritable."

"Yeah, well, he makes *me* irritable. If you stay, you'll save us both from a lot of irritation."

"All right, then," he says with an easy smile. "What do you like on your pizza?"

10.

Dad barely manages to get down two bites of the turkey sandwich before he pushes it away and says he just wants to sleep. He took a painkiller a few minutes earlier, so it's not surprising he's drowsy.

He's sound asleep before the pizza even arrives.

Jacob and I take it over to the small round table in the living room, the one near the window, which means we can look out on that amazing view, although it's subdued at night. The river doesn't sparkle the way it does during the day. It's black and serpentine, and its edges blur into its equally dark banks.

Since we've left the door to Dad's bedroom open in case he calls out, we keep both the lights and our voices low, like teenagers who've come home late from a party and don't want to wake up the parents.

In that spirit, I decide we need to track down some alcohol. I search through Dad's cabinets and finally score something: not the beer I was hoping for, but a couple of bottles of red wine that were languishing in the bottom of the kitchen closet.

I show them to Jacob who says, "You know, there's a chance those are really good. People are always giving him bottles to celebrate some occasion or another."

"So they could be worth, what, like thirty bucks each?"

"Yeah. Or even like a hundred and thirty."

I tighten my grasp on the bottles. "You think I should put them back?"

"It's your call." Then Boy Scout Jacob surprises me. "But he'll never notice they're gone. He didn't even know they were there in the first place—I'm the one who put them away. Let's go for it."

He doesn't have to tell me twice. I find a corkscrew rolling around in a big drawer that's otherwise empty, and we open a bottle.

"Nice," I say after we clink glasses and each take a sip, but it's more of a question than a statement, because I don't really know that much about wine. "Yeah," says Jacob and I suspect he doesn't know any more than I do.

We dig into the pizza, and before long, Jacob is refilling our wineglasses. I get a buzz going pretty quickly, which feels good. It's been a tough week, and I don't think I'll be able to fall asleep in that apartment without being at least a little bit drunk.

We talk about the hospital—which nurses we did and didn't like, how Dad's roommate always had the dividing curtain closed and his TV on, the eternal mystery of why they wake up patients for routine stuff when sleep is so healing—and work our way back to the night Jacob found Dad on the floor of the apartment.

"When I first saw him lying there, I honestly thought he was dead," Jacob says. "I instantly flashed to having to tell your whole family."

"We'd have taken it well," I say with the cheerfulness of the semi-drunk.

"I figured you'd all blame me for it. If I'd just come earlier—"

"Blame's a harsh word. Let's just say we would have held you responsible—legally and morally."

"Thanks." He pokes at the tangle of pizza crusts left on his plate. For a small guy, he can scarf down a lot of pizza. "I don't ever want to have a moment like that again."

"Then the next time you see someone passed out on the floor, run away." The apartment phone rings. I get to my feet and sway there for a moment, waiting for the sudden head rush to pass. "I'll get it."

He rises, too. "I'll go check on your dad."

We head in opposite directions. I go into the kitchen and answer the phone. "Hello?"

"Hey, Keats. How's Dad?"

It's Hopkins. We may not talk very often on the phone, but I recognize her flatly brisk voice almost immediately. "He's doing pretty well, I think. Not that I know anything about anything, but he seems like he's getting better. He's lost a lot of weight, though."

"Huh?" Hopkins's voice fades and then comes back. "—in a cab. Don't know why it's affecting our connection but it is."

I wonder if she heard anything I said.

"I'll have to jump soon, anyway," she says. "Only have a second or two. Is Mom there?"

"She was, but she left. Now only Jacob Corwin and I are here. And Dad, of course."

"Tell Jacob I say thank you. He was the one who found Dad, you know."

I feel vaguely annoyed by her "you know." I'm the one who's there in Boston with Mom and Dad. She's the one who's never around. Of course, I know. "Yeah. He's a good guy."

"Best assistant Dad's ever had. Can I talk to Dad?"

"I think he's asleep. Jacob's in there checking. He's totally paranoid about him now."

"Tell him he doesn't need to be. I looked over all his tests before they discharged him. He's fine. For now. But he is getting old—it's just a matter of time until something more serious takes him down." She says it the way you'd say, *It's nice out now but it might rain tomorrow.* "So where's Tom tonight?"

"Out with friends."

"I didn't know you guys ever spent time apart. Mom says you're joined at the hip."

"She's crazy—we're not like that at all." I realize I'm swaying a little on my feet, so I give into it, and let my body shift from side to side, which feels kind of nice, like being rocked to sleep. It occurs to me I'm a tiny bit drunk, and I don't want Hopkins to know, so I take extra care to enunciate carefully. "How's work these days?"

"Way too busy. That's why I haven't made it to come see Dad yet. I have to, though. Mom keeps saying she won't relax until I've seen him with my own eyes." She gives a short laugh. "It's crazy—she's surrounded by the best doctors in the whole world but doesn't trust any of them. It puts a lot of pressure on me."

"Mom told me you were coming tomorrow."

"That's why I'm calling. It looks like I'm going to have to postpone my trip for another day or two."

I try not to sound whiny as I say, "The thing is...Mom doesn't want Dad sleeping here alone. If you don't come and stay with him, I'll have to keep doing it."

"Ask Jacob," she suggests. "He's the kind of guy who'll do whatever you ask him to."

"That's not entirely true."

"Really? I've always gotten that impression."

"Can't you just come tomorrow? You said Mom needs you to—"

"You know who really needs me?" she interrupts impatiently. "The twenty-seven-year-old mother of three who was brought in here last night having stroke after stroke after stroke. I think the fact that her kids could lose their mother just might take precedence over the fact that you and your boyfriend can't curl up together in your matching jammies for a night or two."

I'm instantly ashamed of my own pettiness. "Jesus," I say. "A mother of three? Really?"

"Yeah, and at the moment she can't talk or move her legs. The dad brought the kids to see her, which was just— Oh, shit, I think I just missed a call I need to take. I better go."

And she's gone, just like that. But the familiar uneasy feeling she leaves me with—insecurity mixed with jealousy—lingers on even after I hang up.

"How's Dad doing?" I ask Jacob, who comes back in the living room a minute after I do.

"Sound asleep. I should probably confess that I poked him just to make sure he wasn't in a coma. He moved a little, which was good, but if he wakes up now, it's my fault."

"He won't. He said those painkillers really knock him out." Hopkins's call has successfully killed my buzz, so I retreat to the corner table, reclaim my wineglass, and refill it. We're on the second bottle now. Well into it, actually.

While I'm at it, I refill Jacob's glass and bring it over to him.

"I better not," he says. "I've got to drive home."

"If you get too drunk to drive, you can crash here." I press the glass on him. "There's this sofa and the pull-out one in the office. We can do rock-paper-scissors to see who gets which one."

"Yeah, maybe," he says, but he puts his glass down without taking a sip.

I'm bummed. I want him to stay. I don't want to be there alone, checking every hour or so to make sure Dad's breathing.

Because what if he's not?

We both look around the room, trying to figure out what to do next. "You want to watch something?" Jacob asks.

"Definitely." I plop down on the sofa while he searches for the remote.

He finds it on top of the TV set—Dad still has the boxy kind you can put things on top of—and comes over to the sofa. I'm sitting right in the middle, so even though it's the only piece of furniture positioned to watch the TV, he hesitates. I slide over a foot and pat the cushion next to me. "Put 'er down," I say brightly.

"Her? Why is my butt a her?" But he sits.

"Why wouldn't it be? You sexist?" I'm still clutching my wineglass. Since it's there, I take another sip. As if in response, my head gives a sudden involuntary bob. It occurs to me I might be pretty drunk. To disprove that theory, I hold myself extra erect and say very clearly: "So what should we watch?"

"Anything that's not set in a hospital." He turns on the TV and flicks past some talking heads and commercials and lands on a show where a handful of overtanned and overmuscled shirtless guys are sitting in a hot tub, shouting at each other and sucking down some beers.

"This," I say and put my hand over his to get him to stop pushing the buttons. "Stay on this."

His fingers twitch under mine. "You really want to watch this?"

"I don't *not* want to watch it."

"You actually like this crap?"

I flutter my eyelids. "I don't *not* like it."

"You going to keep talking like that for the rest of the night? Because nothing's keeping me here now that the pizza's gone."

"I'm not going to *not* talk like this."

"Do I have to leave?"

I promise I'll stop.

We watch in silence for a moment. I realize then that my hand is still on his, on the remote, so I withdraw it. "Am I allowed to change the channel?" Jacob asks hopefully.

"No." I don't know why I'm forcing him to watch some

horrible reality show about people I would go out of my way to avoid in real life. I mean, if I walked into a bar and these characters were shouting and hooting in there the way they are on the screen, I'd turn around that second and leave.

But I guess I'm enjoying the irony of watching Jacob watch these idiots—brilliant academician comes face-to-face with the lowbrow sordidness that's reality programming.

I keep sipping my wine until this glass—my fourth?—is gone. I lean over and put it on the side table. My head's starting to feel a little rolly, like it needs to be propped up on something or it will fall over, so I curl up sideways and rest it on the sofa pillow that's between me and Jacob. When he turns his head to see what I'm doing, his face is just a few inches from mine.

"You okay?" He sounds mildly concerned.

"I'm fine. Just tired. It's been a tough week."

"Poor Keats." His face is a little too close, his light gray eyes a little too intense. So I shut my eyes. It's easier than moving.

I feel his hand on my leg and open my eyes to see what he's doing. He's just patting my knee. All very fraternal and comforting. His voice is low, soothing. "I know how rough this has all been on you. Not just your dad, but all the stuff going on with your mom, too. All the changes. Let me help in any way I can. I'm truly happy to stay over here until your dad's better if that makes your life easier."

It's a good thing Jacob is basically a brother to me, otherwise the whole situation would be awkward, between the wine, the dark, the intimacy—and the fact that on the TV, one of the orange-tanned guys is now feverishly kissing a similarly hued girl who's wearing only a bikini top and the briefest Daisy Dukes I've ever seen. They're at a bar, but it doesn't seem to be restraining them in any way—his hands are going everywhere, under the bra, inside her shorts....

I wonder what it would be like to go out in public in a tiny

pair of cutoffs and a bra. I can't imagine it. I mean, I literally can't even *imagine* it. I'm like those little Orthodox girls
who redress Barbie dolls in modest outfits with long sleeves and
dowdy skirts: I instantly put more clothes on my imaginary
self.

"It's okay," I murmur drowsily. "You do plenty for Dad.
More than anyone else."

"I don't mind."

There's a pause. We sit there very cozy, my head practically
on his shoulder, his hand still gently touching my knee. It occurs to me that if Tom were to walk into the living room right
now, he might not like what he saw. But it's *Jacob*—I can cud-
dle up to him, and it doesn't mean a thing. He's like the sane
brother I never had.

"It is a little weird," I say after a moment.

"I know. She's supposed to be his best friend's girlfriend if
I'm understanding this correctly."

It takes me a second to realize he's talking about the TV
show.

"No, not that." My tongue feels thick in my mouth, and it's
making the words come out distorted. I lick my lips and work
hard to form the sounds correctly. "I mean that you're willing
to spend so much time on my father. It's weird. It's not helping your career any at this point, is it?"

"It's never been about my career," he says. "You know that.
I've told you how much it's meant to me to get to work with
him, even just to spend time with him. If I can pay him back
for all he's given me in some small way by helping out now—"

My eyes hurt. No, it's my head that hurts. It's the part of
my head that's right behind my eyes. I yawn, which makes my
head ache more, which makes me irritable, which makes me say
irritably, "You do know he's not actually your father, right?"

There's a pause. "Yes, Keats, I know that," Jacob says evenly.

"I'm sorry you don't have one of your own, but that doesn't mean you can have mine."

I feel a sudden movement. He's shifted away so abruptly that the pillow he was leaning against falls down, and my head goes down with it. I tumble sideways and have to struggle back to a sitting position.

Jacob's gotten to his feet.

"What?" I say. "Why'd you do that?"

"Nothing." He takes a step back. "It's late. I'm going to take off." Behind him, the scene on the TV changes. The main guy is working out at a gym now, straining to lift more weight than seems physically possible; he's swearing as he strains to raise the barbell, but the curse words are bleeped out with such deliberate clumsiness that every *fuck* is emphasized rather than obscured.

My eyes flit back and forth from the screen to Jacob's face, which looks slightly sinister in the flickering TV light.

He says "bye" and turns.

"Wait, why are you going?" I jump up and stumble over my own feet. I grab onto the sofa arm to steady myself. "The show's just getting good."

"I think I can manage to tear myself away. Don't forget to check in on your dad now and then."

"Wait. A second ago, you were settling in to watch TV with me. What happened?"

He averts his face. "Nothing."

"He says 'nothing,' but he doesn't mean it."

A pause, then, "You know. You deliberately say things . . ." He trails off. "It doesn't matter."

"I'm sorry I said Dad wasn't your father. I was just joking." But the apology seems absurd—Dad *isn't* his father.

Plus it just seems to annoy him more. "Really, Keats? That was a joke? Which part was supposed to be funny? The part about how my own father's dead or the part about how I'm so pathetic and needy that I'm trying to steal yours?"

"I'm sorry," I say again. I want to get him to turn his face back toward me, to smile his good ol' Jacob smile at me the way he always does and not be so angry. I don't like having Jacob angry at me. It feels wrong. I'm allowed to be annoyed at him and to needle him and bug him and ignore him, but he has to be nice to me. That's just how it works with us. "I had too much wine—I don't even know what I'm saying."

"It's not just tonight. You say stuff like that all the time. For some reason you seem to think it's okay to say really mean things to me. I know you get tense around your family, so I try to give you the benefit of the doubt most of the time, but tonight"—he gestures forlornly at the empty living room—"your family's not even here."

"I know." I move closer to him so I can put a consoling hand on his arm. "And you're right: I do say mean things to you sometimes. I don't know why."

Even with his face turned away from me, I can see a corner of his mouth. It tugs upward in a failed attempt at a smile. "I guess I just annoy you."

I'm horrified by the very idea. Jacob doesn't annoy me. He couldn't annoy anyone. I slide my hand up his arm to reassure him. "No, you don't. I swear you don't. You don't annoy me. I like you, Jacob. I always have." And just to prove my point, I rise up on tiptoe and give him a friendly little kiss on his cheek.

He doesn't react, and I'm worried he didn't feel it so I repeat the kiss, only a little closer to that visible corner of his mouth. Then I say, "I just like to tease you, that's all." It makes sense to me. Siblings tease each other, right? And Jacob and I have this brother/sister thing going on. His head rises ever so slightly, and that allows me to press my lips right on the edge of his mouth, where his lips carve into his cheeks.

"Keats," he says hoarsely, only it comes out as more of a question, more like "Keats?"

I make a soothing noise and slide my hand up along his shoulder. He's so much slighter than Tom. Tom works out a lot, and his shoulders are so wide they feel like they go on forever when I try to reach around them. But Jacob's thin, and my arm easily twines around his other shoulder.

"I don't want you to feel bad," I say. "Or to be mad at me."

I can always get Jacob to do what I want him to do. He scolds me sometimes and gets frustrated, but in the end he always does pretty much what I want. And right now I want him not to feel bad and also to like me again.

I press myself against his arm and rise up to give him another sisterly peck. Right before I do, he shifts a little toward me like he's about to say something, and that makes the kiss land almost on the center of his mouth.

"What are you doing?" he whispers in that same low, guttural voice. I can't read his expression. It's too dark in the room, and I'm having trouble focusing my eyes, and anyway he won't really look at me.

"I'm just trying to make you feel better," I explain. "It's the least you can do for someone when you hurt their feelings. Hurt his feelings. That's what my mother would say. She corrects people's grammar all the time. Not yours so much, though—you don't make grammatical mistakes. I really admire that about you." Just to prove how much I admire that, I kiss him on the lips again lightly. "I...Really...Do..." I punctuate each word with another little kiss.

It's kind of hypnotizing kissing him like that, and it's not like he's moving away or pushing me off or anything. He's just letting me do it.

He shakes his head silently, warily, but he still doesn't pull away.

"Now come on back over here," I say and kind of tug him by the waist back toward the sofa. "You've had too much wine and shouldn't drive yet."

"*I've* had too much wine?" he says, but he lets me drag him back. I reach the sofa and pull him down with me so we fall in a tangle on the sofa together. We wriggle until we're side by side, and then I curl up against him again, only even closer this time, my arms going back around his shoulders, my face right next to his.

"Look," I say, nodding toward the TV. "They're at the beach. Who goes to the beach at night?" He obediently watches the show, and I steal the opportunity to nip gently at his ear. You know. In fun. Playfully. Because we're pals.

His next breath is more of a shudder.

The woman and the guy on the reality show start making out again.

"They look like they're having a good time," I point out and flick my tongue lightly at the top of his ear. "I guess she likes him better than she likes the other guy. She seems to."

"I think," Jacob says in a very low voice, "that he should get as far away from her as he can. She's trouble."

"You are an enemy to love." I can feel warmth coming off of his neck, so I nuzzle down into it. In a friendly way.

Something snaps in Jacob. He rears up in his seat and turns on me, and all of a sudden, he's pushing me down on the sofa, and his weight is falling on top of me, his mouth is searching out mine, his hands are grabbing my arms and pinning them up over my head, and I can't tell if he's angry or not. All I know is that I'm aroused, and he's aroused, and I don't really think of him like he's a brother, not really at all, not anymore.

11.

I'm twenty-five years old. I've only ever slept with one man,
which maybe isn't such a remarkable fact. Lots of twenty-
five-year-old girls have probably only slept with one guy.

Well, some anyway.

But I've also only ever kissed one guy on the lips.

Only one guy's hand has ever crept under my top, down my
jeans, cupped me anywhere, nestled under my hair, held my
jaw and pulled my mouth open to his, stroked me, touched
me, entered me, felt me, known me.

Until now.

I think about that briefly, about how the only other guy
who's ever touched me is Tom, the man I'm going to spend
the rest of my life with, but the transient *Should I think about
this more?* moment quickly disappears in a rush of other sensa-
tions. Jacob feels so foreign on top of me, so new and different.
It's exciting. I want to think about *that*. I'm wild with curios-
ity, each new type of contact making me wonder what the next
will feel like.

Tom's lips are thick. When he kisses me, I feel like my
mouth is losing some kind of war with his. He sucks at my lips,
absorbs them, surrounds them. Jacob's kisses are completely
different. As wild as his sudden attack on me was, the kisses
that follow are gentle and tentative. I feel like I should give him

some encouragement, so I tongue his mouth open, and that seems to give him the confidence to use his own tongue, which I like, so I respond with even more enthusiasm...and things just keep building from there.

I'm warm with Jacob on top of me, but his weight—so much less than Tom's—isn't nearly so heavy as the alcoholic lethargy that's making my eyelids droop and my limbs swoon into the sofa. My arms, my legs, my neck, my feet, my captive hands—they're all quiet for now, but my mouth is wide awake, and my breasts and hips are eagerly arching up toward him. I don't feel like I'm in control of those parts of my body. They're doing what they want.

I'm not sure I'm in control of anything at this moment. Maybe I started this, but now Jacob's taken the lead, and he's surprisingly strong for someone so slender. He's still got my arms pinned, and his legs are lying along the whole length of mine so I can't move those, either.

I'm fine not being in control. I like it.

He rises up a fraction of an inch and then lets his thighs settle back on me; my hips rise up to grind against his, and even though we both still have our jeans on, he groans. It's an animalistic sound, not consciously formed, not knowingly uttered. The sound of it unhinges me, and I make my own involuntary noise, low in my throat.

It's like we're having a dialogue on some basic, animalistic level, and it's almost funny—it *is* funny—but I have no desire to laugh, not when he's so deathly earnest, not when I'm so desperately aroused.

He finally releases my arms and rolls sideways—but only so he can unbutton my top. I leave my arms where they are, like I'm being held up by an invisible mugger. Jacob shoves aside the fabric of my now-unbuttoned shirt and buries his face in my chest, rubbing his cheeks and mouth across and then down.

The soft cups of my demi bra put up a poor defense, easily yielding to his inquisitive nose, his seeking tongue, his hungry lips. I shudder, arch my back, close my eyes, give over to the pleasure his mouth is giving me.

Then he stops. I open my eyes. He's hovering, up on his elbow, gazing at me, eyes dark and unfocused. "Keats," he says in that strange, unfamiliar voice. "What do you want?"

I don't exactly understand the question. I think it's pretty clear what I want at this particular moment, but since he seems confused, I say soothingly, "'S okay. I have an IUD."

The male libido is a thing of mystery to me, and even though I don't think I've said anything particularly seductive, Jacob gives another helpless groan and lowers himself back onto me, covering my mouth with his.

I finally lower my arms, but only so I can wrap them tightly around his body. My legs reach up around him, too, and we roll back and forth for a minute like that, our bodies so tight against each other that I can feel the sharp bones at his hips and the hardness between them.

Then he takes his mouth away from mine, lifts his body up, pulls blindly at his belt and button and zipper. Underneath him, I'm squirming, doing the same thing (minus the belt, I don't wear one) trying to shimmy my jeans down, only he's in the way—we're both in each other's way, the sofa's too small for us to get undressed there—so he rolls completely off of me and onto his feet for a moment and steps out of his pants while I stay on the sofa and shove mine the rest of the way off.

In the dim light, I get a quick glance at him, just enough to see how swollen and excited he is—which makes me breathe in sharply—and then he's back on top of me. I wonder if he snuck a peek when I did and what he thought and feel a very brief moment of fear that my stomach's too round, my legs too pale, my hips too wide—but there's nothing turned off about the way he's gripping my shoulders, nudging my knees aside, pressing his hot mouth against mine, and burying himself deep inside of me with a long, shuddering sigh.

* * *

I'm so excited that I come almost instantly. And then I come again. The violence of his thrusts, the feel of him inside of me, the way his body aligns with mine—the newness of it all arouses me like nothing has in the past few years, not since the early months right after I lost my virginity and could trace the growth of my pleasure every time Tom and I had sex—pleasure tinged with wonder at the strange novelty of it all.

And now it's new and wondrous again.

I hope my dad is asleep because I can't seem to control the noises I'm making. Jacob is quieter than I am, his face closed and intense. At the end, he does cry out, but it's a muted, careful cry. Still, the sound of it gives me one last whole-body thrill. I arch up into his final thrust, and then we both collapse down, his weight on mine.

We catch our breath like that, but after a minute or two, he shifts sideways, slipping out of me. He burrows his head into the space next to mine but doesn't say anything. His arm is across my exposed chest, his bare legs curled up across mine.

I don't say anything, either, content just to lie there, not moving. When I close my eyes, I feel the sofa tilt and spin under me.

Jacob murmurs something I don't catch. I make a *huh?* sound, but he doesn't repeat it and so I just smile politely, my eyes still closed. My head reels. I focus on the spinning sensation for a while. My body feels spent in a good way, floaty and on fire at the same time. I know I should probably run to the bathroom and clean myself up, but Jacob's legs are across mine, and that makes it hard to move, so I sleepily give in to the inertia.

Maybe I doze. Maybe I'm just drifting. It's hard to know. Some time definitely passes. I don't think either of us is actually asleep, but we're lying there quietly, our breathing regular, our thoughts taking their own paths.

I start to feel uncomfortable.

At first I think it's a physical thing, and I squirm, trying to find a better position. Jacob says, "Sorry." He wiggles around until he can slide off the sofa and onto his feet. He reaches for his pants. I avert my eyes and pull a cushion over my lap and drag the pieces of my shirt back over my chest.

"Be right back," he says and heads toward the hallway. To use the bathroom, I assume. Or maybe to check on my dad. That would be like him.

I have the sofa to myself. I move around, trying to get more comfortable. I can't find a position that works. The uncomfortable feeling grows.

It's like an ache. Only nothing actually hurts.

I try to will myself back into that dozy, sleepy, lazy haze, but that little bit of achiness won't let me relax.

The achiness takes on a shape. Three shapes actually. Three letters.

Tom.

The bad feeling is shaped like the word Tom.

As soon as I realize that, it blossoms into something bigger, something that makes me curl up in a fetal position, my heart thudding wildly.

What have I done?

I swivel to a sitting position, grab for my pants, fish my underwear out of them and put both on with shaking hands, then adjust my bra and button my shirt back across my chest. Then I curl up against the corner of the sofa, making myself small, my arms wrapped across my chest. The gnawing, aching feeling has spread throughout my whole body. And now I know nothing I do will make it go away. It can only get worse.

I've done something horrible. Something that can't be undone.

I've woken up from a lot of nightmares feeling this way—all sick and worried—and then realize it's a dream and everything is okay again. For a brief moment, I let myself hope that that's what's going on, that I fell asleep on the sofa and had a weird sex dream. But then Jacob walks back into the living room and I see the expression on his face. He's nervous and exhilarated.

More exhilarated than nervous.

"Hey," he says softly. I don't respond. He comes over, sits down next to me, not hesitating or asking for permission this time, just doing it, like now he has a right to. "That was nice." He's peering at me, looking for confirmation.

I turn my face away from him, don't say anything.

"You okay?"

I shake my head and press myself harder against the side of the sofa.

"What's wrong?" he asks.

"Are you serious?"

A silence falls. I hug myself harder. I want to turn into a hard, small knot and then disappear forever.

What have I done?

Jacob says slowly, "I asked you if you knew what you were doing. I stopped and asked you. I tried to make sure you...For god's sake, Keats, I *asked* you, and you just kept on—" He stops.

"I know," I say morosely. "I know. I'm not blaming you. It was my fault. I'll take all the blame. That doesn't make it any better for me, just so you know." The words are slurring. I'm drunk. I've been drunk for the last hour. That's why I let this happen.

But then I think, *That's not an excuse. You had wine, not a roofie.*

I have no idea whether Jacob's looking at me or not because I can't bear to look in his direction. I'll never be able to look at him again. I'll never be able to look in a mirror again, either. Or into Tom's loving, loyal eyes.

"Is it really so bad?" Jacob says after a long moment. "It's not like you're married."

"He got a tattoo." My throat is swelling up, and tears are coming to my eyes. I can't believe I've done this. I can't believe I can't undo it. I rub my cheek against the sofa cushion. "He got my name tattooed on his arm. It's *permanent.*"

"Jesus," Jacob says and then there's silence.

Tears are rolling down my cheeks now. I let them spill onto the sofa arm. They soak in, leaving little dark marks in the velvet.

After a moment, he says, "Did you want him to do that?"

"What difference does that make?"

"A lot. Maybe this happened because you're not ready for things with him to be permanent."

"'This' happened because I got drunk. Because I'm a horrible human being, and I got drunk and did something Tom would never ever in a million years do to me."

This time, the pause is much longer. It goes on so long that I eventually peek around my shoulder at Jacob. His head is resting back on the sofa cushion, his neck exposed, his eyes closed. His chest is rising and falling regularly, but the muscles in his face are taut, and he's clearly not asleep. He just looks weary and miserable. His eyes open, and I immediately turn my head away again. "I should go" is all he says.

I think of how he tried to leave earlier and how I stopped him. Why had I done that? What was I thinking? If I had just let him leave, none of this would have happened.

I draw my knees closer to my stomach, curling up even tighter.

I feel something on my ankle. I look down. It's Jacob's hand. I instantly and viciously jerk my foot away, and his hand disappears.

Then he stands up.

"I'm sorry you're so unhappy." His voice floats down to me from up above. "Do you want me to go?"

"Yes. Please."

"All right." For a few seconds, it's so quiet I can hear him swallow. Then he says, "I'll just check on your dad first."

I don't respond, and after another second or two, I hear him moving toward the back hallway.

I stay in my fetal position. The world has stopped spinning. It's settling back into hard-focused reality, a reality where I cheated on the guy who's stood by me for a decade, who waited patiently for me when I was too young, and who gave himself entirely to me when I was ready.

There's no consolation for me anywhere. Not only have I betrayed Tom, I've also ruined my friendship with Jacob. Can I ever be in the same room with him again? Not once Tom knows about this. He probably won't ever let me get within ten miles of Jacob. He might not even let me visit my father anymore, since Jacob's around so much.

It's a mess. It's a huge, huge mess of my own creation. God, I'm an idiot. An idiot and a bad person. There's no other way to look at it.

When Jacob comes back into the living room, I still can't look him in the eyes, but I sit up and manage to gaze somewhere in the general direction of his T-shirt. "Is Dad okay?"

"He's fine. Slept through…everything."

"Good."

There's a pause, and then we both start to say something at the same time. "I'm sorry," he says. "You first."

I say dully, "I just need you to know we can't tell anyone about this. Not that I thought you would. It's just . . . I'm not going to tell anyone." I can't bring myself to say Tom's name in front of him. "Not anyone."

"Okay."

The indifference of his tone annoys me. "I hate lying. Just so you know." I yank hard on a strand of my hair. "I'd tell him if I didn't think it would only hurt him. That's the last thing I want to do."

"He'd survive."

"I know he'd survive," I snap, glad he's said something I can attack. I want to attack Jacob. Badly. This is all his fault. I mean, it's all my fault. But it's *his* fault for being here tonight— no one even asked him to come over. Those stupid turkey sandwiches ruined my life. "But he'd never forgive me."

"He'd forgive you in about three minutes," Jacob says. "He wouldn't like it, but he'd forgive you. The guy knows how lucky he is to have you at all. You're a thousand times smarter and funnier and more interesting than he is, and you can see the panic in his eyes every time someone has a conversation with you at your level because he can't keep up. He'd forgive you. The bigger question is why you'd want him to."

For the first time since he's rolled off of me, I actually look at Jacob. He meets my gaze levelly, his face pale and tense.

I say desperately, "I love Tom. I'm going to be with him for the rest of my life. And you're wrong. He's a much better person than I am. I mean, he'd never do this to *me*—"

"Because he can't afford to risk losing you."

"I'm the one who can't afford to risk losing him! God!" I grab hair at both sides of my head now and pull even harder. The pain on my scalp is a relief compared to everything that's going on under it. "You know how long we've been together, how close we are, how good he is to me. You're only saying all this bad stuff because of what just happened."

"No. If I really thought you guys belonged together, I wouldn't have—" He halts, then finishes lamely, "—wouldn't have let this happen."

"It happened because of that." I point to the two empty wine bottles on the table. "Let's just be honest. We got drunk and I screwed up. That's all."

He stands there, his shoulders hunched forward like they're protecting his thin chest. "That's all," he repeats tonelessly.

"I'm sorry." I hate myself. "I know I sound like a jerk right now. I don't mean to. It's me I'm really mad at, not you."

"Well, that's a relief," he says. "I feel so much better."

"Please," I say miserably. "Don't be angry. This is all bad enough."

"'Bad enough.'" He gives a short laugh. "The sad thing is, that may be my best performance rating from a girl."

"You know what I mean." Part of me thinks I should reassure him—the sex had been great, hadn't it?—but to tell him so would only be more of a betrayal of Tom. And I can't bear to think about how much I liked it, how aroused I was. That feels more wrong than almost anything else. I never want to think about that again. "I hope this doesn't change things with my family. For you, I mean. That's another reason not to tell Tom. So long as he doesn't know—"

"Yeah," he says. "It's not like there'll be any awkwardness if you and I run into each other now."

I lift my hands helplessly and let them drop. "What do you want from me?"

"Nothing," he says, but at least the sarcasm is gone. Now he just sounds weary and sad. "I don't want anything from you that you don't want to give me."

I stand up. I put my hand out. "Friends still?"

He sighs, but he briefly touches my hand with his. "Sure, Keats. We're still friends." He turns to go.

I say to his back, "For what it's worth, I'm really, really sorry."

"For what it's worth, I'm not."

The door opens and then shuts behind him.

12.

Lady Macbeth had nothing on me. I get under the shower and scrub myself over and over again, letting the water run as hot as I can bear it. Another man has touched me, has been inside of me. I'll never be clean again. *O, that this too too solid flesh—*

No, wait, that's Hamlet, not Lady M. My parents would be disappointed in me. For so many reasons.

Morning takes its time arriving, forcing me to suffer through long hours of lying awake on my father's office sofa with only a towel to cover me because I don't deserve to pull open the bed inside and use actual bedding—no, that's too cozy, too comfortable for someone who's betrayed the person who loves her most in the world.

Anyway, it's not like I'm actually going to fall asleep. There's no way.

I wonder if I'll ever sleep again.

At some point during the long, lonely night, I segue from Lady Macbeth to Hester Prynne. I'm marked for life. A scarlet letter is carved across my heart, my head, my memory.

Tom has his tattoo, and now I have mine.

I've lost something I didn't even appreciate while I had it, something fine and rare and intangible, something I don't even know the word for, something that goes beyond fidelity and devotion and honesty but encompasses all of them. A few hours ago, Tom was the only man in the whole world who'd had access to my body. I'll never be able to say that again and have it be the truth. I've lost that forever.

And knowing that Tom would still think it was true but it wasn't, that I'd be living a lie with him from now on...that makes me want to throw up.

At three in the morning, I check on my father. He's asleep. At five, I check on him again. He's awake. He says, "Is it morning? It still looks dark out." I tell him the time, and he says, "You should go back to sleep." I go back to the office sofa, where I toss and turn and loathe myself. I'm getting really good at that.

At seven, I get up and make coffee.

I bring Dad a slice of toast and a cup of tea. He's sitting up now, reading a book. He peers over his reading glasses at me and says, "You look exhausted. Couldn't you sleep?"

"Not really."

"I'm sorry. It's my fault you're not at home in your own bed."

"It's not your fault I didn't sleep."

"Isn't it?"

"No," I say. "It's mine."

"How so?"

"Guilty conscience," I say and force a smile. *Some joke, eh, boss?*

* * *

Mom shows up around eight thirty. I tell her I'm running late and race out the door so her sharp eyes don't have time to notice anything.

Tom calls me a few minutes later, catching me in the car. He says I sound weird. I tell him I'm exhausted, that I couldn't sleep in Dad's apartment. I also tell him that Hopkins isn't coming so I'll probably have to spend another night or two there, and he says, "If you sound this exhausted after one night—"

"I'll be okay." I ask him about his evening, and he says it was fun, that he and Lou went bowling and had a real guys' night out.

"Where was Izzy?"

"Lou said she was all PO'ed about something and didn't want to come with us."

"Really? Izzy?" Izzy is the last person I think of as a sulker. "I've never seen her angry about anything."

"Yeah, me neither, but Lou says she can really get going when they're alone—that he's the only one she lets loose on. He asked me once if you're like that, and I almost felt bad because I had to say no. Guess I got the one perfect girl in the world."

When we hang up, tears of self-loathing and regret are pricking at the space behind my eyes.

* * *

Mom calls me around lunchtime from Dad's apartment to say she's been there all morning and he's fine, but Jacob's coming soon to relieve her. "I think this taking shifts thing is really going well," she says almost happily. "And when Hopkins comes—"

"*If* Hopkins comes."

"She's coming. She just had a medical emer—"

"I know, I know." I'm too tired and too dispirited to hear about how Hopkins is performing some kind of miracle back in New York. "How was your date?"

"Strange. Sometimes when we're together it feels like our spouses are just waiting in the next room, and we'll all join up again in a minute. And then I remember that it's just the two of us. But Irv is good company."

"Does Dad know you're dating him?"

"Not unless you told him."

"I haven't yet, but I'll keep it in mind when the conversation feels like it's dying."

"I'm sure he'd be fine with it."

"No, he wouldn't." I have no patience today. Not for this. "Don't fool yourself, Mom. He wouldn't be fine with your dating anyone. *You* may have moved on, but he hasn't."

She doesn't say anything.

"So when do I have to show up tonight?" I ask.

"Jacob said he can stay until about five. I can come back then if it's too early for you."

"Kind of. I was hoping to have dinner with Tom tonight."

"That's fine. I'll cover from when Jacob leaves until you arrive."

I hang up relieved. I don't want to overlap with Jacob.

* * *

I manage to get home before Tom and immediately take a shower. Another long hot one. Now I'm OCD Lady Macbeth. Every time I go to turn the water off, I hesitate and rinse off again.

When I decide my behavior is verging on psychosis, I get out and towel off, rubbing my skin so roughly that it stings and turns red.

I'm still in my bathrobe when I hear the door open. I race across the apartment and throw myself at Tom, hugging him tightly around his waist. I push my head hard against his chest, wishing I could burrow all the way inside and just stay there.

"Whoa," he says, pulling back with a laugh. "That's what I call a greeting!"

I look at his handsome, kind, smiling face, and I almost

blurt it all out, right there and then. It's unbearable. I have to tell him. I can't keep a secret from him. It's too agonizing. I'll burn up with the agony of it.

But of course, I *can't* tell him. For his sake, for Jacob's sake, for my family's sake. It kills me that I can't. Absolution would feel so good, so much better than this wrenching guilt that makes me shudder in his arms and bury my face on his shoulder so he can't see my expression.

But I don't deserve absolution. I deserve to suffer.

And I do. All through dinner—we go out to our favorite local restaurant, a small Italian place that may not serve the best food in town but is dark and quiet and always has a table available—and during the walk back to our apartment, I suffer as we talk about his work, my work, my father, the upcoming weekend, all the stuff we'd normally talk about, only it's like the world is melting around the edges and nothing's quite real. Everything's different, but I'm the only one who knows it.

It's lonely being the only one who knows it.

I get why unfaithful husbands show up with flowers and chocolates. I want to do something nice for Tom. I want to show him how much I love him. So back at the apartment, I pull him onto the bed, fondle and kiss him, pull off his jeans, and give him a blow job.

It's not just to be nice. It's also so we don't have sex. I can't yet. I still feel unclean.

Afterward, he pulls me up next to him, ruffles my hair, and thanks me. "That," he says, "was unexpected. To what do I owe the honor?"

"Just wanted to do something nice for you. I missed you last night."

"I missed you, too." He rubs his temple against mine. "I kept reaching for you all night long and you weren't there. Made it hard to sleep."

"I guess we're just addicted to each other."

"You really have to stay at your dad's again tonight?"

"Mom wants me to. But I swear this is the last night. He's doing so much better. And someone's coming tomorrow to set up one of those Lifeline alarm thingies so he can call for help if he needs it."

"I've fallen and I can't get up," Tom says and chuckles.

"Exactly." But it doesn't amuse me the way it does him.

Later, I give him a shoulder massage and fetch him a beer. It's stupid of me to wait on him like this—he actually wonders out loud why I'm being so unusually nice to him—but I can't seem to help myself.

When I leave to go to my father's, Tom gives me a cheerful wave good-bye. I go down to the garage, get in my car, drive away...

And feel a shameful, overwhelming sense of relief.

* * *

Mom's watching a news show on PBS with Dad when I arrive but jumps to her feet the second I enter the bedroom.

When I walk her to the door, she asks me if I can come out to the house on Saturday. The real estate agent's coming to talk strategy, and she wants another set of ears.

"Is anyone else coming?" I ask warily.

"Why?"

Because I can never be in the same room with Jacob Corwin again. "Just wondering," I say.

"Well, you're the only one I've asked. But I'm still hoping Hopkins might make it to town by then, so it's possible she'll be around."

I tell her I'll come.

We say good-bye, and then I go sit on the edge of my father's bed. During a commercial, he tries to convince me to go home to sleep. "I'm fine," he says. "All of this well-intentioned hovering is starting to get on my nerves. I just want life to go back to normal for all of us."

"It will, soon. This is the last night I'll stay here. I promise. Even if you collapse on the floor in a pool of your own vomit, I'll leave you alone tomorrow."

"But for tonight...Don't you have a boyfriend who wants you to come home?"

It's an effort to sound lighthearted. "Hmm. Let me think. Tall guy? Dark hair? We had dinner together tonight, Dad. It's fine."

"I haven't always been his biggest fan," my father says. "I never thought he was good enough for you. I know fathers always feel that way about their daughters' beaux, but this felt fairly objective. In all honesty, your mother and I both assumed you'd outgrow him."

"Well, I haven't. And I won't."

"He's good to you?"

"Very." I feel close to tears. Not because of this conversation, because of everything. "*So* good to me, Dad. He's the kindest, most loyal guy. I don't know what I'd do without him."

"Those are good qualities. Kindness. Loyalty. Sometimes I think we undervalue that kind of thing in our family." He sighs, or maybe just breathes in unevenly, and his face contorts a little.

"You need a painkiller, Dad?"

"A couple of Advils will suffice."

"You sure you don't want something stronger?"

"I like a little edge of pain. Reminds me I'm not dead yet."

"My company doesn't do that?"

"Ah, it's far too heavenly to convince me I'm still alive."

We're not a demonstrative family so when I give in to the

sudden urge to lean forward and brush a loose strand of gray-white hair off his forehead, I quickly straighten back up and reach for the bottle of Advil.

I feel his gaze on me as he swallows the pills. I busy myself straightening up the items on his night table. I toss some dirty tissues into the wastebasket, stack up some old mugs and glasses, pile books on top of one another.

"You're a good girl, Keats," he says as I carry the cups toward the door. "The best."

"Thanks," I say, but I don't believe him. I'm not the smartest or the most talented kid in my family—and as of about twenty-four hours ago, I stopped being honorable, which was the one thing I had going for me.

The phone rings as I bring the cups into the kitchen. I put them in the sink and answer it on the third ring. My stomach lurches when I hear Jacob's uncomfortable response to my hello, and I feel a burst of fury at my father for not having Caller ID on his phone. Not that he even knows what that is.

"Oh, hi. How's it going?" I say awkwardly.

"Fine, thanks. You?"

"I'm good, thanks. What can I do for you?" We both sound like we're speaking a foreign language we've gotten very rusty in.

"Sorry to bother you. Your father asked me to look something up for him, and I just tracked down the information. Could I please talk to him? If he's not asleep, of course."

"Yes, of course. Just a moment." But then I stop playing the game for one second. "Are you okay? Really?"

He doesn't stop playing the game. "I'm fine, thanks," he says in the same stilted, overly polite way, and I tell him to hold on while I put Dad on the phone.

13.

Keats?" Rochelle snakes her head around the opening to my cubicle the next day. "How busy are you?"

"Less than a bee, more than a beaver. Or should it be the other way around?" I'm in the middle of getting competing restaurant bids for a retirement dinner for the arts and culture instructor who started teaching at WCC before the dawn of cable TV. "What's up?"

"I wanted to ask you for a favor."

"Yeah? How's that going?"

"Great," says Rochelle, coming the rest of the way into my office. "You're very enthusiastic and would love to help me out." She's got a whole menswear look thing going on today: a long narrow tie and a white button-down shirt over linen pants. On someone else it would look costumey. On her, it looks fabulous. It must be nice to be five foot ten and rail thin—not that I'll ever know.

She takes a deep breath. "Okay, in all seriousness, here's the thing: I'm getting an article published. It's just a stupid trade journal, but since it's my first piece, I'm kind of nervous about it. You're so good at editing—would you be willing to just check it over for me before I send in the final draft? Just make sure there aren't any glaring grammatical errors? I don't want to make a fool of myself."

"I doubt that's likely, but I'm happy to read it for you."

She beams. "Thanks! I'll send it to you right away. I'd say no rush, only it's due on Wednesday, so there's totally a rush. But it's not too long. Fifteen hundred words."

That sounds long to me, but I just say, "No problem. Send it on over."

"Thanks again. You're the best."

So a little while later, when I check my e-mail, I get one from Rochelle with a lengthy attachment, which I download to look at when I have time.

I also have an e-mail from Cathy Miller. "Two things" is the subject line.

The first thing is that she's wondering if I want to grab lunch sometime. That's probably just an excuse for the second thing, which is a request for Jacob Corwin's e-mail. *You're right—I might as well give it a try. Worst that happens, he rejects me and I'm right back to where I am now, alone on Saturday nights.*

I feel unreasonably annoyed at her. She has lousy timing. Why didn't she ask me for this earlier? Now it's just weird—weird for me to keep engineering the fix-up and weird for her to blithely e-mail Jacob with a *So Keats said I should contact you . . .*

But if I don't give her his e-mail, she'll wonder why.

I propose a day for lunch and include Jacob's e-mail address. Now it's out of my hands.

I go to the vending machine in the back of the building and get a Snickers bar. I don't usually eat candy at eleven in the morning, but I'm craving consolation, and chocolate seems to be the only form it's going to come in at the moment.

I have another e-mail waiting for me when I get back, a thank-you from Cathy—*Here goes nothing! Wish me luck*—and also an IM from Tom: *Lou and Izzy were free tonight so I invited them over and said we'd order in.*

Great, I write back and it is. It saves me from being alone with Tom for the whole evening, which is a relief.

And this wave of relief makes me feel guilty all over again. I love Tom more than anything else in the world, and now I've created a situation where I can't bear to be alone with him because I feel so freaking guilty.

I wander back to the vending machine, but I already know that the achy, sad feeling in my stomach isn't hunger and no amount of chocolate will make it go away.

* * *

The boys are several beers into a baseball game, so Izzy and I volunteer to go pick up the Thai food we ordered—the place we like best doesn't deliver. When we get there, the food's not quite ready yet, so we settle into a couple of padded pleather chairs bookending an oddly ascetic-looking Buddha.

"Maybe we should just stay and eat here without them," Izzy suggests with a wicked grin. "They'll never even notice that we haven't come back. At least not until the game's over." As usual, she looks fantastic. Tonight she's wearing a striped minidress with knee-high leather boots. A guy who enters the restaurant does a total double take and stops to take a longer look at her. Once he's given her a good once-over, he nods with approval, winks at us both, and moves on to go pick up his food.

Izzy settles back in the chair, fluffing out her blond hair with her bright red fingernails. Bangles clink around her wrist.

She's used to getting attention like that.

I say, "I think the guys would eventually miss us—but only when they need someone to bring them another beer."

"That's about what it takes to get Lou to notice me these days. I should make a dress out of beer cans. He'd look at *that*."

"Is everything okay with you guys?" I ask. "Tom said some-

thing about the other night—that you didn't want to go bowling with them for some reason?"

"Well, part of it was I knew you wouldn't be there so I figured they'd have a real boys' night out without me." She screws
up her nose. "But to be totally honest, I was also majorly pissed
at Lou." Part of what I love about Izzy is how straightforward
she is. Her frankness is disarming because it's combined with so
much amiability: usually people wield honesty like some kind
of a weapon, but she's just happy to share.

"What was it about?"

"Oh, I was all PMSy, and it was making me nuts. Lou said
something that annoyed me, and I just lost it."

"What'd he say?"

"Honestly, I don't even remember. That's how crazy I was
being."

"I can't imagine you getting mad at anyone."

She opens her big blue eyes wide. "Seriously? I can be the
hugest pain in the ass sometimes! I don't know why Lou puts
up with me."

"Because you're beautiful and wonderful?"

"Aw, you're sweet," she says, dismissing what I just said with
a fragrant wave of her hand. She uncrosses her legs and leans
forward. "We're so lucky, Keats. Most girls our age can't find a
single decent guy to date, and meanwhile there's Lou and Tom,
best guys ever, and they love us. Half of my old friends won't
even talk to me anymore, they're so jealous I'm already married
to the man of my dreams while they're out there dating losers."

I murmur something polite in agreement, but I still think
Lou's the lucky one here. He's okay, but I like Izzy better.

"You and Tom are planning to get married one day, right?"
she says, then quickly adds, "If I'm prying, you can just tell me
to butt out."

"No, it's fine. We definitely plan to be together forever.

We're just in no rush to do the ceremony thing. Too much dealing with family."

"I was younger than you when we got married, but part of it was I felt like I couldn't move out and leave Mom and Dad to deal with Stanny alone unless I was married. It just wouldn't have felt right." Stanny is her brother with special needs. "That wasn't why we did it, though," she adds quickly. "We just really wanted to."

"Planning a wedding seems so overwhelming to me right now. And there's no rush."

"You're right," says my always-agreeable friend. "There's no rush at all. But when you do get married, I want to be a bridesmaid, okay?"

"I don't know," I tease her. "Then everyone will be looking at you instead of me."

"Don't be silly. The bride's always the most beautiful woman there." Izzy takes the subject of weddings seriously. "And I want to be in charge of doing your hair or at least of telling a professional how it should be done. You know how much I love your hair. And I've already decided how you should wear it for your wedding—half up—"

"Kate?" calls out the woman at the cash register. "Your order's ready."

"—half down with some ringlets pulled out on both—"

"Hold on," I say, standing up. "I think that's our food."

"She said 'Kate.'"

"I know," I say with a sigh, and we go up and get the food I ordered.

* * *

Cameron Evans can't stop staring at me. "Wow," he says. "Keats Sedlak. I'd recognize you anywhere. I sat right behind you for all of ninth grade English." He circles around me. "The back of your head hasn't changed at all."

"Thank you," I say since it seems to be meant as a compliment.

His father, who pumped my hand energetically when they first arrived, now beams delightedly at both of us. "You don't forget hair like that!" he says, then turns to my mother. "Look at them. Two minutes ago they were little kids, and today they're all grown-up and smarter than we are. How'd that happen?"

"Time passed?" my mother suggests drily.

"Ex-act-ly." He looks like a blown-up version of his son. They're both tall with big heads and straight, fair hair that's parted and brushed down, but Cameron is superthin and his father's shoulders and waist are padded with flesh under the wool suit jacket he wears. His shrewd, dark eyes dart around, assessing the house, assessing my mother, assessing me. "So do you remember Cameron as well as he remembers you?" he asks me.

I nod. He's changed, though. He was awkward and self-effacing in high school, but he's become slick and outwardly confident.

He swipes his hand through his hair, smooths it down on top, leans his hip against the dining room credenza, and says smoothly, "You were a lot more memorable than I was."

"I doubt that."

"No, you were. She was," he tells my mom. "She was just so smart. The teacher loved her. Everyone waited to hear what she had to say. If Keats didn't know the answer, no one did."

"That is so not how I remember it." I'm trying to be a good sport, but I'm finding this conversation excruciating. This guy is a salesman, just like his dad. It's the house that's exciting them, this big old house that my mom is dying to get rid of and doesn't owe any money on—it should be an easy sale; she won't hold out for an impossible price. They've got the scent of it, and it's clearly giving them both a hard-on. They'll say anything right now to make us happy.

But my mom seems enthralled by all this reminiscing. "Yes, teachers always loved Keats."

"No, they loved Hopkins," I say. "Sometimes they loved me for being her younger sister."

She shakes her head. "Hopkins drove most of her teachers nuts."

"Only because she knew more than they did before class even started."

Mom shrugs. No argument there.

"Oh, I looked up that article you mentioned," Mr. Evans says to Mom. "The one in *Harvard Magazine*. And the one in the *Wall Street Journal*, too. Sounds like your daughter's doing some groundbreaking work." Mom's clearly told him a lot about Hopkins. He turns to me. "And what are you up to these days, Keats? You must have graduated from college a few years ago, yes?"

Mom's clearly told him nothing about me. Well, what is there to tell?

"I work over at Waltham Community College."

"Teaching?"

Mom answers him. "Keats manages their English department."

"The English department office," I correct her sharply. "I don't run the department. I run the office."

"Interesting," says Cameron, even though it really isn't.

"What do you do?" I ask to be polite. Then I realize what a stupid question that is.

"Um...this?" He gestures around us, indicating the house.

I flush. "Right. I knew that."

"Cameron didn't come with me last time," Charlie says. "He

hasn't gotten a good look at the property yet. How about you give him the grand tour while I sit down with your mother and start throwing some boring numbers at her?"

Oh, great. It occurs to me that maybe Mom had me come out today just so she could fix me up with Cameron. But all I can do now is try to sound cheerful as I tell him to follow me. As we walk out into the hallway, I hear Charlie saying, "We're truly honored that you chose us to represent this amazing property, Eloise. I can see that this is a house that's been cherished, and I promise you that we will find a buyer who'll love it just as much as you have."

"They can set fire to it so long as they give us our asking price," Mom replies.

I trot Cameron swiftly through the downstairs. I'm a little bummed to see Mom hasn't made much progress since the last time I was here. There are some boxes scattered around, so I guess she planned to start packing, but they're still empty, and the shelves and tables are still crammed with junk.

"I love the way your house rambles," Cameron says as we head up the stairs. "It has so much character."

"It always felt kind of rabbit warreny to me. Not necessarily in a good way. But I will say, there are lots of excellent places to hide here."

"Did you hide a lot when you were a kid?"

We're upstairs. "Not really hide. I just liked to crawl into tight places where no one could find me."

"How is that different from hiding?" he asks seriously.

"I'm not sure." I point down the hallway. "That's my brother Milton's room—he still lives here—and the one next to it used to be mine, but he's spread into it, and over there—"

"Wait—spread into it? Did he break down any walls?"

"No, he just leaves the doors to the shared bathroom open."

"Let me see." He's already at the door, turning the knob.

"Wait! We have to knock first. He's probably in there."

"Oh, I didn't realize he was home."

I knock and Milton says, "What?"

"It's me. And"—I hesitate, not sure what to call Cameron—"and a real estate agent. Can we come in so he can see your room?"

"Do you have to?"

"Yes," I say and open the door.

Milton's sitting at his computer. He's got some major bed-head, but otherwise looks adequately presentable in sweats and a T-shirt. "Hi," he says, swiveling in his chair. My companion starts to introduce himself when Milton cuts him off. "You're Cameron Evans."

Cameron blinks. "Yeah. How'd you know that?"

Milton shrugs. It's something he's always been able to do—remember virtually every person he's ever seen. He used to read through the school yearbook once a year just so he could put a name to each face. And from then on, he knew who everyone was. It's an unusual skill, and I'm jealous of it. People remember me because of my red hair and weird name, so I'm at a disadvantage at parties.

"You're a real estate agent now?" Milton says to Cameron.

Cameron reaches into his jacket pocket and pulls out a small silver business card holder. (Really? A business card holder? The guy is *my* age. Why is he pretending to be fifty?) He extracts a card and hands it to Milton.

"Evans and Evans?" Milton reads.

"My dad and me. Although the company name predates me. He and my mother were the original Evans and Evans, but now she uses her maiden name professionally."

"Why?" Milton asks.

"They got divorced and don't work together anymore." He says it easily. I wonder if it's a function of how much time has elapsed or if it just wasn't all that traumatic for him.

"Ours are in the process of getting a divorce," I say in the spirit of unity.

"Your mom mentioned that. It's one of the most common reasons for people to sell their houses, you know."

"Did yours?" asks Milton.

"What?"

"Did your parents sell their house when they got divorced?"

"Actually, no. Mom still lives in it."

Milton hands him back the card even though he was probably supposed to keep it. "Home prices are down about twenty percent from four years ago," he says. "That must be rough on your business."

"We're doing okay." Cameron's smile is looking strained.

"How much do you think you can get for this house?"

"My father's discussing that with your mother right now."

"I've checked out the comps," Milton says. "A house two streets over sold for one point five million eighteen months ago, but since then, two similar houses in the neighborhood have gone for less than a million, and there are about four currently on the market. Several of them have lowered their prices more than once. What do they call that? Chasing the market? Don't you represent one of them?"

"We represent quite a few houses in your neighborhood." Cameron wipes his hand across his forehead. "Not sure which one you're thinking of.... It's a moderately slow market right now, but you guys don't have to worry about that. This house is unusually stunning, and with no mortgage—"

Milton shakes his head condescendingly. "Perrin Barton in the *New York Times* said a few weeks ago that no one should be selling right now. Hold on to your real estate, she said. If anything, buy more. Every sign says prices are depressed below market value because buyers are nervous about the economy, but in a couple of years, real estate should regain some momentum."

I'm listening, amazed as always at how Milton—the guy who can't boil water for pasta or run a simple errand—can easily track down, synthesize, and remember information. It's no wonder he was a straight A student, but it's easy to forget his strengths when I only ever see him fading into the background here at home.

"Huh," Cameron says. I can literally see the sweat beading on his forehead. To be fair, it *is* warm in Milton's room. He never opens a window. "Interesting. I'll have to read that article. But no one really knows what the future will bring. The important thing to remember is that sometimes it's just the right time in your life to sell, no matter what the market's doing, and that's where your mother seems to be right now."

"She owns this house outright," Milton says. "No mortgage means she's not paying out every month, and the taxes are low since they bought it so long ago. It doesn't cost her much to carry it. In fact, any place she moves, even an apartment, would probably cost her more per month. Seems to me it makes sense to hold on to it until the market gets stronger."

"That's definitely a conversation you should have with her." Cameron's edging toward the door. "My sense is she's ready to just be rid of this big, old house. But it's always a personal family decision—"

"Come on," I say, taking pity on him. "I'll show you the upstairs office." I grin at my brother behind his back. "I'll be back later to talk, Miltie."

"Bring some toast with you," he says and swivels back to his computer.

* * *

Later, after the Evanses leave, I tell Mom what Milton said about waiting to sell the house.

She shakes her head. "He's not the one who has to take care of this monstrosity. I just want to get rid of it at this point."

"I know. And I think Milton knows that, too, but he's not losing his home without a fight. Oh, and also? He wants some toast."

Mom follows me into the kitchen. "So Cameron seemed very happy to see you again," she says pointedly.

"Only in your imagination."

She goes over to the refrigerator, studies its contents, closes the door without taking anything, and whirls around, her skirt billowing up. "If he calls you, you should at least have coffee with him. It wouldn't kill you."

"Tom wouldn't like it," I say flatly. I put the bread in the toaster and press it down.

Her eyebrows go way up. "How medieval of him. And of you to think that means you can't do it."

"I'm not saying he'd *forbid* me. He lets me do what I want. But I'm not going to do something that makes him uncomfortable." Good thing she doesn't know what a hypocrite I am.

She folds her arms across her chest. Then unfolds them and fingers the dangling silver earring in her right ear. "This is the time in your life to be meeting lots of people, Keats. I understand the attraction of a steady boyfriend, but you're losing out on so many opportunities by playing house too soon."

"Mom, no one's playing at anything here. Tom's the guy I'm going to spend the rest of my life with and you need to—"

She cuts me off. "The rest of your life? You're not old enough to know anything about the rest of your life. I'm not sure *I'm* old enough to make those kinds of statements, and I've got thirty years on you."

"Fine," I say. "As far into the future as I'm capable of seeing, I expect Tom to be at my side, first as my boyfriend and then as my husband and eventually as the father of my children. When we do get married, I hope you can find enough affection for me to congratulate us and to accept Tom into our family." My voice is breaking, but I don't even know what's making me emotional, whether it's my mother's attitude or my own recent screwup. I open up a cabinet to get out a plate, hoping it'll hide my weird overreaction.

"All I want is for you to be happy, Keats. And if I were certain that your happiness lay with Tom, I wouldn't say another word. But given how young you are, there's a very good chance that he's not the right man for you, and if that's true, I want you to realize that sooner and not later, when you have kids and a house and a mortgage and a life together that's painful to untangle."

I whip around. "You're judging me because of *your* mistakes. And that's not fair. I'm completely different from you."

"Not as different as you might think. When I was twenty-five, I thought I knew everything, too."

The toast pops up. "How wonderful for you that you're so much wiser now." I throw the slices onto a plate. "I'm going to go hang with Milton for a while."

"Good," she says. "He needs the company."

"You think?" I take the toast upstairs. Milton and I play several rounds of *Call of Duty*, and then I come back downstairs and Mom says, "Your father just called."

"How's he doing?"

"Much better. He's starting to really sound like himself. For better or worse. He did have a request for us, though. Since Hopkins is supposed to get in late tonight—"

"Oh, is she? I didn't know that. No one tells me anything."

"—he asked if we could all have an early dinner together tomorrow. Says he has something important to discuss."

"Can I bring Tom?"

"That would be up to your father. He's the host."

"And he invited *you*?"

"He said I *had* to be there. I want to see Hopkins, so that's fine with me. Oh—I'll have to cancel my other plans."

"Another date?" She nods. I raise my eyebrows. "Who is it this time? Donald Trump?"

"It's Paul again."

I wrinkle my nose. "Paul? Yuck. What happened to Michael?"

She laughs. "And you accuse me of intruding into *your* personal life."

14.

In the midst of my misery, there's one small ray of relief. I never told Tom what happened in this very apartment last week, so he can calmly walk into the room where Jacob and I rolled around naked together. If he knew—

He doesn't. Thank God.

This proves I was right not to tell him.

But it doesn't help with my internal distress. To be back here so soon with Tom...the guilt and shame rise up again as sharp as they were that very first night.

It almost ruins my excitement at seeing my sister. It's been about four months since I last saw her on Christmas Day, but that was brief—Tom and I were at the house just long enough to open gifts, and she was gone the next day—and so much has gone on with Mom and Dad since then that it feels like it's been a lot longer.

She greets us at the door to Dad's apartment and gives me a hug, then tells me I look tired.

Hopkins is tall and thin, angular like Mom but without Mom's unexpectedly wide hips. She's narrow all over. Even her face is long and narrow, and so are her nose and elegant eyebrows and her ponytail. She's pretty—at least *I* think so; Tom doesn't agree, maybe because she's so decidedly ungirly. I've never seen her wear makeup or do anything with her hair other than wear it straight down on her shoulders or up in a ponytail. And she dresses terribly in shapeless dresses or dowdy skirts or jeans that are too short. Right now she's wearing khakis that gape at the waist and sag at the butt and a dark blue oxford shirt that looks like it came from the men's department. Everything about her screams, "Notice my brains, not my looks." She doesn't need to fuss over her clothing or wear mascara: she's Hopkins Sedlak, the smartest, most powerful person in any room, no matter what she's wearing.

She shakes Tom's hand and gives him a cool kiss on the cheek. "I can't believe you guys are still together after all these years," she says before leading us over to the coffee table area, where Mom and Dad are already sitting.

Milton's not there. I ask Mom about it, and she claims he "almost" came, which probably means that she asked him to come, he said he'd "think about it," and then when it was time to leave, he said, "Not this time but maybe the next." It's never the next time. I wish she'd just confront him, force him to realize he's always postponing joining the human race, and then just drag him along. But she never seems to have the energy or the time—or maybe the inclination—to do that.

Dad's apartment is a lot messier than when I was there last. There are papers, journals, and electronics (a laptop, a Black-Berry, an iPad) scattered over every surface and even some dirty clothing on the floor. Hopkins has changed the landscape of the place.

I had forgotten what a slob she is. When she lived at home, she'd shove off her shoes the second she didn't want them on her feet anymore, and I spent most of my childhood either tripping over her sneakers or picking them up and putting them to the side. No one else ever bothered. It wasn't just her shoes, either. She left a trail of food and tissues and papers behind her wherever she went. I once complained to Mom that Hopkins made the biggest messes in the house and never helped clean up, and Mom shrugged and said, "She has more important things on her mind"—like she was *proud* of Hopkins for not taking the time to toss out her own peach pits.

Dad's enthroned in one of the armchairs. His face is still pale and thin, but he's sitting up straight, he's dressed, his hair is combed, and he looks better than he has in weeks. I ask him what this meeting is about, and he says, "All will be revealed in time."

I offer to clear the coffee table, but when I pick up Hopkins's laptop, she instantly jumps up and grabs it from me. I pile up some of her papers and follow her into the office where the sofa bed is open, sheets all rumpled, the blanket tangled. While we're alone in there, I ask her why she thinks Dad wanted everyone to come tonight.

She says, "You'll see," in a way that makes it clear Dad has already told her. He told the daughter who *wasn't* by his side when he was hospitalized. It hurts, but it's not Hopkins's fault, so I swallow the hurt and ask her what's going on at work these days.

"It's been absolutely—oh, hold on a second." She pulls her BlackBerry out of her pocket and peers at it. "Sorry, Keats, I have to take this. You go on and join the others and I'll be right out." I had forgotten how different her voice is from mine. It's low and flat with very little intonation. It's a lecturing voice, not a conversational voice. As I leave the room, she's rapping out a toneless "Hopkins Sedlak" into the phone, which I guess is how she answers it.

I usually just say hi.

"Ever hear the one about the prodigal daughter?" I say to Tom when I come to sit down next to him on the sofa.

"Isn't it a son?"

"Not in this case."

"Huh?"

Before I can explain, the door opens and Jacob walks in with two restaurant takeout bags.

I stop breathing for a second. I had no idea he was coming. I'm paralyzed with horror at the thought of how this moment would have played out if I had told Tom about what happened. Thank god I didn't. Thank god I didn't.

Mom rushes forward, takes one of the bags, and kisses Jacob on the cheek. Hopkins wanders out of the guest room with the BlackBerry clamped to her ear and waves at him. I stay on the sofa with Tom who calls out a genial greeting.

When Tom settles back down, I feel the sofa cushion shift ever so slightly under me, and unwillingly, I flash back to the other night, Jacob's body on mine, my hands pinned, my mouth and legs open and eager. There's an alcoholic haze over it all, but I remember it pretty clearly.

I reach for Tom's hand and put my head on his shoulder. That's when Jacob comes to join us around the coffee table. I want to sit up straight but am worried he'll think I'm moving away from Tom because of him, and that's the last thing I want him to think, so I keep my head on Tom's shoulder, but it's getting uncomfortable—my neck is aching—and I feel stupid, so I finally go ahead and sit up, but I can't look anyone in the eyes.

I leap gratefully to my feet when Mom says she needs someone to help her set the food out. I follow her into the kitchen where she worries out loud that Indian food might be too rich and spicy for Dad, but as we peel back the foil tops to the containers, she sees that Jacob ordered mostly plain tandoori chicken and white rice. "I should have known he'd be careful," she says, pleased.

"Because he's so perfect?" I say. "Because he never does anything wrong? Oh no, not *Jacob*."

She stares at me. "What are you talking about?"

"Nothing." I avoid her eyes, pretend to be busy folding up the tinfoil. "It's just—why is he always at our family get-togethers?"

"Ask your father. He's in charge tonight, not me." She pulls a stack of paper plates out of a bag. "Oh, good—Jacob got these, too. There aren't nearly enough plates here for all of us— I'm sure it never even occurred to Larry to think about that." Napkins and forks come out of the same bag. "I'm so glad Hopkins made it, aren't you? I feel like there's a huge weight off my mind. The other doctors might have missed something, but if Hopkins says he's fine, he's fine."

I murmur something, an assent, I guess.

She goes on. "I've got to take her to get her hair cut, though. Did you see how long that ponytail is? I bet it reaches her waist when it's down."

"She's old enough to get her own hair cut if she wants to, Mom."

"I know, but she never gets around to it. She's too busy do-ing other things. I always take her while she's in town."

Why does this bother me? As I put serving spoons in the food, I try to figure it out. It has something to do with the weird mixture of idolatry and infantilizing that my mother shows toward Hopkins, like she's someone whose brain is so overdeveloped she can't be expected to function like a normal human being. Mom's that way with Milton, too.

It's like the very fact that I'm able to take care of myself proves how not brilliant I am. How ordinary.

It's not fair. Do I need to be incompetent to be considered in their intellectual league?

I'm still seething about this when my mother tells me to call the others in to eat.

I go back into the living room. Hopkins is sitting at the

edge of the sofa, talking in her rapid, expressionless way to Jacob and Dad, who are in the armchairs. Her back is basically to Tom, even though he's sitting next to her and listening. "Neurologists owe all their knowledge to the nail gun," she's saying. "If it weren't for stupid people shooting nails into their own heads, we'd never have figured out the different regions of the brain."

"You'd still have strokes," Jacob says.

"Strokes are good," she concedes. "Bullets help, too."

"Strokes are good?" Tom repeats from behind her. "How can a stroke be good?"

No one responds to that.

"Who was the guy who got the iron rod through his head and lived?" Jacob asks Hopkins.

"Phineas Gage," my father instantly cuts in. "It's such a great name. So memorable. A novelist couldn't have come up with a better one."

"*That* he remembers?" my mother says to no one in particular. She's come up behind me without my noticing. "He can't remember my maiden name or anyone's birthday, but he can remember that?"

"Wait, who's Phineas Gage?" Tom asks.

No one responds to that, either. It's like he's not even there. Hopkins just keeps addressing Dad and Jacob. "If you really want to learn something new about the brain, you should just hire someone to run down to a construction site and start shooting nails at every head he sees."

"That must be why they wear those yellow helmets," Jacob says. "To protect themselves against rogue neurologists."

Hopkins laughs. "Some people just don't appreciate the spirit of scientific inquiry." Those two seem to be getting along well.

"Some people don't like taking nails to the head," I say.

"Anyway, isn't that the point of all our modern imaging equipment? To learn about the brain without actually damaging it?"

"Where's the fun in that?" Hopkins says, and now it's Jacob's turn to laugh. A little too generously, like he's making some kind of point about where his allegiance lies, about which Sedlak daughter he approves of.

"Fine," I say. "You go shoot some nails into someone's head. Just come eat first. Dinner's ready."

Tom's up and across the room before the words are out of my mouth. He has his plate filled before the rest of us make it to the kitchen. Once we've gotten our food, we all gather around the coffee table again, Tom and Mom and I at one end, the three others at the other end.

I chow down mechanically, not particularly enjoying the food, eating out of nervousness, not pleasure. As soon as I stop shoveling in rice and chicken, I feel sick to my stomach.

Hopkins is ignoring her own barely touched plate in favor of punching away at her BlackBerry—e-mails or texts, I assume. They're probably all wildly important. Every time she hits *send*, she's probably saving someone's life or at least his memory.

I keep reminding myself of that as the meal continues and I find myself wanting to snap at her to stop playing with her phone and actually eat *something*, for god's sake. It's not just that her food is getting cold. If I'm being honest, I have to admit that I'm jealous of the fact she's so much thinner than I am, jealous that she seems to be indifferent to eating. It's always been like that. She's never cared about meals, had to be reminded to eat when she got busy or was studying. I've never in my life forgotten to eat, and if food's in front of me, I'm eating it. It's why I can't remember a time in my life when I didn't wish I could lose five pounds.

She finally puts the phone down, and starts telling Jacob and Dad about the case she's been working on (and probably e-mailing about)—the young mother with the repeating strokes. I can tell Mom is dying to hear what she's saying. She keeps her head cocked in that direction, and while Tom tells her about some of his plans for his dad's business—he wants to expand more in the direction of supplying uniforms and linens instead of just laundering them—her nod is more impatient than interested.

Tom and I clear our dishes together. In the kitchen, he asks in a low voice how much longer we have to stick around.

"I haven't seen my sister in ages," I say. "What's the rush?"

"I know," he says. "I'm sorry. Take your time."

But he's clearly not having fun, and I feel bad about that, so when Tom and I retake our seats in the living room, I interrupt Hopkins to ask Dad if he's ready to get on with the business of the day, whatever that may be.

"I guess now is as good a time as any to have the conversation." His eyes are much sharper now than they were when he was ill. They flit from face to face, surveying us all under his fly-away eyebrows. "I suppose you're all wondering why I asked you here tonight," he says jovially.

"Please tell me it's not to solve a murder," I say.

"Solve one? No. But possibly to commit one." He chuckles, pleased with some private joke. "Let me explain. We're here to talk about my death—or more accurately, my living will. Recent events have convinced me it's wise to put my affairs in order."

Tom says, "You don't need to worry about any of that, Larry. You look great—right back on track."

I cringe inwardly. My father hates glib reassurances.

Sure enough: "Thank you," my father says coldly. "I appreciate the sentiment. However, I still hold the belief that I will die some time in the not-terribly-distant future. Do you disagree with that supposition, Tom?"

My boyfriend fidgets uncomfortably and glances desperately

at me like he needs some help. "Well, I'm sure it won't be soon."

"Your certainty on the matter is invaluable." Dad's contemptuous of anyone who skirts the subject of the inevitability of death. Like most people, Tom knows on some level that everyone dies, but he doesn't particularly like to acknowledge that fact. My family revels in acknowledging that fact. My parents think it shows a sophisticated intellect to discuss your own mortality—and that of your loved ones—calmly and rationally.

I flash a smile at Tom that's meant to be reassuring. He gives me a weary shrug that says, *I get points for trying, right?*

"You already have a living will, Larry," my mother says, her brow furrowed with confusion. "We made them together."

"I know. And if you remember, you're my health care proxy."

"And you're mine."

He settles back in his chair and eyes her. "All things considered, perhaps it makes sense to update them?"

"Worried she'll be too eager to pull the plug, Dad?" Hopkins asks with a short hoot of laughter.

"I had my chance," Mom says calmly. "And I encouraged those nice doctors to keep him alive."

"I'm not the slightest bit concerned that the plug might get pulled too soon," Dad says with a shake of his head. "My fears all run in the opposite direction." He turns back to my mother. "Your life, Eloise, will soon be diverging from mine in ways that lead me to believe it might make sense for us to find other proxies. I don't want you ever to have to come rushing back from wherever you might happen to be—and whomever you might happen to be with—because a decision has to be made about my health."

Mom opens her mouth like she's going to argue, then closes

it again. She reaches out and gently touches his hand with hers. "Thank you," she says. "In all honesty, I would be relieved not to have to make that kind of decision."

"Let's save you some energy for dancing on my grave, shall we?" Dad says with a painful jocularity. He surveys the rest of us. "That means someone else will have to step up to the plate. By not being here, Milton forfeits the honor, which I'm sure will come as a huge disappointment to him. Jacob, I'm including you because—" His voice actually falters a tiny bit. Is my father getting emotional? He clears his throat and goes on perfectly steadily so I'm not sure, "—because you've proven during these last few weeks something I've suspected for quite some time, that you are far more than an assistant to me, more even than a friend. I can trust you—quite literally—with my life."

Crammed onto the sofa between Hopkins and my mom, I feel safe enough to dart a glance at Jacob to see his reaction.

He flushes. But all he says is a simple "I'm honored."

A satisfied nod from Lawrence Sedlak. "That leaves me with three people who could potentially take on this responsibility." Three? That means Tom isn't even in consideration, which I guess isn't a surprise, but it feels like a slap in his face, given that he's sitting right here with us and is more closely connected to Dad than Jacob is—he'll be his son-in-law one day.

I pat Tom's hand. He meets my eyes and surreptitiously raises his watch wrist. He's not hurt, just bored.

Dad's gaze flickers back and forth between me and Hopkins and Jacob. "So who would like to volunteer to make the final, crucial decisions about my health care and possibly the length of my life?"

"Are your wishes laid out pretty clearly in your living will?" Hopkins asks. "Have you defined what *quality of life* means to you?"

"As clearly as I can. None of this is simple, as you know better than anyone. I can say to you, 'I don't want to be kept alive if I'm not cognizant,' but it's still up to you to define cognizance."

"Hopkins is a neurologist," Jacob points out. "It seems to me if any of us can come close to figuring out whether a mind is active or not—"

"Hopkins is the obvious choice," Dad agrees. "But she's also a busy professional who lives in another city. Whereas—" He stops and everyone looks at me.

"I'm a loser who's always around," I supply brightly. "I can't say I *want* the job, Dad, but someone's got to do it, and I'm willing to."

He studies me thoughtfully. "My only question for *you*, Keats, is do you really have it in you to call an end to my life? Could you be ruthless enough? Because I'd much rather die too soon than linger on in some vegetative state."

"Leave me all your money, and I'll promise to kill you whenever you want. Today even." I try to sound lighthearted but I'm hurt. This is the second time in an hour that he's made it clear he trusts Hopkins much more than me.

"I'm serious about this. While you have many fine qualities, Keats, I'm not convinced ruthlessness is one of them."

"I'm ruthless!" Hopkins says cheerfully.

"Ruthless, yes, but seldom around, which brings me to you." Dad nods at Jacob. "Do you think you could say enough is enough on my behalf?"

Before Jacob can answer, I cut in. "Dad, this could all happen a decade or two from now. We don't know where Jacob might be by then."

"He's told me he intends to stay in the area."

"But there aren't all that many jobs opening up these days, and every academic in the world wants to live in the Boston area. Realistically he might just not be able to get work nearby. He'll have to follow the job. And it's not fair—and probably not realistic—to expect him to come back if you get sick." The truth is, the idea of having Jacob permanently connected to my family because of something like this freaks me out. A week ago, I think I would have been fine with it—relieved even because this isn't a job I want. But back then, Jacob's presence wasn't an embarrassment and a rebuke to me the way it is now.

"I'm getting the sense you'd rather the choice stayed in the family," my father says to me.

"It just makes more sense, doesn't it?" I toss a quick "no offense" in Jacob's general direction without meeting his eyes.

Hopkins flings up her hands. "This is stupid. I'll do it. It's not like there aren't telephones and airplanes. Wherever I am, I'll either get here or tell Keats what to do."

Dad says, "And if I'm alive but not capable of coherent thought?"

Hopkins grins at him and draws her finger slowly across her neck with a *kkkkkkk* sound.

"Excellent," my father says with real satisfaction. "Jacob? Call my lawyer tomorrow and tell him to change my proxy."

15.

"Your family's sick," Tom says when we're out in the hallway. "The way you all talk about your dad dying like it's a joke. It's not normal."

"I know. But Dad's right to take care of this."

"My dad could never talk about his own death that calmly. Then again, my father's a lot younger and healthier than yours, so he doesn't have to."

"He'll have to someday."

"Well, if he does, I'm not going to be making jokes about finishing him off, that's for sure. It's not funny. And I forgot how weird your sister is. She's impossible to talk to."

"You don't talk to Hopkins," I say. "You listen to her."

"I don't want to do either. I don't even know what she's talking about half the time. And she treats me like I'm a moron. I'm not crazy about the way she treats you, either."

"I'm her little sister. You know how that is. You're not always that nice to *your* little sister. But you love her."

"My little sister is a jerk. You're great. Hopkins doesn't appreciate you enough." The elevator pings and the doors open. "Meet me downstairs in ten minutes, okay?"

"Thanks for getting the car." We had to park a few blocks away.

"No problem—I'm happy to give you a few more minutes with your family." He steps inside the elevator.

"You mean, you're happy to have an excuse to escape early."

The doors close before he has a chance to deny that. Not that he would.

Right as I'm turning around, Jacob emerges from my dad's apartment, a bag of garbage in each hand. "Oh," he says and looks like he's almost ready to retreat back inside, but then he just says, "Garbage chute," and keeps going.

"I think it's behind that door." I point.

"Yeah, I know."

Of course, he does. He's spent more time here than anyone except Dad. And I'm sure he's taken out the garbage many more times than Dad has. In fact, I doubt Dad ever has, probably just lets it pile up until Jacob or the cleaning lady takes care of it.

I could wiggle past him and go back into the apartment, but both of his hands are full, and the door to the utility room is closed.

And in all honesty, I'm a little bit curious about what he's feeling toward me right now. I mean, the last time we were together, we were...together. We haven't seen each other since then, unless you count the miserable conversation we had right after. He hasn't looked at me or spoken directly to me once this evening. Some part of me wants to know if it's anger or circumspection or frustrated desire—or all of the above. This is probably my only chance to be alone with him to find out.

So instead of returning to the apartment, I open the utility room door for him. A light comes on, triggered by the door, and illuminates the tiny room. I follow Jacob inside and pull open the garbage chute for him. The door closes behind us.

He tosses in the bags, one after the other. I keep the chute open so we can hear them rolling all the way down. It takes a while. "That never grows old," I say.

"It is oddly satisfying."

"We don't have one in our building. We just put the trash out in the back hallway, and someone collects it."

"Sounds like luxury. The only one taking the garbage out to the street at my place is me."

So. We've made conversation. I'm encouraged by this and try to think of something else to say. I need him to know I'm ready to get back to our old footing, where we were simply pals. So I say—oh so casually and good-naturedly—"Hey, did my friend Cathy e-mail you about getting together? She told me she might." I figure this way he'll know I'm cool with his seeing someone, that whatever happened between us can and should be ignored.

His face darkens. He says in a low, vicious voice, "I'm not going to discuss my romantic life with you, Keats. Not now. Not ever."

I take a step back. "I thought you said we were still friends."

"In retrospect, that might have been an exaggeration." He pushes past me, opens the door, and leaves. The door swings shut again. I'm alone in the garbage room. And I'm stunned.

I could always bully and tease Jacob into doing what I wanted—and into forgiving me when I pushed him too far—but apparently I've lost that ability.

* * *

I follow him back to my Dad's apartment. He doesn't hold the door for me. I catch it before it's completely swung shut, just as my phone buzzes in my pocket. I check it.

Got the car. Be there in 2 mins.

I put it back in my pocket.

The others are still sitting around the coffee table. Someone's put out a box of chocolates, probably a leftover gift from when Dad was in the hospital. Hopkins is talking, and Mom and Dad are leaning forward like they don't want to miss a single word. So is Jacob, who's sitting next to Hopkins. I can only see his face from the side, but it looks intent and interested—no trace of the angry man who stalked away from me a minute earlier.

I move closer, curious to hear what's keeping everyone so enthralled.

"So this guy sits down every day at the same table in the rec room and writes. Pages and pages. He fills up one notebook, then another, then another. He barely moves, except to eat or when we make him get some exercise. But he always closes the journals when he's done and writes 'private' all over them. We want to respect his privacy, but we're dying to see what he's writing. Maybe he's the next Anthony Trollope, right? Of course, it could also be pornography. Or random words. And then his shrink decides, well, maybe we should have a peek, just to make sure that—" Hopkins stops because of the ringing.

Ringing that's coming from the phone in my pocket. Everyone turns to look at me. I hold up a finger, mutter "excuse me," and move away to answer it.

Tom says, "Did you get my text? I'm pulling up in front. I'll have to circle around if you don't come out soon."

"I'm coming." I hang up and tell the others I have to go.

Hopkins gets up. "I'm leaving first thing in the morning, so I probably won't see you again on this trip," she says. I can feel her phone vibrating in her hand as we hug briefly.

"I wish we'd had more time together," I say.

She agrees as she looks down at her cell.

"Can't Tom find something else to do?" Mom says. "So you can stay longer? I took the T in, but Jacob, you have your car here, don't you? Could you drive Keats home if she stays?"

Before he can even react to that suggestion, I quickly say, "I should go anyway. It's—I need to get home." I have no excuse beyond that.

Mom looks disappointed. "It's so rare that I see you girls together like this."

"Well, we're busy people," Hopkins says, still peering at her BlackBerry.

"When are you going to get out to the house to go through your stuff?" Mom asks her.

Hopkins doesn't even look up, just says absently, "I don't know. I'll try, but it might not happen. You have my permission to just throw everything out."

"That's just not practical."

I cut in. "I really have to go. Tom will kill me if I'm not downstairs soon." I quickly lean over to hug my dad and then my mom, but then I don't know what to do because in the past I'd have given Jacob the same kind of familial embrace, and now if I don't, it might look weird, but after that last exchange in the garbage room, I don't feel like I should even go near him. I just kind of wave my fingers in his direction. He doesn't respond.

"Good-bye, guys," I say and get my purse, which I'd left on the little round table. I head toward the door as Hopkins sits back down on the sofa and says, "Where was I?"

Jacob says, "The shrink said you guys should go ahead and look at the journals."

"Oh, right. So now we feel like we have permission, but we can't let any of the patients see us do it. The last thing we want is to make them—"

As I close the door behind me, Mom, Dad, and Jacob are all listening eagerly. I feel shut out, like they don't want me there because I'm not a member of their little clique, even though I know it was my decision to leave early.

What bothers me the most is the way Jacob was ignoring

me and paying so much attention to Hopkins. Was he doing it to teach me some kind of lesson? To prove that he has a great relationship with every other member of my family, but I've blown it with him? Or is he just that fascinated by my big sister? Which would make him exactly like everyone else in the whole freaking world.

It's not until I'm in the car that it occurs to me I'll never know if the crazy patient was a good writer or not.

* * *

At home, I change from the dress I've been wearing all day into sweatpants and a T-shirt. I pull my hair into a ponytail and crawl onto the bed next to Tom. He's watching some ESPN highlights show but he says, "You want me to change it so we can watch something together?"

"No, it's fine. There's something I need to do on the computer." I get up, fetch my laptop, and bring it back to the bed with me. By the time I have it open and am peering at my e-mail, there's a commercial on.

Tom slides to his feet. "I'm going to grab a beer. You want anything?"

I shake my head. He leaves, and when he comes back, I point to the computer screen. "I can't believe this."

"What?" He eases back down on the bed, leans over to see what I'm working on.

"Rochelle asked me to read this thing she wrote—an article for a journal for educators. She said it just needed a light proof-reading, but it's a total mess. I mean, her ideas are good, but there's no organization. Like here, on this page, she's talking about how gender roles play into the teacher's expectations, but then she talks about basically the same thing two pages later. It's like she never even sat down and read it through."

"Huh." Tom leans back on his pillow and picks up the remote. "Guess that's why she asked you to look at it."

"It needs a complete rewrite, but she said to just check it over." I gnaw on my fingernails for a moment, then add, "I want to help her, but it would take me hours to *really* fix it."

"Do whatever you think is best." He turns up the volume.

I scroll rapidly through the article for another minute or two. "Listen to this." I read a passage out loud. When I look up, Tom's twirling the remote in his hand. "Were you listening?"

"Yeah. It sounded okay to me. What's wrong with it?"

"Are you kidding? She had like three different topics and six metaphors going in that one paragraph alone. And she says the teacher has to 'literally work her fingers to the bone' if she wants these results."

"She's just saying that she'd have to work really hard."

"I know what she means," I snap. "But you can't say it like that."

"Why not?"

"You can't *literally* work your fingers to the bone, Tom. Not unless you're sticking them in a jigsaw."

There's a pause. I've gone back to studying the article when Tom breaks the silence. "You always treat me like I'm some moron after you spend time with your family."

I look up. "What are you talking about?"

"It's true. You know I'm not a genius, but most of the time it doesn't bother you. It's only when we see your parents or your sister that you start acting like I'm a total idiot."

"That's not true." I close my laptop and put it on the table next to the bed. "Just because I said that thing about centrifugal force? That doesn't mean anything—Rochelle's brilliant and *she* got it wrong, so obviously it's no big deal."

"I just don't like when you get that tone in your voice—

like you're so sick of having to explain everything in the entire world to your stupid boyfriend."

"I don't think that at all." I curl up and put my head on his chest, but he doesn't put his arms around me. "Tom, if I get impatient with you after seeing my family, it's not because I think you're stupid, it's because my family puts me in a bad mood. If I take some of the tension out on you, I'm sorry. I'd rather be with you than with them any time."

He relaxes then and puts his arm around my shoulder and rests his head on top of mine. "Yeah, I know it's hard on you to be with them."

"If I hadn't met you when I did, I'd probably be as crazy as they are. You saved me, Tom."

"Don't forget that." His hand wanders down along my back, cups my ass. "I like these sweatpants. They're nice and soft."

"You sure that's the sweatpants?" It's an effort to keep my voice light. We haven't had sex—other than the blow job I gave him, which doesn't count—since I slept with Jacob. I know there's no way for him to tell, but it's like "The Tell-Tale Heart": there's something hidden away that could betray me. And it's my own guilt.

"Let me check," he whispers, and his hand comes back up to the waistband of the sweats and then sneaks inside, under my underpants. "Soft here, too."

He gets the sweatpants off of me pretty soon after that. I'm pliable and passive, willing if not eager. The sex is fine. I wish I had nothing to compare it to. The fact that I do makes me sick.

Excitement will always fade, I tell myself as Tom slides inside of me. Rack up enough years with any guy, and the sex will eventually become routine. Excitement fades, but it's stupid to chase after it—you'll just end up alone. Excitement fades, but other things take its place and that's how it should be. I'm ahead of most girls my age. They're still making themselves crazy looking for the next best thing. Me, I've found the forever best thing.

My body slides up and down on the comforter as Tom pushes in and out of me. Up and down. I hold on to the bed frame and pretend to come.

* * *

In the end, I do a moderate edit on Rochelle's journal piece, cutting and pasting to bring some order to the whole thing but not actually rewriting much. She's very grateful. I feel vaguely annoyed with her, not because of the extra work, but because I'm sick of always being the organizer, first for my brilliant family and now for my brilliant boss. Part of me wants to be brilliant and sloppy, too, and let someone else bring order to *my* messes, but I didn't get the brilliant part, and there's no gain in just being sloppy.

Mom e-mails me. She doesn't quite get that e-mails are supposed to be informally dashed off. This one reads like it should have been written on scented paper with a pen that's been dipped in an inkwell.

Dear Keats,

That was a lovely evening at your father's. I'm sorry you couldn't stay longer. Hopkins has returned to New York, and life seems to be getting back to normal for all of us, although there's what they call a "caravan" at our house on Sunday morning and I'm supposed to get every room cleaned up and looking its best before then. So perhaps "normal" isn't the right word.

Could you do me a favor and read the e-mail I've attached to the bottom of this one? It's from Michael Goodman and

*I have to admit I'm somewhat uncertain of its implication.
Would you please read it and call me when you have a free
moment to discuss it?*

*Love,
Mom*

Okay, now I'm curious. I scroll down and read the e-mail she's
forwarded (she doesn't know the difference between *forward*
and *attach*). This one is a lot less formal than hers.

*Eloise—just wanted to let you know things are heating up at
work and I'm going to be snowed under for a while. I'll give
you a call when I see the light at the end of the tunnel. Stay
well. M.*

I read it a couple of times, then reach for the phone. When
Mom answers, I say, "It's not good."

"What?"

"The e-mail from Michael. I think it might be a brush-off,
Mom."

"I was wondering about that. That's why I asked you to read
it."

"I'm sorry. It's possible I'm wrong." I scan the e-mail. "But
I don't think I am. When people go out of their way to tell you
they won't be in touch, it's not usually a good sign."

"Shoot," she says. She sounds sad. Resigned, but sad. Makes
me want to offer her some hope.

"But it's also possible he really is just letting you know he
won't have much free time for a while, and he'll resurface in a
few weeks and—"

"No, I think your first reaction was right. I was getting a
strange feeling the last time we went out. It was harder to talk.

He seemed a little detached." She sighed. "You know, when I first sent him an e-mail—through that dating service—he admitted he was looking for someone significantly younger. But then we hit it off, and he said he'd give it a try. It's not like he didn't warn me."

"At least you have those other guys, right? Paul and Irv?"

"Unfortunately, he was the one I liked the most." She gives a small mirthless laugh. "From what I remember of my school days, this is how it always goes: you're always in love with the guy who doesn't want you, and the guy who wants you is never the one you want."

"It doesn't *always* work that way. The guy I like has always liked me back."

"That relationship has definitely insulated you from any rejection."

"I don't feel like I'm missing out on anything."

"I'm sure this is a personal growth experience for me," she says drily. "Painful things usually are."

* * *

A couple of days later, Cathy Miller comes by the office to meet me for our scheduled lunch.

"I need to stop at Costco either before or after," I tell her as we try to figure out where to go. "I have to stock up on coffee and snacks for the office."

"You're in charge of the shopping?"

"I'm lucky to have a job," I say more sharply than I intend. It's just...I'm sick of having to defend what I do.

Cathy puts her hands up. "Oh, believe me, I'm not criticizing. You have a great job. I'm jealous of it—I'm terrified I won't get hired anywhere after all these years of school and debt."

"Something good will come along."

"Do you ever think about going back to school?" She can say she thinks my current job is "great" all she wants, but just by asking that question she's implying I'm wasting my time here. Just like my family always does.

"Sometimes." The truth is that lately I've been thinking about it more and more. I'm getting bored at WCC, and it's not like there's any promotion track. Going back to school seems more appealing now than it did right after I graduated, but I don't know what I'd study, and I certainly don't want my family to know it's even a thought. They'd jump on it like a dog on a piece of dropped meat. I don't really want to discuss it with Cathy, either, so I add, "Not seriously, though. I'm pretty happy here. So should we eat somewhere close or drive separately somewhere farther so I can go on to Costco after?"

"Can I go with you to Costco? I've never been there. I've always wanted to go, and I have the afternoon free. Plus it gives us more time to talk."

I drive us to a deli near Costco ("You don't want to go in my car—you can see through the bottom to the street, it's so old," Cathy says cheerfully) where we both order tuna melts.

"This is nice," she says, gazing around contentedly after the waiter's taken our orders. Then she leans forward across the table. "So I'm dying to tell you something. You're going to be so psyched. I went out with your friend Jacob last night!"

It's weird what a shock it is to hear her say that. And not a particularly good one. But I force a smile and do my best to feign enthusiasm. "Great! How'd it go?"

"I *really* like him. I don't know why I didn't realize how cute and smart he was at dinner that night. I think you're right that we were all paying too much attention to your dad. Or maybe I'm just slow."

"So the date went well?"

"I think so. The only thing is—" She hesitates, glancing at me then down at the table. "I know he's your friend, and I don't want to make you reveal any secrets or anything—"

The fake smile freezes on my face, and I feel sweat pricking at my temples. Is it possible he said something to her about what happened between us? He wouldn't have done that, would he? He promised he wouldn't. "What do you mean?"

"It's just that I'm kind of curious about him. He said something about how he had a rough childhood. And he seems kind of..." She stops and plucks at the corner of the paper napkin in front of her. "I know this sounds awful, so forgive me, but I don't know how else to put it. He seems kind of damaged. Not in a crazy or mean way. Just like he's been hurt a lot and that makes it hard for him to open up to people now. You know what I mean?"

While I try to figure out some response, the waiter puts our drinks down in front of us. I sip mine gratefully. My face feels hot, but the iced tea makes me shiver with a sudden chill. "Both his parents died when he was still pretty young. You don't recover easily from that."

"Oh my god," Cathy says. "Poor guy. No wonder he seems so sad. Maybe your dad's heart attack brought back some of his worst memories."

"Yeah, probably."

"What about his romantic history? Do you know if he had a bad breakup recently or anything?" Something about the expression on my face makes her quickly add, "I swear I don't mean to pry. You don't have to tell me anything you think is confidential. It's just that I really do like him, and so I want to figure him out."

"He doesn't talk about his private life much," I say. "It just doesn't come up. And my dad's not the type to ask."

"How's he doing? Your father, I mean?"

I tell her Dad's doing great and fill the time waiting for our food with hospital anecdotes. Part of me wants to steer the conversation as far and as fast away from the topic of Jacob Corwin as possible, and part of me wants to ask Cathy tons of questions about the date.

Did he kiss her? They wouldn't have done anything more, I reassure myself—neither of them is the type to speed things along physically.

Although Jacob sped things along pretty quickly in my father's living room.

That was different.

I wonder if they've already made a plan to get together again.

Do I care?

I should. I should be rooting for this relationship to work out, because if he and Cathy fall in love, I won't have to worry about his hurt feelings anymore, or about how long things will be awkward between us. He'll have his girlfriend and I'll have my boyfriend, and that would create some kind of emotional Venn diagram where we can be friends in the overlap.

But I feel a tiny little stab of hurt somewhere in my head when I think of him and Cathy talking together or sitting together or holding hands or anything like that. Just hearing her talk about him like she has a right to, like he's not just my friend but someone who's potentially important to her—that's a stab right there.

The waiter puts our sandwiches down, and Cathy tucks eagerly into hers, which gives me a moment to let my mind wander, and I picture Jacob looking at Cathy the way he used to look at me.

That stab is the worst one so far.

It's the first time I've admitted to myself that I've known for a while that Jacob liked me and that *I* liked the way he'd jump to get whatever I needed or come over to talk to me if I was sitting alone. That I could tell he liked looking at me. That I could tease him and even take advantage of him, and he'd put up with it—maybe with exasperation, but he'd endure it and come back for more.

It's why I knew he wouldn't push me away when I kissed him.

It's why I kissed him.

"Aren't you going to eat?" Cathy asks me, and I realize she's inhaled half her sandwich already, and I'm still just staring at mine.

"Oh, sorry. I was just thinking about the stuff I need to get at Costco. I should make a list before I forget." I busy myself getting some paper and a pen out of my purse and spend a minute or two staring off into space and occasionally writing things down. It buys me some time to think my own private thoughts for a little while longer.

I've enjoyed soaking up Jacob's admiration more than I've ever acknowledged, even to myself. Not that realizing that changes anything. I have a boyfriend, a great one, and Jacob's free to see anyone he likes, even Cathy, even if she's really too tall for him, and too bony and earnest—

I stop myself. Cathy's great. I'm being a jerk.

Jacob's free to date whoever he wants. Because I'm satisfied with Tom.

But if I'm satisfied with Tom, why did I sleep with Jacob?

And then it hits me: it's because Tom got that tattoo! That's why I slept with Jacob.

My body almost crumples with relief. I've figured it all out.

Tom made it clear our relationship was permanent, and right after that I slept with another guy for the first time ever. Those two things *have* to be connected.

I know I want to be with Tom forever, but the fact I'd never been with another guy was probably flipping me out on some unconscious level when he showed me that tattoo and we celebrated an entire decade of being together. I would never cheat on a fiancé or a husband, so I needed to get something out of my system while Tom and I were still just girlfriend and boyfriend.

I slept with another man so I could commit myself wholeheartedly to Tom for the rest of my life and never cheat on him once it mattered.

This revelation makes me feel so much better.

I heave a big, relieved sigh and put my paper and pen away.

"Make your list?" Cathy asks.

"Yep," I say and pick up a sandwich half. My appetite's back.

16.

Rochelle is mildly annoyed that I forgot to buy Splenda. We're completely out, and she can't drink her coffee without it.

"Can I make a suggestion, Keats?" she says. "Tape a piece of paper to the cabinet in the kitchen—or even better, mount a dry erase board. Then we can all write down whatever we need as things run out. Don't you think that's a better system than just trying to pull together a list at the last minute?"

She means well. I know she means well. But I'm not in the mood for a lecture on organization, not from Rochelle. When I first started working for her, the kitchen was a mess, just a grungy old coffeemaker and a couple of half-eaten boxes of stale cookies. I cleaned it up, stocked it, labeled, shelved, and jarred everything, and made sure there was always a fresh pot of decent coffee for anyone who wanted a cup.

Also, I just made her article a lot better.

Then I wonder why I'm reacting this way. Rochelle's decades older than I am. She has a PhD in English. She's poised and stylish and married with children. And she's my boss. She has every right to give me advice, and this particular bit of advice is practical and easily implemented. So why am I chafing under one well-intended suggestion?

I don't know.

Maybe I'm just sick of my job. Or of my life.

That evening, Tom and I are driving to meet Lou and Izzy for drinks and a movie, when I ask him if he thinks I should take the GREs in the fall.

"Why would you do that?"

"I don't know. Just to see how I'd do on them."

"I already know how you'd do. Great. You totally killed on the SATs, remember?"

"I did okay." Not as well as Hopkins or Milton—they both got perfect scores. "I was just thinking that if I did *really* well on them, I could think about going back to school."

"Where?"

"I haven't gotten that far yet. Maybe get an MA in English literature somewhere. Or maybe think about law school."

"Those are two really different things—don't you have to take a different test for law school?"

"Yeah, I guess. I haven't put that much thought into this yet. I just feel like I want a change. I'm starting to hate my job."

"I thought you loved it."

"I do."

"You're not making any sense."

"It's a perfectly fine job." I finger a tiny imperfection on my jeans leg. "I just don't know if it's what I want to do for the rest of my life."

"It won't be." He reaches over and pats my knee. "You'll probably end up running the whole college. Or another place will hire you away for a much more important job." He squeezes my thigh. "Plus you know...Someday you might not want to be going to a job at all. You might want to stay home with the kids."

"Oh, am I having kids?"

"I certainly hope so." He grins. Man, he's handsome.

"Someday," I emphasize. "Not for a while."

"Right. Anyway, I'm not saying you shouldn't take the GREs. If you want to, you definitely should. I'll even help you study—we can make flash cards and I'll quiz you."

I put my hand over his on my leg. "Thanks. You're a pretty sweet guy, Tom."

"Only *pretty* sweet?"

I lean over so I can give him a kiss on the cheek. "Very sweet."

When he smiles and tilts his head like that, he still looks exactly like the guy who gave me a ride home when he was in college and I was fifteen.

* * *

After we've gotten our drinks, he announces to Lou and Izzy that I'm thinking of taking the GREs.

"God, that's like my worst nightmare," Lou says. "Test taking is not a strength of mine."

"I hear you, man," says Tom, and they clink beer mugs.

"I did okay on mine," Izzy says. "I mean, I'm sure nowhere near as good as Keats did, but okay. It didn't really matter, though, because my parents wanted me to stay at home and go to community college, so I could help with Stanny."

"Your phone's ringing," Tom says to me. The bar is crowded, and the four of us are crammed into a booth that would have been an intimate table for two. "I can feel it vibrating."

I get to my feet so I can work the phone out of the pocket of my jeans. "It's my mom."

"Ignore it," Tom says.

"I'll just see what she wants." The bar is noisy and hot, and I don't mind having an excuse to walk outside onto the cool, quiet street for a second.

"Am I interrupting something?" Mom asks.

"We're just at a bar with Lou and Iz. No big deal."

"I need your help."

"What's up?"

"It's just...I wanted Milton's room to look halfway decent since all the real estate agents are coming to see the house. So I asked him to straighten it up, and he threw a fit."

"What do you mean 'a fit'?"

"Well, he threw something at me."

"Seriously? Are you okay?"

"I'm fine. It was just a pillow."

"A pillow?" I laugh. "That doesn't even count as throwing something, Mom."

"He was seriously angry. He also hurled a book across his room and put a dent in the wall. Just when I'm about to start showing the house and need it to look its best."

"So what do you want me to do?"

"Come out here this weekend. Please? Tell him he has to accept that this house is being sold, whether he likes it or not. And maybe get him out of his room for a little while so I can clean it up."

"I could come on Saturday. Tom's playing golf with his dad all day. His mom wanted me to have lunch with her at the club, but I wouldn't mind having an excuse to skip that." Eating at the club with Tom's mother is an agonizing experience. She talks too loudly for the hushed dining room, and people are always turning to stare at her. I don't know why the Wellses were so desperate to join this particular old-money club. They don't really fit in there.

Actually, that's probably why.

"Tell Tom's mother that I need you at the house. Because I do. I haven't made a dent in the packing. I could really use as much time and help as you can give me."

"You mean I get to pack, too? I can't wait!"

When I get back to the bar, Lou is telling Tom about a TV show they're "totally addicted to." I slide in next to Tom, who whispers a quick "Everything okay?" and I nod.

Lou is describing the main guy on the show and how he works out and tans and has this on-again, off-again relationship with some trampy girl, and I realize that they're talking about the show Jacob and I watched that night in my dad's apartment. I can only remember it in flashes, but those flashes swirl around me now: the comically huge biceps on the best friend, the skimpy clothing, the deep kisses the girl kept giving the guy, Jacob's saying they looked like siblings. Or did I say that?

Jacob and I used to be like siblings. Now we're not even friends.

I fidget, cramped on the small bench, and massage my temples.

"You okay?" Tom asks, half shouting in my ear the way you do at a noisy bar.

"It's hot in here, don't you think?"

"Want me to get you an ice water?"

"That would be great." I slide out of the booth so he can get up.

"Anyone else want anything?" he asks.

"Two more Coronas," says Lou. "Oh, and did you want something, too?" he says to Izzy and laughs. He makes the same joke every time.

After Tom moves away and I sit back down, Izzy leans across the small table. "You're so quiet tonight, Keats. Is everything okay at home? What did your mom want?" Her big blue eyes are concerned, the thick layer of mascara fanning her lashes into star points.

"Everything's fine. She's trying to sell the house, but my brother—he lives at home—doesn't want her to."

"How old is he?" Lou asks.

"Twenty."

Lou snorts. "A guy that age shouldn't be living at home anyway. I mean, unless he's like Stanny."

"*You* lived at home until you were twenty-five," Izzy points out.

"That was different. There was a separate entrance, and I paid rent."

"Well, maybe her brother does, too."

"He doesn't," I say. "He's not very independent. He's got some issues."

"Like Stanny?" asks Lou.

"No," I say. "He's got different issues. He doesn't like to leave the house. I mean, he *really* doesn't like to leave the house—I don't think he walked out the door once this year. And I'm not too sure about the year before that."

"Things are probably too comfortable for him at home," Lou says. "Someone should just kick him out of there. Show him a little tough love."

I realize I'm rubbing my temples again. "You're probably right," I say wearily.

Izzy pats my hand. "It'll all be okay, Keats."

Her reassurance is meaningless but her intentions are kind, and I thank her. When Tom comes back, I tell him that my head is aching and I'll have to skip the movie. I urge him to go on ahead with Lou and Izzy, but he says he'd rather just go back home with me. When we get back, he turns on the TV, which just makes my head hurt even more.

* * *

"Okay," I say to Milton on Saturday. He's in his desk chair, working on the computer, and I'm sitting on his bed, watching him. "What's this about your throwing something at Mom?"

He stares at the computer screen and types something. "Huh?"

"Stop doing that and look at me."

"Hold on—this is important."

"Why, are you winning?"

"It's not about winning," he says. "It's about creating. You don't understand."

I get up. I forcibly swivel his chair around so he has to face me. "Do you have any idea how much she does for you?"

"Mom? Yeah, I guess. Let go."

"She told me you threw a fit last night."

"It wasn't a fit. I was just mad." He won't meet my eyes. Then again, he never does. "She keeps saying she's going to sell the house, and it's a bad idea. I've tried to tell her why, but she won't listen to me."

"That's because she's going to sell it no matter what you say."

"She shouldn't. It's not a seller's market. I've looked at the comps—"

"That stuff doesn't matter, Milton. Mom doesn't want to deal with the house anymore. Hopkins and I and Dad have all moved out—"

"Dad would move back in a second."

"But that's not what Mom wants. She wants to live in a nice small apartment."

"What about me?"

"What about you?" I hold on to the chair, certain that if I let go, he'll spin away from me again.

"I don't want to live in an apartment. This is my home."

"I know, but it's not your decision to make. It's hers. And it's not like she's going to throw you out on the street. You're just moving somewhere new." I let go of the chair and stand up. "Now get up. Come keep me company downstairs. I want a cup of tea."

"You're just trying to get me out of the room so Mom can clean it before the real estate agents come."

I shake my head, laughing. "How did you know that?"

"It's obvious."

"Well, come on anyway," I say and tug on his arm, pulling him up out of the chair. "Give Mom a break for once."

Mom must hear us coming down the stairs because she suddenly appears at the bottom with a vacuum, a can of Pledge, and some rags.

"Don't move my stuff," Milton says to her as she passes us.

"I wouldn't dream of it," she says without pausing.

"She's going to move my stuff," he tells me as we make our way into the kitchen.

"She's just going to make it look neater. It's a pigsty in there. You don't want strangers seeing it like that, do you?"

"I don't care. I don't want them in my room anyway." He sits down at the booth. "Will you make me something to eat?" His assumption that the rest of us will wait on him always astounds me.

And yet, of course, we *do*. "What do you want?"

"An egg in a frame?"

That sounds good actually. I decide to make one for myself, too. We still have over an hour before the agents come—plenty of time to clean up any mess we make. I find bread in the freezer where Mom keeps it, defrost a couple of slices in the microwave, pull out butter and eggs, and turn the burner on under the pan. I haven't cooked in this house for a while, but everything's where it's been for the last two and a half decades.

Milton watches me as I cook. "Make it crispy but not burned," he says. "I hate when it tastes burned. And keep the yolk runny. Not raw, just runny. It's safe to eat so long as it's pretty hot. Salmonella's killed at fifty-five degrees. Celsius, not Fahrenheit."

"What's that in Fahrenheit?"

"One hundred and fifty degrees."

"And what's boiling again?"

"Are you serious? Two hundred and twelve. Come on, Keats."

"Right. I knew that—I just forgot for a second." I cook our eggs and take them on plates to the table.

"Celsius is so much more logical than Fahrenheit. I wish the U.S. would switch over to it already. Can I have a glass of milk?"

"Get it yourself. I made the eggs." He doesn't get up, just starts eating. I eye him. "You have it pretty good here. I don't blame you for not wanting to leave. You get half the house entirely to yourself, Mom waits on you hand and foot, and you don't have to work or study or do anything."

"I study," he says. "I'm taking courses."

"Right."

"I am. Seriously, Keats. I'm working toward a degree."

"And then you'll get a job?"

"Yeah, probably," he says but without a lot of conviction. "And I work, too, you know, it's just on stuff you guys don't appreciate."

I raise my eyebrows skeptically but don't respond to that. I stick my fork into the middle of my egg in a frame and the yolk runs out dark yellow and steaming, just like Milton wanted. I feel absurdly pleased with my success. "I'm thinking of going back to school myself and getting a graduate degree," I say idly.

"You should."

"Why do you say that?"

He shrugs, forks some more bread and egg into his mouth, and chews noisily, his mouth open. There's yolk at the corners of his mouth and a fleck of white on his chin. His manners are atrocious. He says with his mouth still full, "You're too smart for that stupid job."

"It's not a stupid job. As jobs go, it's a good one, but you wouldn't know since you've never had one."

"Mom thinks it's a stupid job. She says so all the time." He stuffs the last bite of yolky bread into his mouth, chews, and burps. "I'm really thirsty now."

"Then get yourself something to drink. You're a grown man, for god's sake."

He's so startled that for a moment his eyes actually meet mine. "I know," he says. "I was just about to." He rises to his feet. As he gets a glass out, he swings the out-of-joint cabinet door back and forth a few times and says, "Maybe no one will want the house anyway. It's kind of falling apart."

"Someone will want it. It's a big piece of property in a great neighborhood in a good school district. The house doesn't matter that much—I wouldn't be surprised if the new owners tear the whole thing down."

Milton puts the glass down on the counter still empty and turns to me. "Mom should put in the contract that they can't do that."

"Once it's not our house anymore, what difference does it make?"

"So long as it's not destroyed, it will still be the same house we grew up in. I was even thinking that maybe one day I could buy it back with my own money."

"Come on, Miltie. Be realistic. Is that ever going to happen? You buying this house with your own money?"

"It could."

"It's going to sell for over a million dollars."

He shrugs. He stares down at the empty glass, his face morose.

I get up and touch his arm. "I know you love this house. I do, too. It's our home. But that's going to change. And it *should*. Just because you're used to things being a certain way doesn't mean that's the way they should stay. Change is scary, but it isn't necessarily a bad thing." He keeps shaking his head. I can't even tell if he's really listening, but I keep going anyway. "You can't just cling to something because it's all you know, Milton. Being an adult is about making new choices, accepting that what was right for you once might not be right anymore, that sometimes you have to give something up to move on to something better, that—"

I stop. Milton's staring at me.

"What?" I say.

"Why are you crying?"

"I'm not crying."

"Yes, you are. You have tears in your eyes. And your voice is all shaky."

"I'm just frustrated that you can't see this."

"No," he says. "You're not just frustrated. You're crying. Why?"

"Will you just go get your milk?" I don't want to admit that he's right, I'm crying, because I can't explain it. It's just weird.

He obediently walks away and opens the refrigerator door. I take the opportunity to rub my face hard against my sleeve. It helps. The tears stop.

"The milk's all gone," Milton says, almost in amazement. "But I know we had some this morning. Mom brought me a glass."

"She must have used it up."

"Rats." He shoves the door closed again. "I really wanted some."

"Yeah? Then let's go get some."

"You can," he says, backing away quickly. "I have some stuff to do. Don't forget: I like two percent."

"You have to come with me."

"I'm not even really dressed, Keats."

"You're fine. People go out in sweats all the time. You just need shoes."

"I don't know where mine are."

I believe him. It's probably been months since he's worn them. Maybe years. "I'll run up to your room and see if I can find them. You wait here." I don't trust him to get within a few feet of his computer and be able to tear himself away again.

"It'd be faster for you to just go by yourself."

I get up close to him and fix him with as steely a look as a short, curly, red-haired girl can pull off. "You are going with me to the supermarket if I have to kick you in the butt every single step of the way. Do you understand me?"

"Yes, I understand you," he says in an aggrieved tone. "I just don't see what your problem is."

"My problem is that my brother never leaves the house. But that's going to change right now. Don't move, or I swear I'll make Mom promise never to run an errand for you again." Before he can respond, I'm racing out of the kitchen and up the stairs, yelling for Mom, telling her that I need Milton's shoes.

She meets me at the doorway to his room. "What are you talking about?"

"He's coming with me to the supermarket."

Her mouth falls open. "Really?"

"If I can find his shoes."

"He hasn't left the house in two years."

"I *know*. Help me find his fucking shoes before I lose my chance!" I don't think I've ever sworn in front of my mother before. Her eyes grow big, and then she nods quickly and helps me find the shoes.

17.

An hour later, Milton's safely back in his room, two large glasses of milk under his ever-expanding, always-elastic waistband, and Mom and I are up in the attic, hiding from the real estate agents who are crawling all over our house.

I'm telling her about our supermarket expedition. "He tried to stay in the car, but I wouldn't let him. I had to literally open his door and haul him out. I think I pulled a muscle in my back." I reach back and rub my knuckle against the sore area.

"But then he went in with you?"

"Yep. I marched him in. I was practically shoving him."

I'm curled up on the daybed, but Mom is prowling the room, ducking her head when the ceiling gets too low and then circling back around. "I can't believe you got him out. I don't know how you did it."

"By not giving him a choice."

"You have more power over him than I do. He listens to you."

"What are you talking about? You're his mother. I'm just his sister."

"He respects you more."

"This wasn't about respect," I say. "It was about a combination of physical force, threats, and verbal abuse. I *bullied* him into going."

"How do you think he feels about it?"

I consider that. "When we got to the milk section, he said there's really only one kind he likes and he was glad he could pick it out. He said you get the wrong one all the time. And he liked doing the scanning at the self checkout. But he was still pissed at me for making him go."

"You have to keep doing this," she says, and I scowl at her because she's not saying, "*I'll* keep doing this." No, it's "*you* have to keep doing this."

"I'll do what I can, Mom, but I'm not the one who lives with him."

"I'm just so busy these days. And it sounds like it wasn't easy." She's already back to her excuses.

I sit there for a moment, running my hand absently along the worn-out sofa arm. It's a mess, all holey and bumpy. I close my eyes and see Milton's face pale with anxiety as we walked into the brightly lit supermarket and people swirled around us. *But he'll be less afraid next time,* I think. And even less the time after that. It's the unfamiliar that's terrifying. "Mom?" I say after a moment or two.

"What?"

"Is it scary?" I ask. "Being on your own? Dating random men? Not knowing if any of it's going to work out or not?"

"A little bit." I'm looking down, but I hear her step closer to me. "But once I realized your father wasn't the person I wanted to grow old with, the thought of staying with him was a lot more terrifying than of being alone."

"But Dad's a good guy. He's not perfect, but he's *good.*"

"I told myself that for years. It wasn't enough."

I don't say anything else.

* * *

When Mom thinks most of the real estate agents are gone, she heads down to the main floor. I stretch out on the daybed and stare up at the ceiling and think about my life.

I must fall asleep at some point, because I wake up to my mother's voice calling up the steps. "Keats? Everyone's gone."

"Even the Evanses?" I call back with sleepy suspicion. I'm in no mood to make small talk with that smarmy duo.

"It's just us."

I rouse myself and go downstairs. There's some leftover cheese and crackers from the caravan. We snack on that, and I bring a plate to Milton, who doesn't thank me, and then I help Mom tackle the cabinets in the family room, which are crammed full of old board games, drawings, homework assignments, photos, and other crap, including—inexplicably—an old cheese knife and a troll doll with pink hair.

"I didn't think I needed to bother cleaning these out yet since the doors hide everything," Mom says as we get to work. "But Charlie said an agent opened one of the doors to see what it was like inside and a chess set fell on her head. Charlie said, 'The house doesn't have to be perfect, but it shouldn't be *dangerous.*'"

We both giggle at that. I'm not sure why it's funny, but it is.

Mom's easily distracted from the task at hand. Sometimes she stops to read the papers she pulls out; sometimes she excuses herself to make a phone call or to use the bathroom, and doesn't come back for a while; and sometimes she just wanders around the room, grumbling about what a huge chore it is to sell a house. But I keep working steadily and make pretty good progress. I stop only once, and that's because Mom makes me look at something she's just unearthed.

"You have to read this," she says, nudging my arm.

"What is it?" My hands are dirty from all the pencil and crayon dust in the cabinet, so I swipe a lock of hair out of my eyes with the back of my wrist and peer over her shoulder.

"Hopkins wrote this. She wanted me to give it to Mrs. Rieper."

"She wrote Mrs. Rieper a letter?" We'd both had her as our second-grade teacher, only years apart, of course.

"At the beginning of the school year." Mom tilts it so I can see it more clearly. "But I never gave it to her."

I read the note.

Dear Mrs. Rieper,

I know you and I had what you might call our differences when I was in your second-grade class. If I remember correctly, you once told me, "You think you know everything, but no seven-year-old knows everything, so maybe you should just listen and learn once in a while." Does that ring a bell for you? I'm writing now because my sister is about to be a student in your class, and I want to assure you that despite her last name, she's nothing like me. Keats is a very sweet and good-natured little girl, and her teachers always love her. In fact, her preschool teacher once told my parents that she would adopt Keats if she could. (She was joking, of course, and simply meant she enjoyed Keats immensely.) She deserves to be judged on her own merit and not as the sister of a student you frequently showed a lack of patience toward. Please try to keep an open mind and make her feel welcome in your classroom.

Yours,
Hopkins Sedlak

I read it twice, torn between laughter and horror. "Is this for real?"

Mom nods and folds it up and puts it in the *Save* pile. "You can see why I didn't send it on."

"Yeah, good choice." I turn back to the cabinet but then just stand there for a moment, thinking. "It was kind of sweet of Hopkins. Misguided, but sweet."

"I think she really did mean well. Can you believe she was only thirteen when she wrote that?" Mom laughs. "Only Hopkins... Do you remember Mrs. Rieper at all?"

"Vaguely. She was perfectly nice to me."

"I told you before: teachers liked you better than they did Hopkins."

"Only because I didn't challenge them, and she did. They had to appreciate how brilliant she was."

"I'm sure they tried to," Mom says drily.

It takes us—me, really—several hours to get through the cabinets, but finally we have two huge bags of trash, one bag of papers to be recycled, three stacks of drawings and stories that seemed worth saving (one for each child), and a box of games and toys in decent shape that Mom wants to donate to a hospital or shelter.

I carry the trash and recycling out to the sidewalk and load the box into Mom's car. Since we never had a real lunch, we're both starving by now, and we figure we've earned a nice meal out. I ask Milton if he wants to come with us, but I'm not surprised when he says we should just bring something back for him. I don't push him to go. He made it all the way to the supermarket today. That's enough for now. It's more than he's done in two years.

He tells me to close the door on my way out of his room.

So Mom and I go out alone to a local Italian restaurant, where she gets a seafood salad and I get pasta marinara and a call from Tom, who wants to know when I'm coming home. I tell him I'm at dinner with my mother.

"You're eating with her? But it's Saturday! And it's not even six yet! Why didn't you wait for me?"

"Because I was hungry." I tell him I'll meet him at home in an hour or so and get off the phone quickly.

I drop Mom back off at the house. She's got one foot out of the car when she stops and turns back to me. "You know, Keats, wherever I live, if you ever need a place to stay, for any length of time... You know you're welcome to come stay with me, right?"

A month ago, a week ago—maybe even yesterday—I would have gotten annoyed at her for even saying that.

But today I thank her and say, "It's good to know."

She doesn't ask me any questions, just nods and gets out of the car.

* * *

As soon as I enter the apartment, Tom turns off the TV and jumps to his feet. "I'm starving," he says. "Let's go to Jo-Jo's. I'm dying for a burger." He's changed from the golf clothes he was wearing that morning into a T-shirt and jeans.

"Do you mind going without me? I've already been to one restaurant tonight."

He crosses his arms over his chest. "Come on, Keats. The least you can do is keep me company—I still can't believe you blew me off without even checking. You knew I'd want to have dinner with you."

I go with him to Jo-Jo's. It seems easier than arguing. He orders a double burger, and when it comes, he shoves his plate toward me. "Take some fries—you know you want them."

But I really don't.

He comments on how quiet I am. "Your mother bug you about something?"

I shake my head. "She was fine."

"Then why are you so out of it?"

"I'm not."

Fortunately the TV's on at the bar, and he can see it from his seat, so he's happy to just go back to sucking down the hamburger and cheering whenever someone gets a hit.

I watch him eat for a while, and then say, "I made Milton go to the supermarket today."

"Yeah?" His eyes are on the TV. "Why?"

"Because he never leaves the house anymore, and I decided he should."

"Oh. Good for you then. How'd it go?"

"It wasn't easy for either of us. But it's a good thing, I think. Something needed to change."

"He's a nutball, your brother," Tom says genially. Then he winces and says, "Damn it—I can't believe he didn't catch that!"

I sink down lower in my seat.

"Split a sundae with me?" he says when his plate is cleared.

"Still not hungry."

"Please tell me you're not trying to lose weight. You're so miserable when you're on a diet. And you know I think you look great the way you are."

"I'm just full from dinner." But it's not really that. It's something else that's making me feel sick to my stomach. Some sense that I've made a decision. Or that a decision has been made for me.

Tom orders dessert anyway—with two forks—and eats it quickly, staring at the TV over my head. I don't use the extra fork.

On the walk back to our place, he hooks his arm through mine. "Sorry if I was in a bad mood before," he says. "I was just hungry."

"It's okay."

He tries to see my face, but it's dark out, and we're walking side by side. "You sure your mom didn't say anything to upset you?"

I try to answer but I can't. I'm trembling and I'm scared he'll feel it.

I'm about to do something awful. And frightening. And probably wrong.

I'm about to jump off a cliff.

* * *

In the apartment, I take Tom by the hand and lead him to one of the armchairs and tell him to sit down.

"What's up?" he asks.

I don't sit down. I stand in front of him, biting my lip while I try to figure out how to say what I have to say. Eventually what comes out is, "I'm thinking I might go stay at home for a little while."

"Really? Why? Is your mom okay?"

I stare down at the floor. The carpet is classic rental apartment wall-to-wall stuff: beige, easy to walk on, easy to vacuum. "She's fine—she just needs help getting ready for the move. Lots of people were looking at the house today. I think she'll get an offer soon, and then she won't have much time to pack up."

"With the money she's going to get for that house, she can hire people to help her."

"It's not that simple. We need to sort through it all and figure out what to keep."

He shrugs. "So help her. That doesn't mean you have to live there. It's close enough you can go over there whenever you need to, and I hate when you're gone at night. I don't sleep well when you're not here." He reaches for my hand but I move it away.

I say, "I think maybe it's good for us to get used to sleeping apart."

"What do you mean?"

I don't respond, just stand there in front of him, not meeting his eyes, feeling my throat swell up.

After a moment, he says, "You've got to be kidding me."

I whisper, "I'm so sorry. I think I need some time to myself."

"No," he says again, and his voice is rising with real panic. He stands up and grabs my arm. "Keats. I don't know what this is about—whatever it is, tell me and I'll fix it—but for god's sake, don't start talking like you're going to *leave* me."

"I'm so sorry," I say again because I don't know what else to say. I can feel silent tears slipping out, clinging to my eyelids before dropping onto my cheeks.

"You're always saying we'll be together forever. Just last night we were talking about our *kids*, for god's sake. What happened since then? What's changed?"

"Nothing. Nothing's happened."

"Was it something your mother said? I know she doesn't think I'm good enough for you—no one in your family does. But you've said a million times that you're glad I'm not like them."

"I know. I am. And there's nothing wrong with you at all." My voice keeps breaking. It's hard to get the words out. "You're great. I just feel different now. I don't even know why. I just do."

His eyes search my face for more information, but I have none to give him. "I'm sorry I yelled at you about dinner," he says so humbly that it breaks my heart. "I shouldn't have done that. I know I get impatient sometimes. I've been taking you too much for granted. I won't anymore, I swear. I'll wait on you hand and foot if that's what it takes to keep you happy."

I'm shaking my head, whispering, "No, that's not it," but I don't think he hears me.

"There's something you're not telling me." There's a suddenly suspicious tone to his voice. "Were you really with your mother tonight? Or with someone else?"

"My mother and I had dinner alone together." I recite the facts tonelessly. "We went to Ceci's. She had a salad. I had pasta."

"Give me your phone." He holds his hand out.

"What?"

"Give me your cell phone."

"Why?"

"I want to see who's been calling you."

"No." I step back. "No one's been calling me, Tom. Not the way you mean. That's not what's going on."

"Then why won't you just give me your phone? Show me you're not hiding anything."

I hand it to him reluctantly. "Don't do this, Tom. Please."

He pokes at the phone. "Who's Mark?"

"No one important."

He throws the phone across the room and grabs me by the wrists. "Who is he?"

"Jesus, Tom! Mark's a guy in my office—you've met him a bunch of times, and if you actually read those texts, you'd see they were all work related."

He grips my hands tightly. "Tell me the truth, Keats. Who did you have dinner with tonight?"

"I already told you: my mother."

"Have you been seeing someone behind my back?"

I'm tired. I just want to curl up somewhere and go to sleep until this is all over and done with. "I'm not leaving because there's someone else," I say wearily. "I'm leaving because it's time."

He tugs me closer to him, tries to put my arms around his waist, but he has to hold them there because I won't. "Please, Keats," he says, and he doesn't sound angry anymore, just devastated. "Please don't do this. You're the only thing that matters in the whole world to me. I can't lose you. I won't have anything." He burrows his face into my neck, presses his mouth against the skin there, then moves his lips up over my jaw and across my cheeks and then back into my neck again.

I don't know what he's thinking. That his passion will reignite mine? That sex will solve the problem, convince me to love him again? But I don't want to be kissed right now. I don't want to have sex. I just want to leave.

He lifts his head to see how I'm reacting, and I extricate my hands and turn away from him. "I have to pack," I say.

"Wait," he says. "Wait. You can't." His fingers scramble at his shirtsleeve. He pulls it up and shoves his arm right in front of my face so I have to see what's written above his elbow. The sight of it scrapes something raw inside of me. "You *can't* leave me," he says desperately. "See? This is forever."

I shake my head and whisper, "I'm so sorry. You shouldn't have done that."

There's a moment where we're both silent.

Then he falls down to his knees on the floor and buries his face in his hands.

18.

I can't stop shaking. My fingers are wrapped around a mug of tea, but I'm not drinking it, just using it to warm my hands. I have chills, even though it's a warm spring night.

My mother greeted me very calmly when I showed up at her door. She just took my suitcase, put it at the foot of the stairs, then walked me into the kitchen where she sat me down in the breakfast booth and busied herself making tea.

"Okay," she says, settling across the table from me. "Now tell me what happened."

"I left Tom."

"I gathered that from the suitcase. What brought about this decision?"

I stare down at the mug. The tea bag's still in it. I should take it out before the tea turns bitter, but even that simple act seems beyond me. I've never felt so exhausted in my life. "I don't know."

"Something must have made you want to leave tonight."

"It wasn't anything he did. I just didn't want to be there with him anymore. Does that make sense?"

"More sense to me than to anyone else probably." There's a pause. "You know how I've always felt about Tom. He wasn't—"

I put a hand up. "Don't start saying mean things about him. Please."

She falls silent.

I put the mug down so I can pull my knees up to my chest and wrap my arms around my legs, which helps steady the shaking a little. "He was crying when I left."

She reaches across the table and touches my arm gently. "That sounds miserable. But you did what you had to do."

"All he's ever done is be nice to me. He doesn't deserve to be treated like this."

"That doesn't mean he deserves to be with you."

"I'm nothing special, Mom. I'm no Hopkins."

"You say that like it's a bad thing." She leans back in her chair. She's wearing an old terry-cloth bathrobe over a night-gown. She was getting ready for bed when I rang the doorbell.

"You know what I mean. Hopkins is brilliant. I'm not. She saves lives. I . . . do Costco runs."

"She's a little crazy," Mom says calmly. "You're not. She lacks most social graces. You make people gravitate toward you. She'll probably never have a husband or a family. One day— but not too soon, I hope—you'll have both."

I stare at her, jolted briefly out of my misery. "You're just trying to make me feel better."

"When do I ever do that?" she says, and I'm surprised to hear myself actually laugh. She shakes her head, rakes her fingers through her gray-threaded dark hair, shifts in her seat. "I've never understood how you, of all our children, could have such an inferiority complex. Can't you see that you're the lucky one in this family?"

"If you call not being extraordinarily brilliant lucky."

"If you'd stop feeling sorry for yourself for two seconds, you'd see how much easier most things are for you than for your siblings. Have you seen either of them at a cocktail party? It's a disaster."

"I know Milton can't deal. But everyone adores Hopkins."

"Many people admire her. Even more are grateful to her. But they don't want to confide in her or go out for drinks with her." She fingers the handle of her mug. "I've spent years watching you both when other people are around. People may listen to Hopkins because she's got the stories and the expertise. But you're the one everyone wants to sit next to. Like"—she casts about for an example—"like Jacob, for instance. The second you walk into a room, his face lights up. And he's not the only—what's the matter?"

I've buried my face in my hands. Words burst out of me before I can stop them. "I slept with him! With Jacob! At Dad's apartment the night I stayed over. He was there, too, and we slept together. Right on Dad's sofa!"

There's a pause. And then my mother laughs. "Did you really?"

"It's not funny! It was a huge mistake. A total disaster."

"It does explain why he seemed a little off at dinner the other night."

I grab a napkin off the table and wipe my nose with it. "He hates me."

"I'm sorry I laughed," she says. "But honestly, Keats, this is exactly what you're supposed to be doing at your age. Trying things out. Sleeping with the wrong guy. Making stupid, unforgivable mistakes—and then forgiving yourself. I mean, if not now, when?"

"You've been doing a pretty good job of doing all that. And you're not exactly twenty-five."

"I know!" she says, clasping her hands to her chest with sudden delight. "It's like that book we read when you were a kid, about the mother and daughter who change bodies—"

"*Freaky Friday*?"

"Right. You've been living the life of a middle-aged woman. I mean, that job of yours..." She sighs. "That job was meant to be done by a sixty-year-old woman who's just happy to get out of the house because her husband was forced to retire and has nothing to do and is driving her crazy with all his little projects around the house, and she can't take it anymore, so—"

"You've thought about this way too much. And it's really a perfectly good job."

She shakes her head. "Between that and being with Tom since forever, you've been living older than your years for too long. You need to get your youth back."

"If I do, will you start acting *your* age? Let Dad move back in? Get a boring office job? Knit and bake?"

"God, no. I cut my own wild years too short. I'm owed a few more." She cocks her head at me. "See? This is what happens if you don't act out when you're young—you do it when you're my age. And I'm the first to admit it's not a pretty sight."

"You're fine." I release my legs and put my feet back on the floor. I start to say something, then stop.

"What?" Mom says.

"It's just…" I hesitate, then say in a rush, "Why'd you call him the wrong guy?"

"What? Who?"

I evade her eyes and play with my mug, pushing the handle back and forth, watching the liquid slosh gently up the sides. "Jacob. You said I slept with the wrong guy."

"I did?"

"You said that I was doing exactly what I should be doing at my age, like sleeping with the wrong guy. So that implies you think Jacob's the wrong guy."

"Oh, right. I guess I did say that. I just meant it in a general sense."

"So you *don't* think Jacob is the wrong guy?"

She waves an airy hand. "Oh, I love Jacob, you know that. And if you want to marry him in ten years, I'll perform the ceremony myself. But any man is the wrong man for you right now. You need to spend some time alone, Keats. Get to know yourself. Seek out new experiences and new possibilities. Then, when you're thirty—or forty—you can think about finding the right guy."

"Thirty or forty?" I repeat with horror.

"There's no rush."

"Most women your age would want grandchildren."

"I do," she says. "I really do. And let's be honest—you're my best and possibly my *only* hope for them. But I can wait."

"Hold on." My phone's vibrating. It's been doing that on and off since I got there, but I've been ignoring it. I pull it out of my pocket and see I've missed four calls and seven texts. All from Tom. I show Mom. She sighs but doesn't say anything. I put the phone back in my pocket.

Eventually I say into the quiet of the kitchen, "Was it awful, telling Dad you didn't want to be married to him anymore?"

"I suspect," my mother says slowly, "that it wasn't all that different from what you just went through. Minus the tears—your father isn't the crying type. But the anger, the resentment, the hurt—all pretty much what you experienced. It was the most difficult thing I've ever had to do."

"I'm sorry I made you feel bad about it."

She salutes me with her tea mug. "Welcome to the Heartbreakers of America Club, Keats. It reads a lot better than it lives."

"I never want to go through that again."

"Me neither."

I close my eyes and let my head rest back on the chair. "I'm exhausted. I want to crawl into bed and sleep for a million years."

"Go ahead. You'd better use Hopkins's room, though, since Milton's taken over yours. I have no idea if the bed's made or not."

"I'll check." I get up, but she catches at my arm.

"Keats, I'm serious about this. I don't want you to become one of those women who go straight from one guy to the next because they're afraid of being alone. Sooner or later in life, everyone's alone. You need to get comfortable with yourself now while you're still young, so you don't make unnecessary compromises later out of fear."

I promise her I'll try and go up to bed.

There isn't a single book in Hopkins's room that I can read to get my mind off of Tom, just stacks of the comparative religion tomes, anatomy textbooks, and science journals she was already reading back in junior high. I'd kill for the distraction of a junky romance novel, so I slip into my old room thinking I'll steal one off the shelves, but Milton's asleep on the bed in there—still wearing his sweats and the shoes he put on that afternoon, like he was suddenly overtaken with exhaustion—so I leave quickly and empty-handed.

As tired as I am, I can't get to sleep until past dawn. The mattress is awful—both thin and lumpy—and I'm not used to sleeping alone. I toss and turn for hours and then fall asleep so late that by the time I wake up again, it's almost noon, and when I make my way downstairs, Mom's rushing around, getting ready to meet Irv at a museum.

"A museum?" I say, sitting in my sweatpants and tank top at the breakfast booth, idly watching her search for her purse and coat. "That's your idea of a date? Walking around a museum?"

"What's wrong with that?"

"It's boring. It's what old ladies do."

"Just check in on Milton, will you? Make sure he gets some lunch at some point." She leaves.

I watch some TV and think about doing some packing, but I'm not really in the mood to poke through dusty old books and papers. I'm bored and restless. And lonely.

I have my MacBook with me, so I fool around online for a while, but when Izzy IMs me, I quickly close the computer. I have no idea if Tom's talked to Lou yet, and I don't want to have to pretend everything's normal—or tell her I left him.

I try talking to Milton, but he's playing some incomprehensible (to me) online game and says he can't stop until he either wins or dies. "Kind of like life," I say. He doesn't respond, just peers at the screen and taps at the keyboard. I don't blame him. I don't know what I meant by that, either.

* * *

So you see, it's not fear that makes me get in the car and drive to Jacob's that evening.

It's not what Mom's worried about, that I'm afraid of being alone. It's nothing like that.

It's boredom. I'm so bored I could bang my head against the wall just to be doing something.

And also I want to see Jacob. I want to be face-to-face with him and tell him what happened. I want to see his expression when I say I left Tom for good.

Just thinking about it makes me feel kind of light-headed and excited.

See? Not fear. Other emotions entirely.

I've never been to Jacob's apartment, so I have to look up his address in my mother's address book. She must be the only person left in America who doesn't have a computerized contacts list. The book literally says "Addresses" on its felt cover and has a tab for every letter of the alphabet, but that's where the organization stops. Mom has crossed out and rewritten so many phone numbers and addresses for people over the years that entire pages are scribbled out.

There are three addresses for Jacob. One's an apartment in

Somerville—that one's been crossed out—and one's in Texas. That must be his real home. Or the closest thing he has to it. The third one is also a Somerville apartment, but this one isn't crossed out, so I assume it's still viable and copy it down.

I shower and blow my hair dry and take some time picking out a pair of jeans and a silky top from the stash of clothing I brought over the night before.

I stop by Milton's room to let him know I'm going out. He nods indifferently and doesn't look up.

I lock the front door behind me, go out to my car, put the address in my GPS, and feel more nervous than I think I've ever felt in my life as I drive the twenty-five minutes it takes me to get to Somerville. Once I'm off the Turnpike, I see lots of couples out walking or waiting in front of restaurants.

I feel lonely. With Tom, I was part of a couple. I was normal. Without him, I'm something alone and strange and different.

A Sedlak.

It takes me a while to find a parking space near Jacob's building. It's that kind of neighborhood—tons of graduate students crammed into small apartment complexes. Every tenant has a car, but each driveway only has room for one or two, so the streets are packed with the spillover.

I finally find a space two blocks away that may not be entirely legal—it's right on the edge of someone's driveway, maybe goes over it a couple of inches—but they can definitely get out and I'm sick of circling.

It's a cloudy, gray twilight, and I feel underdressed without a jacket. I shiver a little as I walk the two blocks to Jacob's place. Even so, it feels good to be outside after being stuck in the grimy house all day.

I make my way back to his building. The door has been

propped open, so I go in and then up a flight of stairs and find his apartment. Its number is spray painted on the door with the kind of stencils you can buy at a hardware store.

I take a deep breath. I feel winded, but not from the steps. From forgetting to breathe. The truth is I'm scared, which is silly. It's just Jacob.

I knock. I wait.

Footsteps. So he's there.

The door opens. Yes, he's there. Wearing his usual button-down shirt (blue this time) and khakis.

I'm glad he looks like himself. I'm glad to see him. I'm glad I came.

"Hi," I say, nervous but glad.

He looks startled. "Keats? What are you doing here?"

Before I can answer—"Keats?" says another voice. Someone else is there. She comes forward. It's Cathy.

Wait—it's their second date, and she's already hanging out at his place?

But maybe it's more than their second date. I haven't spoken with her recently about him. Maybe they've seen each other a lot in the last week. Maybe they're always together when they're not at work.

Maybe they're in love.

I want to throw up.

"Hey!" she says enthusiastically. "I didn't know you were coming over!"

"I didn't, either," I say. They both look confused.

I don't know what to do now. I wasn't expecting him to have any guests, let alone this one. I say, "I, uh, just needed to ask Jacob about something."

Jacob is studying my face. I probably look pretty distressed. I know I *feel* pretty distressed. "What's wrong?" he says anxiously. "Is it your father?"

I grab blindly at the excuse. "Yes. Dad is—" I stop. Dad is *what?*

"What's wrong?" he asks again, more urgently.

"I don't know. He asked for you." I lick my lips because they've gone dry. I can't believe I'm lying. Why am I lying? I'm just so thrown by Cathy's presence, I don't know what I'm doing.

I thought Jacob would open the door, and his face would light up, and I'd tell him about me and Tom, and then things would just work themselves out somehow. But instead Cathy's here, and all Jacob can think about is my father—the one Sedlak he truly cares about.

And now I'm deep into crazy and have to keep going. "He—it's almost like he was having some kind of breakdown. He got really upset and said he had to see you. I don't even know why." I realize there's a hole in my story, so I make a clumsy attempt to cover it. "I tried your phone, but you didn't answer."

"Really? You tried me?" He's pulling the phone out of his pocket. "I didn't feel anything." He checks it. "No missed calls. . . . You sure you have the right number for me?"

"I thought I did." This is what happens when you lie. You stop making sense, and impossibilities pile on improbabilities. "Weird. Anyway, I figured I'd just check to see if you were home, but since you're busy—hey, Cathy—I'll just go back and tell him you can't come right now. No worries."

"But you said he's really upset about something?"

"Yeah, but it's okay, really. I'll just deal with it."

He turns to Cathy. "Would you be okay if I just run over and come back as soon as I can? I know it's rude, but—"

"Oh god, of course you should go." Man, she's sweet. Her large bony face is radiant with generosity and a genuine desire to help out. "I'm also happy to come with you if you think I could help in any way."

I say quickly, "I think—given how Dad is tonight—maybe it should just be family." Then I remember Jacob isn't actually family. "You know what I mean."

"I completely understand," says Cathy.

I flash her a forced smile. "But seriously, Jacob, you don't have to—"

"Come on." He grabs some keys from a little table near the door. As he shifts, I get a glimpse of the apartment. It's small and dark, and the few bits of furniture in it are ratty looking. Then Jacob's back in the doorway, blocking the view. "Let's go."

Oh god, what a *mess*.

I say good-bye to Cathy and apologize to her for interrupting.

"Are you kidding me? It's so totally fine. Take your time, both of you. I've got a book in my bag. I'm happy to curl up and read. Sounds kind of nice actually."

"Thanks." Jacob smiles at her. "I'll be back as soon as I can."

"Oh, and Keats?" she says. "Do you want to join us for dinner afterward?"

"I'll probably stay with my dad," I say faintly. "But thanks."

"Well, there's plenty of food if you change your mind." She waves us out the door and then closes it behind us. His casa is her casa apparently.

We walk down the stairs in silence. Once we're on the street, Jacob says, "We better drive separately. I'll meet you over there," and starts to head toward his car, which is parked in one of the two driveway spaces. I'd say that meant he was lucky except it probably means he's stayed in these student apartments the longest of anyone there, which doesn't seem particularly lucky at all. Just sad.

"Wait." I can't let him go all the way to my father's. I wonder who'd be more confused once he got there, Jacob or Dad. "I need to tell you something first."

"What is it?"

"Come here." I don't want to be where Cathy can look out of a window and see us, so I lead him around the corner.

"What are you doing?" he asks.

I turn and face him. "I lied," I whisper.

"What?"

I'm so embarrassed I want to crawl under the nearest house foundation. "I lied. I didn't come here because of my dad. As far as I know, he's fine."

"I don't understand."

"I came to see you. To talk to you. But then Cathy was there, and you asked me if it was about my father, and I didn't know what to say."

He takes a step back and runs his fingers through his hair. "I am so confused. So your father wasn't asking for me tonight?" I shake my head. "Why did we just go through all that then? Why didn't you—" He stops. His eyes narrow. "What's going on, Keats?"

I wish it were dark out so he couldn't see my face, but it's May and the sun is taking forever to disappear completely. "I just wanted to talk to you."

"You lied about trying to call me first, didn't you?"

I nod, my face turning hot with shame.

He crosses his arms. "Why'd you come over then?"

I wish he'd show some sign of softening toward me. It would make this so much easier. But his look is hard, his body language is hard, his expression is hard.

I swallow hard. "I wanted you to know that I broke up with Tom."

He registers this with a slight raise of his eyebrows, but the rest of his expression doesn't change. His face stays stony, his eyes cold, his voice flat. "I'm sorry. I know what a long relationship that was. It can't have been easy."

"No, not easy. But it was what I needed to do."

"Then I'm happy for you."

I don't know what else to say. This wasn't how it was supposed to go. He was supposed to be overwhelmed with joy at the news.

I thought he was waiting for me, hoping I'd come to him. I thought he wanted me and the only thing keeping us apart was my loyalty to Tom. I thought all his previous anger was simply frustrated desire.

Apparently I was wrong.

"I've moved back in with my mom," I say because the silence is going on too long. "For now, anyway. I don't know what I'll do when the house gets sold."

"Your father might like the company."

"Yeah. I guess."

Another pause. He glances up the street. "I should go back up to Cathy, but I don't know what to tell her."

"You can tell her I lied if you want."

"Thank you," he says politely. "But she'll want to know why. And I don't have an answer for that."

"You know why," I say almost angrily. "You can pretend you don't, but you do."

He uncrosses his arms and sticks his hands in his pockets. "Maybe. Not entirely. I'm gathering it has something to do with your being bored or lonely and thinking I'd come running when you called. Something like that?"

"No." Although he's not actually wrong, is he? Except it's more than that. "It's more than that," I say.

"Time for another round of torturing Jacob?" he suggests. His tone is lighthearted, but his expression isn't. "The game that never grows old?"

I put my hand on his arm. "I've never meant to torture you. If I have, I'm sorry. Really, really sorry."

He looks at my hand on his arm, like it's something he's never seen before, something foreign and a little repellant. I remove it. He says slowly, "I'm not sure you're capable of understanding this, Keats. But that night at your dad's...What happened there mattered to me. A lot. But you made it instantly clear it didn't matter to you." He shakes his head. "No, it was even worse than that—you couldn't look at me afterward. You couldn't even *look* at me. Do you know what that felt like?" He stops for a moment, his jaw tightening. He's fighting for control. He gets it. His voice is calm as he says, "And now you're here because you're feeling lonely? What's that phrase again? *Fool me once, shame on you. Fool me twice—*"

"Yeah, I know the saying." This is painful. He hates me. "It wasn't deliberate. What I did. I was a mess. You know how upset I was, how guilty I felt—"

"It must have been very hard for you." His voice drips with sarcasm. Whatever happened to good ol' Jacob? He's gone.

I killed him.

"I said I was sorry." I catch my lip under my teeth to hold it steady—it's trembling.

"I appreciate your apology. It's a little late, and it doesn't change anything, but I appreciate it." He uses the same tone my father does when he talks to Tom: polite contempt. He glances at his watch. "I'm going to go back. I'll think of something to say to Cathy. Maybe I'll just tell her your dad called and told me not to bother coming over. What's one more lie?" He starts to move away.

"Do you like her?" I ask in a small voice.

He whips around. "And that's another thing," he says harshly. "You fix me up with someone else. Knowing how I felt about you. You were so eager to get rid of me, in such a rush to make sure I wouldn't bother you again, that you instantly threw someone else at me. Thanks for that, Keats. Did you think you hadn't crushed me enough? Just making sure the job was complete?"

"That's not fair. I fixed you two up before we…before all this. Remember? At my birthday party?"

"You gave her my e-mail just last week."

"Because she asked me for it. I didn't want to. I swear. I thought it was the right thing to do." I hug my arms to my chest. My face feels like it's on fire but the rest of me is freezing. "It hurt to think of you two going out. That was part of what made me realize that I had to leave Tom. I was jealous at the thought of you and Cathy being alone together. I knew that wasn't right, that I shouldn't be feeling that way about someone who wasn't Tom."

He steps closer. His voice lowers. "So it hurts to know I'm going back to spend the evening with her? Maybe even the night?"

"Yes," I say. "A lot."

"Good," he says softly and walks away.

19.

Somehow I make it to my car and get inside of it. I fold down over the steering wheel and think I'm going to cry, but I don't. I just stay like that, frozen, feeling sick to my stomach. I ache all over. My teeth keep chattering. It's like I have the flu but I know I'm not really sick.

I'm not sick. I'm an idiot.

Every memory makes me cringe. How I treated Tom, how I treated Jacob, how I've hurt them both, how I'm continuing to hurt them both.

No. Right now I'm only hurting Tom. Jacob's fine.

But the truth is that even my remorse is selfish. I wouldn't care who I had or hadn't hurt if I were alone with Jacob in his apartment right now.

It's only because I'm all by myself that I'm guilt ridden and sad and regretful.

I'm not just an idiot—I'm a selfish idiot.

Deep down, I'd assumed that because Jacob had wanted me so much before and for so long, he'd still want me, and I'd be making a simple substitution: Tom out, Jacob in. It hadn't even occurred to me that maybe Jacob wasn't sitting around waiting for me to change my mind, that maybe he'd gotten over me, that I'd *helped* him get over me by hurting him so deeply. Nothing like a little hatred to burn away affection.

But still...

I wonder.

What if I got out of the car now? What if I screwed up my courage and went back to Jacob's place?

Cathy invited me to dinner once already. If I came to the door, she'd tell me to come in and join them, and in front of her, Jacob would have to say, "Yes, please stay," even if he didn't want me to.

He'd have to.

And if I had dinner with them . . .

I'm funnier than Cathy. I can make Jacob laugh so hard he can't breathe—I've done it a million times. I'm prettier, too—I mean, I know it's not nice even to think stuff like that, but I am. It's just the truth. And Jacob and I have a past together. I could keep reminding him of that. I could remind him of all the times we've celebrated Thanksgiving together or rolled our eyes at something together or fled from my father's temper together.

We've done a lot together.

I hurt him, and he's mad at me... but the only reason I was able to hurt him so deeply was because he *liked* me so much. How hard would it be to get past all that hurt and get him to like me again?

I'm prettier and funnier and sexier than Cathy. If I force a contest, I'll win. The only thing she has going for her is that she's nicer than I am.

And that's when I stop myself.

She is. Nicer than I am. Maybe not in any major global sense. I'm not killing puppies or anything. But if you just look at us from Jacob's perspective...

There's this girl who seduced him, knowing he had had a thing for her for a very long time, and who then instantly— almost angrily—rejected him. Not just rejected him—made it clear that sleeping with him was the biggest mistake of her life.

And then there's this gentle, innocent girl from the Midwest who thinks he's cute and smart and wants to get to know him better and who doesn't have a mean bone in her body.

If he were my real brother, not my pretend one, which one would I be urging him to go after? The girl who's already hurt him once or the one who'd never hurt him?

Even if I'm right, even if I could bully and provoke and tease him into choosing me over Cathy, the bigger question is *Should I?*

And I know the answer to that one.

* * *

I hear a honk and jump in my seat. Someone's trying to get out of the driveway that my car is blocking. Admittedly I'm only over by those couple of inches, but the guy is honking and glaring at me like I've bricked him into a dungeon for all eternity.

I wearily sit up and start the car and drive away from the curb.

Only . . . where do I go now?

My mother's?

I picture my arrival there: It's dark and the house is chilly because that house is always chilly, except in the middle of summer when it's briefly sticky and hot. The only light that's on is the one in Milton's room, but his door is closed. I let myself in, maybe eat a cracker or two in the empty kitchen, maybe watch some TV by myself, then eventually find my way up the stairs to Hopkins's room, where the bed is lumpy and the sheets are old and every object in it reproaches me for not being as brilliant as she is. My mom's either lost in a book or still out on her date with some guy who actually likes her, who thinks she's wonderful.

No one thinks I'm wonderful.

No, that's not entirely true. I stop at a light, and as it switches to green, it's like something also switches on in my head.

I could go back to *my* apartment—the one that I've lived in for the last four years. The one that's warm and clean and bright. The one that belongs to a guy who thinks I'm the center of the universe, who'll run to the door when he hears me come in, who'll throw his arms around me and beg me never to leave again.

I picture that homecoming now: the lit-up warmth of the apartment, the way Tom would drag me into the living room and kiss me over and over again, and then just collapse with me on the sofa and hold me against his chest and tell me he's never been so scared in his life, that I can't ever do this to him again. We'd have sex, and it would be more exciting than it's been in years because of the fear in his heart and the relief in mine.

We'd go out to dinner. I'd feel safe and relaxed, and the food would taste better than anything's tasted in the last forty-eight hours. He'd constantly be petting me, rubbing my shoulders, my knee, my arm, checking to make sure I'm really there, that I've come back to him. And then we'd go back to our apartment with its big comfortable bed, and we'd watch TV all curled up together until it was time to sleep. And I would sleep soundly again, back in my own bed, with his familiar weight next to me.

I get off the Mass Pike at Waltham and follow the turns that take me to our street. It's easy and automatic. I've driven this route a thousand times.

When I'm near our building, I count up eight flights of windows, and sure enough, the light is on in our living room. He's there. Probably stretched out on the sofa, watching TV, feeling lonely, missing me. He's left me three more texts and two more voice mails today. I don't have to listen to them to know that he just wants me to come home. When I walk through that door, he'll fall at my feet.

I signal left to pull into the garage. I slow down. I brake.

But I don't turn.

The car behind me honks loudly. I raise my hand in sheepish apology and take my foot off the brake. I accelerate past the building, then change lanes too suddenly and get honked at again by someone else—third time tonight, and I've deserved it every time—and take a right at the corner.

I head back to the Turnpike.

It kills me to admit it, even to myself, but my mom is right: I'm afraid of being alone. And that's the only thing that's making me think about going back to Tom.

I don't love him anymore. I don't want the life he and I have created for ourselves. I want something different. If I went back now, the evening would be lovely. Maybe even the whole next month would be lovely. But eventually the glow of reuniting would fade, and I'd be right back where I started, bored and frustrated, and then either I'd leave him again—and that would be far crueler than anything I've done so far, even crueler than what I did to Jacob—or I *wouldn't* leave him again, and my life would stall in a place I've already outgrown.

I drive back to my mother's house—the closest thing I have to a home for the moment.

It's exactly the way I pictured it: dark and cold and lonely. Mom isn't there.

For a while, I sit alone in the kitchen, feeling sorry for myself. I think about crying. I think about getting into the liquor cabinet. I think about eating chocolate.

And then I haul myself to my feet, go upstairs, and knock on Milton's door.

"What?"

I open the door. "I want to go to a movie."

"So go."

"I need you to come with me. What do you want to see?"

"I don't want to go to the movies."

"We can see whatever stupid-ass science fiction fantasy movie you want. I don't care. So long as there's popcorn and trailers."

He swivels toward me in his chair. "Science fiction and fantasy are two completely different genres. Science fiction is based on actual science. It's usually futuristic, but it incorporates real scientific principles we already know or at least can conceive of, whereas fantasy—"

"I don't care. Just look online and see what's playing."

"I can get movies streamed instantly to my computer. That's what Mom and I do when we want a movie night. She makes microwave popcorn."

I walk over to his desk and bend down so I can put my face right in front of his. "Here's the thing, oh brother of mine. I have had a spectacularly shitty weekend. I broke up with Tom and got rejected by . . . someone else, and I'm bored and lonely and depressed and on the verge of a nervous breakdown, and all I want right now is to see a movie, and for once in your freaking life, you are going to do something you don't want to do as a favor to someone else, to your big sister who loves you and who used to give you your bottles and get you ready for school and who's had a spectacularly shitty weekend as she mentioned earlier. You got that?"

Milton's mouth has fallen open. He closes it, but his eyes are still wide with shock. "You really broke up with Tom? Mom said so, but I didn't believe her."

"I did."

"Wow. I never thought you'd leave him. What happened?"

"It was time for me to grow up," I said. "And I'm dragging your sorry ass along with me, whether you like it or not."

"To the movies, you mean?"

"For a start," I say grimly.

* * *

The next morning, I wake up early and can't get back to sleep. I go down to the kitchen and start the coffeemaker. I'm sticking some bread in the toaster when Mom comes in from the garage. "Oh, hi," she says a little uncomfortably. She's wearing the same outfit she had on last night.

My eyebrows shoot up. "Look who's doing the walk of shame!"

"The walk of shame?"

"You're wearing your clothes from the night before." I wag my finger at her. "Don't deny it, Mom. You had a sleepover."

"Is that what you young people call it now?"

"Only the under ten crowd. So is this meaningful?"

"Not really." She puts her purse down and runs her fingers through her hair, which is looking a little bumpy and unkempt. "To be honest, I'd had too much to drink last night and didn't think it was safe to drive home."

"So...you slept on his sofa?"

"I didn't say that." She smiles and jerks her chin at me. "How are you doing? I tried calling you a couple of times last night to let you know I wasn't coming home, but you didn't answer."

"Sorry. My phone was off. We were at a movie."

"We? Who's we?"

I grin. "Milton and I."

She's reaching for a cabinet door, but she halts, her hand frozen in midair. "Are you serious? Milton went *out* to see a movie?"

I nod. "We saw *Androids of Titan* at the General Cinema."

"How was it?"

"The movie was awful, the popcorn was great, and the company was extremely decent."

To my surprise, she darts forward and throws her arms around me. "You're incredible," she says.

"You better look the word up," I say. "You're using it wrong."

She breaks away and sniffs the air. "Oh, good, you're making coffee. I'm dying for a cup." She's whirling around, the way she does, darting to the cabinet, then coming back by me to go to the coffeemaker, her voluminous skirt flaring up around her.

I reach out. I grab a fold of her skirt. I hold on to it tightly. She stumbles and grabs the edge of the table to steady herself. "What are you doing, Keats? Let go of me!"

"I've just always wanted to do that," I say, and then I release the fold of her skirt and let her fly away.

* * *

Over the next week or so, I get a lot of sad e-mails from Tom, a few more texts, and one truly heartbreaking, drunken, sobbing phone call one night, but I refuse to see him or talk for more than a minute or two, and eventually he stops trying to contact me.

Meanwhile, Izzy, who's always kind, always compassionate, always agreeable, calls me a "heartless bitch" in an e-mail. She writes, *Tom came over last nite and cried like a baby. I thought I knew you. I thought we were friends. But maybe you never cared about any of us. You must be a good actress. Sorry if I don't feel like clapping for this particular performance.*

It hurts, but there's not a lot I can do about it. I send her back a note that says, *I'm sorry. I miss you.* She doesn't respond. So I guess I've lost my closest friend.

I left most of my stuff at the apartment, so I pick up a load one day when I know Tom will be at work. I leave behind anything that belonged to both of us. The big items were all really Tom's: the apartment, the furniture, the TV set and sound system. I had made myself part of his life, but now I want my *own* life.

I'm just not sure exactly what that will be.

So far I'm just a twenty-five-year-old single girl living in her sister's old room, working at a job that's not really leading anywhere.

For a few days I give in to self-pity. Then I get sick of the self-pity and decide to improve whatever parts of my life I have control over.

The first step I take is the simplest. I tell Milton I'm reclaiming my old room. He asks me why I don't just stay in Hopkins's room. "Wouldn't that be easier?" he says hopefully.

"I like mine better."

I have nothing but free time on the weekends now, so I spend the next one cleaning out his trash and moving his equipment back into his room. Then I go through all of my old stuff, putting aside what I want to donate to charity, which includes a lot of little gifts that Tom gave me during our first few years together.

I'm tossing into the Goodwill-destined box a small purple teddy bear he gave me for my sixteenth birthday when I'm suddenly struck by how truly weird it is that a guy in his twenties pursued a girl so much younger than him. At the time, I was so convinced ours was an epic Love for the Ages that I never questioned our age difference, just wished other people would see how irrelevant it was.

But now I wonder: why did he feel so much more comfortable with me than with girls his own age? Was there something wrong about that?

And that makes me wonder how different my own life would have been if I hadn't had the same steady boyfriend from fifteen on. Would I have met more people, made more friends, been more involved in high school and college? Would I be stuck in a dead-end job and living with my parents at the age of twenty-five? Had I stopped growing and challenging myself because of Tom?

I thrust the thoughts away—what's the point of asking myself these questions _now_?—and focus on making my room neat and organized. One thing at a time. A small step forward is better than none. And until very recently, I hadn't taken even a small step forward in a long time.

Once my room's organized and packed up except for the stuff I'm actively using, I tackle Milton's room over his objections. He calms down when I tell him he can keep working on the computer while I clean up around him. Once I start making a dent in the chaos, he stops objecting and even admits he likes it better this way.

One day I force him to go with me to Staples, so we can pick out some racks to keep all his computer stuff organized. He's reluctant to go, but once we're there he's impressed by the electronic supplies and in no rush to leave.

Mom's home when we unload our purchases. "Are you actually bringing more stuff into this house?" she asks. "When we're supposed to be packing it up?"

"It's all to get better organized, which will make the house look neater and sell faster, speed up packing, and be useful at the next place."

She thinks for a moment, then says, "Can you do the kitchen next?"

So whenever I'm home, I work on getting the entire house in order. It slowly becomes more and more livable. I throw out huge garbage bags filled with junk and make at least one trip each weekend to Goodwill with a trunk full of clothing, books, and knickknacks.

Once the surfaces and cabinets are cleaned up, I convince Mom to hire a cleaning service to come through. They're there for nine hours, and after they leave, the house smells better than it has in years.

I had forgotten how big this place is, how many corners you can get lost in or read a book in or stare out a window from. It makes me a little sad: I'm falling in love with my home again just as I'm about to lose it forever.

Milton's still fighting that idea. He takes a day off from what he calls his "work" (something about designing a video game) to research what it would take to get the house declared a historic landmark. The results are discouraging—we don't meet any of the criteria—but he keeps sending e-mails to people in the Massachusetts Building Department and even to our local congresswoman, trying to convince them.

The Evanses are thrilled with all the work I've done. "The house looks a thousand times better," Charlie says on their next visit. "It's time to do a huge open house and to advertise the hell out of it." There have been a few showings over the past week or so, but no nibbles yet. They're ready to push harder.

Charlie asks if Mom and I might want to have dinner with him and Cameron to talk about strategies and preparations for the open house. Mom says yes, of course, and they make a date for Friday night.

"Why?" I ask her after they've gone.

"Why not? You need to get out of the house."

"You're telling *me* that? You let Milton be a complete shut-in for the last two years, and you're already nagging *me* to get out of the house?"

She just laughs. "I figure my chance of success is better with you. Seriously, Keats, you should be out having fun."

"That doesn't explain dinner with the Evanses."

"Cameron's cute."

"He's not uncute," I admit, and then my own words give me a jolt. I teased Jacob by talking that way the night we slept together. I brood over that in silence, which Mom takes as acceptance of our dinner plans.

I've gotten several e-mails from Cathy over the last few weeks and seen her once at the office. She seems to be spending a lot of time with Jacob. She keeps inviting me to go out with them and seems genuinely to want me to, but I keep coming up with excuses to say no.

It's not that I don't want to see Jacob. I do. I miss him. Now that my father has completely moved out of the house, Jacob doesn't come by anymore, and the couple of times I've visited my dad, he hasn't been there.

But it's because I miss him and want to see him that I know I have to turn down Cathy's invitations. So far it seems like they're making each other happy. I don't want to get in the way of that. And there's still a selfish part of me that wants their relationship to fail, that still wants Jacob for myself. And it would be wrong to sit across from them at dinner, secretly rooting against their happiness.

* * *

Mom and I go out to dinner with Evans *fils* and *père*. She wears a pretty blue silk top over a black-and-white skirt. I wear jeans and a tank top. "Are you sure that's nice enough?" she asks when I join her at the garage door.

"Positive."

The restaurant is a dark and expensive steak house, and as soon as the waitress hands us our menus, Charlie Evans leans across the table and says grandly, "Order anything you like! It's on us!"

If I look at Mom, I'll crack up, so I determinedly stare at the menu and master my twitching lips.

The men order martinis and steaks. Mom and I each get a glass of wine and a salad.

At first the conversation is general and mostly about the real estate market, but Cameron addresses me directly at one point, and from then on we have two separate conversations, which is fine with me. I like Cameron better than his father— sometimes you can still see a person peeking out from under the slick veneer with Cameron, but veneer is all you get with his dad.

He's curious about why I've moved back home after living away for so long. I explain that I wanted to help Mom get the house ready to sell and that my "previous living arrangement" had fallen through unexpectedly.

I don't feel like going into detail about that.

"Do you know where you'll live once the house is sold?" he asks. "With your mother?"

"I think I'll probably get my own place."

"I can help you find an apartment."

"Thanks. I may take you up on that."

"What neighborhoods are you thinking about?"

"I haven't gotten that far."

"In Boston proper? Or somewhere more suburban?"

"I'm not sure."

"Do you like older buildings or newer ones?"

"I don't really have a preference."

"Do you want a doorman?"

"I'm fine either way."

"What about a pool or a workout room?"

"They'd be nice but they're not crucial. Really, anything decent and affordable is fine with me."

He stares at me with a puzzled frown, like he can't imagine

someone who doesn't care where she lives. He doesn't know what to say after that, and we listen to our parents' conversation in silence.

Mom and I turn down dessert and coffee and head home early. "There's nothing wrong with the Evanses," Mom says on the drive home. "But there's nothing particularly _right_ about them, either."

"You'll leave me alone about Cameron now, right? I mean, I gave it a shot. Sparks didn't exactly fly."

She nods, then sighs. "I think I'm getting tired of all this dating."

"Really? I thought you were having the time of your life."

"It was fun for a while. Now I just want to find someone I can count on spending my Saturday nights with. Enough is enough."

"Anyone seem like a Saturday night candidate these days?"

"Not really. Paul and Irv are good guys, but they're not the men of my dreams."

"I used to say Tom was the man of my dreams. Maybe it's a bad concept. Who can live up to that?"

* * *

The next day, Rochelle says she needs to talk to me. I come to her office, which is a real room, not a cubicle like mine.

"I'm going to hate myself for telling you this," she says, looking up from her desk. "But I heard about a pretty cool job that I think might be right up your alley. I'm e-mailing you the info right now."

"Is this a nice way of telling me you're firing me?"

"That's not even funny. _Please_ tell me you're not interested in it—I'll be thrilled."

"Let me read your e-mail first."

"I'm already regretting this," she says as I leave.

She has more reason to regret it a week later when I give her my notice. She was right: the job is right up my alley, a combined editing and sales job with an international trade journal publishing company. They're based in Boston, but they have offices all over the world, and I'll probably get to travel a lot. I like the guy I interview with and the several fairly young people he introduces me to at the office, and I guess they like me because they offer me the position the day after I interview.

Their journals cover pretty much every category, and when Hopkins hears about the job, she informs me she's on the editorial board of five of their neurology journals.

When Dad hears about it, he says morosely, "Publishing is a dead industry. You might as well apprentice yourself to an alchemist."

"That's what's so great about this company," I say. "They publish even more online than they do in print."

"That's supposed to make me *like* them?"

When Mom hears about the job, she says, "You'll travel a lot for them? I'm so jealous. I want to travel."

"What's stopping you?" I ask.

When I tell Rochelle I'm leaving, she utters a heartfelt, "Shit! I was afraid of this."

"I'm sorry—but thank you for telling me about it. I'm really psyched to be trying something new."

She nods and sighs. "I would be, too, if I were in your shoes."

When I tell my boyfriend about my new job, he . . .

Just kidding. I don't have one to tell.

20.

The week I finish up at my old job (and have a really pathetic going-away party because I'm the one who always organizes those kinds of things, and no one else knows how to do it right, so the cake is too small and there's nothing to drink), our house gets sold to a family of four. They bring an architect in immediately. From the little I overhear, it sounds like he's planning to gut the entire house.

Soon after that, Charlie Evans takes Mom to look at apartments in Boston, and she falls in love with a brand-new building overlooking the ocean.

"They still have two and three bedrooms available," she tells me as we look through the brochure together in the kitchen booth.

"So what are you thinking?"

"I don't know." She puts the brochure aside and settles back in the booth, running her finger back and forth along the edge of the table. "The elephant in the room is Milton, of course. I don't know what to do with him—although he's doing so much better these days, thanks to you. How many times this week have you gotten him to leave the house?"

"Three times since last Sunday. My goal is to get him out once a day every day, even if it's just for a few minutes."

"Great. Anyway, I don't feel like he needs me as much as he

used to. But I also don't think he's ready to be completely on his own. So I guess we'll stay together." She tilts her head at me. "And then there's you—"

"The baby elephant in the room?"

"You need to find an apartment. The timing's perfect—we have so much furniture to get rid of here. You can take whatever you want. Plus there's all the stuff you tagged."

Actually, the cleaning crew had tossed the little dusty Post-its we'd put on the furniture—the ones that hadn't already fallen off. Not that it matters. I remember who got what.

"I have an idea," I say abruptly. It's something I've been revolving in my head for a while, trying to decide whether I'll regret voicing it or not. "What if Milton and I get a place together? Somewhere central, where there are lots of young people around, and he can walk to restaurants and stores? Like you said, he's doing so well right now. I don't want him to backslide."

"Which he might if he lives alone with me," she admits with a slightly pained smile.

"You've said yourself that I'm the only one who can actually get him to do anything."

"But living with him...that's a lot to ask of you, Keats."

"You're not asking, I'm offering. It's not all for his sake, you know. I don't like the idea of being all alone in an apartment every night." Actually, I hate the idea. I'd end up sleeping with all the lights on, terrified of every sound. "And I'm not going to take care of him, Mom. We'll live together, but I'll expect him to do his own laundry, dishes, cooking—everything."

"Good luck with that."

"He's capable of it all, Mom. But since you've always done it for him, he hasn't tried."

She gives a rueful shrug. "It's always been more work to get him to do things than to just do them myself."

"Well, he won't have a choice with me."

"Still, there'll be bumps along the way. And I don't want you to have to deal with them all by—" She interrupts herself. "Wait! I have the perfect solution! What if we get apartments in the same building? That way we can lead separate lives—I promise not to interfere on a daily basis—but if you need some backup, I'll be right there."

"But you want to live here." I tap the brochure. "I think Milton and I should be somewhere that's more of a neighborhood where you can walk around."

She flicks the brochure away. "I'll live wherever you want. Seriously, Keats, this just makes sense. If you need to travel for work, I can check in on Milton, and if *I* need to travel—well, want to—you can get my mail and keep an eye on my place."

Part of me can't believe what I'm committing to. I've been trying to insulate myself from my family for the last decade, and here I am agreeing to live with them.

The amazing thing is I'm not even terrified by the thought. It actually seems kind of nice.

"There's just one thing," I say. "If we're going to be living under the same roof...I promise not to pass judgment if I run into you in the lobby with a different guy every night and you have to promise me—"

"The same thing? It's only fair."

"No, not to pass judgment on me if you see me with the *same* guy every night."

Her look is piercing. "Got someone in mind, Keats?"

"Sadly, no. Just hoping for a better future."

"Date," she says. "Meet lots of new guys. Then meet some more."

"More easily said than done."

"My friend Zinnia said her son just broke up with his girl-friend. Can I tell her to have him call you?"

I wrinkle my nose. "Is he named after a flower, too?"

She's fairly certain he isn't but can't remember what his name is.

* * *

So I go out on a date with Zinnia's son, whose name is Conrad, which isn't a flower but is arguably even worse. He's studying to be a chiropractor and actually offers to realign my spine.

He doesn't ask me a single question about myself, just goes from one monologue to another, holding forth on the subjects (among other things) of bar nuts, men-scarves, and ex-girlfriends.

I'm glad I committed only to drinks and not dinner, because even before I've finished my glass of wine, I'm ready to leave.

"I tried," I tell Mom when I arrive back home before nine.

"That's all I ask," she says. She's on *her* way out to a late date with Paul Silvestri. "The point isn't to find the perfect guy immediately. The point is to get a sense of what's out there."

"What's out there is depressing me."

"Keep trying. Meanwhile, there are boxes to pack."

She's right about that last part. I'm theoretically on vacation right now, on break between the two jobs, but I'm working hard to get us ready for the move.

I'm also working hard to get Milton out of the house on a daily basis. If we don't run errands during the day, then I come up with something fun for us to do at night. We go out for dinner or for frozen yogurt or to the library when it's open late or to the Gap to buy him some new jeans and shirts, which he desperately needs.

At first, I have to generate all the ideas and cajole and threaten him into going, but after a while, he starts coming up with excursions of his own, like driving out to see the apartment building we're going to be living in soon, a recently renovated building on the border between Central Square and Harvard Square. Another day he asks me to take him to a comic book store in Brookline, where he gets into a passionate argument about Jonah Hex with the guy who works there, who has fair hair and blue eyes but otherwise resembles Milton with his pale skin and stooped shoulders and general air of having been living underground for an indeterminate period of time.

"We should go back there again," Milton says when we leave the store.

"You should learn to drive, so you can go on your own when I'm at work."

"There's also the T. I checked it out online. Once we move, we'll be really close to a stop."

"I know. That's part of what I liked about the new place."

"Hey," he says, "I was thinking...I'd like to see Dad's apartment. Since I haven't yet."

So we make a plan to visit Dad the next day. When Mom hears about it, she tells me she has some boxes for him.

"I doubt he actually wants any of this stuff," she admits as she lugs a carton across the kitchen, "but I don't see why I should have to figure out what to do with everything he left behind." She puts the box on the counter and stops for a moment to catch her breath. "Of course, he'll just make Jacob deal with it. But at least Jacob gets paid for his time. I don't."

"True." I'm in the breakfast booth, spreading peanut butter and jelly on a rice cake. We've basically stopped cooking anything fresh for dinner since we're trying to use up all the food in the pantry before the move.

"Speaking of Jacob—"

"Yes?" I say because she pauses.

"I was just wondering . . . Whatever happened with all that?"

"Nothing." I'm glad she doesn't know about my visit to his

apartment. "Actually, he's been seeing my friend Cathy. I hear from her occasionally, and it sounds like it's going pretty well."

"Is she good enough for him?"

"She's great," I say firmly.

"Here's the thing," Mom says. "I want to have everyone come home for one last dinner in the old house, including your father. We'll plan around Hopkins's schedule, of course—"

"Of course."

"Anyway, I've been meaning to ask you: Would it be okay if I included Jacob? Or would it make you uncomfortable?"

"It's fine," I say with a breeziness I don't feel. "Really. He *should* be here after all he's done for us." I struggle with myself for a moment and my nobler side wins. "And you should tell him he can bring Cathy. I think they're probably pretty serious by now."

"I'd like to meet her."

"Seems like this is your chance."

"And you're really okay with this?"

"Mom," I say with a forced laugh. "*He's* not the guy I lived with for ten years. I'd be freaked out if you invited Tom. That would be awkward. But Jacob's always welcome. The thing with us was no big deal. I'm sorry I even mentioned it." There were several truthful phrases in there and maybe a lie or two.

"Good." She takes up the box again. "And don't worry. I'm not inviting Tom."

"I never for a second thought you were."

She shifts the weight of the box onto her hip. "You know, Keats, I have to admit, I was worried you'd go running back to Tom the second you felt lonely or bored. But you've stayed the course. You've been open to meeting new men, and you haven't been desperate or self-pitying. You've been a good sister to Milton and a wonderful daughter to me. I couldn't be prouder of you."

I think about that first weekend after my breakup. How I threw myself at Jacob and how, when that didn't work, I headed back to Tom and only stopped myself at the last second. I'm not nearly as tough or wise as she's making me out to be. One word from Jacob, a moment's less reflection in the car, and she would be shaking her head right now, not congratulating me.

Somehow I stumbled or was shoved into making the right choices. It doesn't give me a lot of faith in my own judgment.

* * *

If I thought Dad would exclaim in surprise and delight at the sight of Milton at the entrance to his apartment, I was in for a disappointment.

He opens the door and says, "Ah, Milton, too," so calmly that you'd think his son visited him every day. He pats our arms as we enter and offers us a half a muffin left over from his breakfast that morning. "I'm afraid I don't have much else. Jacob's going to go to the supermarket for me in the morning."

"How is Jacob?" I ask casually as we all sit down around the coffee table. Dad's gained some weight in the last month, and his gut is spilling out over his belt again, which can't be good for his heart health. So much for Mom's hope that he'd start exercising and getting in shape.

"He's fine. He's hoping to get his dissertation done before December, so he's been working hard and hasn't been around quite as much. But we work quite effectively by e-mail. He's still the best researcher I know."

"Have you met his girlfriend?"

"Jacob has a girlfriend?"

"He does?" Milton says. "You didn't tell me that, Keats. What's she like?"

"She's nice. Oh, wait, Dad, you met her! I totally forgot. She was at my birthday dinner. Cathy. With the red hair."

"Oh yes. The rawboned girl."

Only my father would describe someone that way. "Yeah."

"He hasn't mentioned her."

I'm stupidly glad to hear that. At least she hasn't invaded this part of his life yet. Not that she *shouldn't*. Just...I'm glad she hasn't. Especially since my being glad doesn't hurt anyone.

21.

At first, Hopkins says she's way too busy to come to Boston at all this summer, but Mom puts her foot down and says she *has* to. For once in her life, she's feeling sentimental and needs to see us all under the roof of that house one last time. Hopkins grumbles to me in e-mails about how annoying Mom's being but finally says she can fly in on a Saturday—our last one in the house before we move the following Thursday.

Because we've already packed up her room and thrown out her horrible mattress, Hopkins says she'll stay at Dad's and bring him over to the house with her. They arrive while Mom and I are carrying in the Italian food she picked up for dinner and I run upstairs to tell Milton they're here. He joins us in the kitchen a few minutes later.

Hopkins eyes his clothing: jeans, shoes, a shirt with buttons. "Look at you," she says. "You're practically a member of the human race."

"Practically," he agrees and sits down next to Dad in the breakfast booth.

I laugh.

It's different being with my family now. Easier.

It's funny. I always thought Tom protected me from them, and in a way he did, but only by creating a wall between me and everyone else. Now as I stand in the kitchen, pouring wine into plastic cups because all the glasses are packed, I feel comfortable with my family again. I mean, they're all crazy as lunatics. That won't ever change. But where they are feels like home again.

"It's good to see you down here." Dad pats Milton on the arm.

"Uh-huh," says Milton. "What are we having for dinner?"

"Pasta," Mom says. "But we're waiting to eat until Jacob gets here."

"Can I have some wine?" Milton asks. "I'll be twenty-one in three months."

Mom says, "I thought you'd never ask," and pours some into a small glass. "See what you think."

He takes a sip and makes a face and puts it down. "The reason why I wanted this is that I'm sort of celebrating."

"What are you celebrating?" I ask.

"I won something."

"What?"

He doesn't look at anyone in particular, but he's smiling. "A game design contest. It's cool because professionals look at your work and critique it, and one of them said he wanted to talk to me more about mine." He nudges my arm. "That guy at the comic book store told me about it in the first place."

"He did?" I had been standing there the whole time and hadn't heard a word about a contest. "When?"

"We've been e-mailing."

"Oh. That's great."

"I started making the game a long time ago, but then when I found out about the contest, I started working a lot harder on it so I could get it done in time."

"It's great news." Mom's beaming.

"Yeah, well, I've got even bigger news," Hopkins says, looking up from her phone. "I wanted to tell you guys in person. One of my clients is donating a fortune to the hospital with the condition that they name a conference room after me."

For a moment, I reel from the blast of familiar emotions: awe mixed with jealousy that Hopkins is so amazing and I'm not. She'll have a room named after her, and she's only thirty. By the time she's forty, she'll probably have a hospital wing named after her. By fifty, a hospital. I'll be the sister of the famous Hopkins Sedlak for the rest of my life, and I honestly don't know whether to be proud of that fact or crushed by it.

But then I glance over at Milton and see how his face has gone closed again—no more smile—and something else cuts in. Something new.

Annoyance.

Why couldn't Hopkins just have let Milton have his moment? Why did she have to blow his news away with her bigger news? He never gets to have news. She always has news.

But then I realize that while Dad is exclaiming proudly—if quietly—over Hopkins's announcement, Mom's response is much more reserved. "That's great," she says flatly before turning back to her son. "Milton, I want to hear more about your game. Did you come up with the entire concept?"

"Yeah."

"Are there animals?" I ask. "Is it cute? Or violent?"

"Sort of both."

Mom says, "Please tell me it's not one where people are shooting at each other."

"Just a little bit," he says. The smile is back on his face.

Hopkins returns her attention to her BlackBerry, looking vaguely annoyed that her announcement hadn't caused the stir she was hoping it would.

Milton's deep into describing his game—a Disneyland-like theme park has been hijacked by extraterrestrial aliens so the people who run the rides have to organize a resistance and fight them—when the doorbell rings.

"That must be Jacob!" Mom says brightly and looks at me.

Since moving back home, I've been the official door opener because Milton ignores the doorbell and she's lazy.

I get up and leave the kitchen.

I take a deep breath in the foyer before I pull the door open.

Yeah, it's Jacob. Just him though. No Cathy.

"Hi," I say. I step back to let him in, putting space between us, not sure how to greet him anymore, not sure if a hug from me would be welcome.

"Hi." He enters but lingers by the door uncertainly. "You remind me of someone I once knew. This girl with a crazy name. Keats something-or-other. She probably doesn't remember me. It was a long time ago."

I roll my eyes. "It's been like a month, Jacob."

"Feels longer." He holds out his hand. "Good to see you, Keats."

"Same here." I shake his hand, and then we both lean forward, and I kiss him lightly on the cheek. I gesture down the hallway. "They're all in the kitchen. Come on."

"Hold on." His gray eyes flicker up to my face, then away again. "While we're still alone, can I just say really quickly that I'm sorry?"

"What for?"

"You know." He jams his hands into his pockets. "The last couple of times I saw you...I wasn't very nice."

There are a lot of things I could say now, but I choose the fairest one. "You didn't say anything that wasn't true. I acted badly."

"You were in a tough spot. I could have had more sympathy for that. I *should* have had more sympathy for that."

"Thanks. It helps hearing you say that."

"Good." There's a pause. "That's all. I wanted to clear the air. So we could be friends again. I want to be friends again, Keats."

"Me, too. Very much." We stand there in silence for a moment. Then I say quietly, "I've missed you." I quickly slip away and head toward the kitchen, not meeting his eyes.

*　*　*

We eat on paper plates in the dining room, now stripped bare of everything but the table and chairs, which my mother's taking with her to the new apartment.

After we've done some damage to the pasta, Jacob says, "I can't believe how much packing you've done since I was last here, Eloise. You look like you're in good shape for the move."

"Keats gets most of the credit for that," Mom says. "She's been working like a maniac. My job is to keep her in coffee so she has the energy to keep going."

I hold up my hands. "See? Packer's calluses."

"Packing doesn't give you calluses," Hopkins says.

Does she think I'm a total moron? "I know. I was just kidding."

She shrugs and pushes her plate away—as usual, she's only eaten a few bites—and then sits up with sudden energy. "Oh my god, I can't believe I haven't told you this yet, Keats! Your ex called me the other day."

"Wait—what? You mean Tom?"

She nods and leans back in her chair, everyone's eyes on her, and it occurs to me that she always makes that happen one way or another, that my sister *needs* to be the center of attention. I used to think it wasn't something she asked for, that tribute was just paid naturally to her because of her gifts. But she really can't let a moment pass without being noticed.

"I can't believe I forgot to tell you until now! He wanted to ask me if I'd speak to you on his behalf. Isn't that amazing? He said he knows we haven't spent a ton of time together, but that you've always valued my opinion—thanks, by the way,

I'm honored—and that it would really mean something to you if I said you should get back together with him."

I put my head in my hands. "God," I say. "I'm sorry."

"No, don't feel bad, Keats. I had the best time. We had a *great* talk. I told him that if he wanted me to sell you on him, he'd have to sell himself to me first, and he gave it an *incredibly* valiant effort. There was a lot of really sweet stuff about how much he loves you, how no other guy could ever love you as much as he does—oh, and he promised not to molest any more little girls in the future if you take him back—"

I raise my head. "That's not funny."

"Just kidding about that. Obviously. But the rest is true, I swear. He also said—"

"I don't want to hear it. Seriously, Hopkins. It's all kind of painful for me. I don't want to make fun of him."

"But I wasn't mean at all! I was incredibly nice. I let him talk for like twenty minutes. I even took notes." She starts punching at her phone.

"Please—can we just talk about something else?"

"No, no, wait—hold on—" She's frowning down at the screen. "I promise you this is totally worth it. I want to make sure I get the phrasing right. I think at one point he rhymed *statutory* and *masturbatory*—"

"Shut up, Hopkins."

Someone else said that, not me. I turn, surprised. People don't talk to Hopkins that way.

But Jacob just did.

Hopkins looks up from her phone. "Oh, come on," she says. "That was another joke. *Obviously*. Seriously, Keats, let me read you some of the actual stuff he said—"

"She asked you to stop. So stop," Jacob says.

"He was Keats's boyfriend for like three billion years, right? I don't know why she's suddenly lost interest in him."

"This isn't funny," I say. "I feel bad for him. I'm sorry he bothered you, but please let's not make fun of him now."

She opens her eyes wide—between those big eyes and her angular face and the way her hair is pulled so harshly back from her brow and temples today, she looks a little like a salamander at the moment. "*He* called *me*. If I'm going to be forced to endure the teary lamentations of your idiot ex, I should at least be allowed to get some amusement out of it."

I'm a little stunned. This is my big sister. The one who's loomed so large at every stage in my life and whose praise and attention I've always craved. And she's acting like an asshole. "Fine," I say. "If you're not going to stop, I'm leaving." I stand up.

My father says to my mother, "It's nice of the girls to squabble like teenagers. Makes me feel young again."

"A thoughtful gesture," she agrees absently, her eyes on me. "Keats, sit down."

"If she's going to keep going on like this—"

"She's not." She turns to Hopkins. "That's enough. No one is enjoying this."

"*I* am. Anyway, you should be grateful to me, Mom—you were always complaining about how you had to put up with his boring moronic stories at every family dinner for the last decade."

My mother evades my eyes. At least she has the grace to flush.

"He *owes* you some entertainment. Listen, just listen to this." Hopkins studies the BlackBerry. "I swear these are all direct quotes. 'Keats was my universe.... She made life worth living.'" She looks up. "I know, I know, it's clichéd, but let's not judge him too harshly. It obviously came from the heart. Oh, and then he says—"

Two chairs scrape back in unison. One of them belongs to

me. The other is Jacob's. "Hold on, Keats, I'm going with you," he says as I head out of the room.

"What is everyone's problem?" Hopkins asks with an aggrieved tone to her voice. "Okay, fine. I'll stop."

But I keep going because it feels good to walk away from her. Oddly powerful.

And also...Jacob's following me.

So I keep going, all the way to the stairs and up those, and then down the dimly lit hallway—good thing Milton left his door open and the lights on because it would be even darker there without that—and up the second set of stairs to the pitch-black attic. I grope blindly along the wall at the top of the stairs, trying to feel the light switch.

It's so dark that Jacob actually bumps into me. "Sorry," he says and quickly drops down a step. "Didn't realize you stopped."

"I'm trying to turn on the light." My hand finally lands on the switch, and I flick on the overhead light. I step up into the room, and Jacob follows me.

"Wow," he says, gazing around. "You really cleaned this out." Where there once were stacks of books and journals and old mugs filled with broken pens and partially used pads of paper, there's now just the daybed and the desk and the empty bookshelves. It took me three days to clean it out.

"I'm glad we're almost done packing up. I am so sick of sorting through decades of junk." I cross the room and sit down on the daybed.

"Story of your life?" he suggests. "Cleaning up your family's messes?"

"I make plenty of my own. As you probably know better than anyone."

He shakes his head, comes over to the sofa, and sits carefully at the other end, leaving plenty of space between us. He starts to say something, stops, then just says, "Sorry about Hopkins and all that."

"She was trying to be funny, I guess. But it just seems so sad to me."

"That's the problem with having a heart," he says. "Stuff like that gets to you. Clearly not a problem for Hopkins."

"Maybe she got an extra brain in her chest instead of a heart?" I suggest. "That would explain the supernormal intelligence."

He waves his hand dismissively. "Eh, she's only smart in some ways."

"Yeah, just in the ways that matter."

He shakes his head. "You're the one who's smart in the ways that matter. Nice in the ways that matter, too."

I feel myself blushing. It's a weird compliment—but it feels good right now, right when I need it, right when Jacob is the one delivering it. He's calling me nice. I didn't think that would ever happen again.

"So," I say after a moment of silence. "How's life?"

"Pretty good. I've been working hard. I want to actually finish my dissertation this fall. I'm tired of being a professional student."

"And then you'll look for a new job?"

"I'll look, but it's rough out there right now. I think I can get some kind of instructor position here to tide me over for a while if nothing else comes through. With your dad's help."

"At least you'd stay in the area that way."

He nods. "I don't want to leave Boston, but I'll have to go where the jobs are."

"Anything else going on in your life?" I'm fishing, wanting to ask about Cathy, curious why she's not here when I know Mom invited her—but I'm scared to ask outright, because the last time I did, he said he'd never talk to me about his romantic life again.

"Not much. Classes are over for the year. I spend my time doing research for your father, research for myself, writing, eating the occasional cheap meal…"

He's still not answering the question I haven't asked. I say cautiously, "Any chance we're friends again enough for me to ask what's going on with Cathy?"

"Yeah, we're friends enough," he says evenly. "But Cathy and I stopped seeing each other a couple of weeks ago."

"Oh." It takes an effort to sound sympathetic, not eager. "What happened?"

"I think we just reached a point where it was time for things to either move to the next stage or end. And ending seemed more right. For me, anyway. She claimed she felt the same way." A pause. "It's possible she was just trying to make me feel better."

"She would do that."

"She would."

I hear someone calling my name, and then there's a clattering on the stairs and Hopkins appears. Today she's wearing an oversized Oxford shirt—maybe from the men's department?—which might have looked chic over leggings, but she's got on baggy jeans, and the whole outfit just looks too big, like she pulled her clothes out of someone else's closet that morning. "There you are," she says. "What are you guys doing up here?"

"Talking," I say.

She raises her eyebrows. "What a nice secluded spot to have a conversation in. Anyway, Mom told me I had to apologize to you. Apparently I was rude. Jacob, could you help me with something?"

"Hold on," I say. "Was that your apology?"

"Clearly."

"I just wanted to make sure. It didn't really sound like one."

She rolls her eyes. "Whatever. Jacob, there are a couple of boxes for me downstairs."

"Yeah, I packed those," I say.

She ignores me. "I need to mail them to my apartment, but I have an early flight tomorrow so I can't do it. Would you mind?"

"What time's your flight?" I ask before Jacob can respond.

"Eleven."

"The post office opens at seven thirty. You have plenty of time to do it yourself."

"I can't risk missing my flight—I have patients who need me. Anyway, it's none of your business. I'm asking Jacob." She turns back to him. "You don't mind, do you?"

I wait for his resigned acceptance of the task. He always does everything we Sedlaks ask him to do.

But then he surprises me. "I agree with Keats. Just get to the post office early enough, and you'll be fine."

She scowls. "It's going to make my morning really rushed."

"Some mornings are like that," I say.

"I'm supposed to do an interview with a reporter from the *Globe*. I said maybe we could talk tomorrow morning. But if I have to go to the post office—"

"You'll figure it out," I say calmly. "You're a supergenius."

"Well, at least help me load the boxes into the car." It's not clear which of us she's talking to. Whoever will actually do it, I guess.

"In a minute," Jacob says without moving.

She folds her arms across her chest. "Dad and I need to get going pretty soon."

"They're not that heavy," I say. "I know because I packed them and carried them downstairs in the first place. If you can't wait for us, feel free to load them yourself."

She throws her hands in the air, annoyed, but with no good argument left to make. "I don't even know why you guys are all the way up here," she snaps irritably. "You planning to make out or something?"

What is she—thirty going on fourteen? "Maybe," I say.

"Thanks a lot." She flings herself angrily down the stairs, done with us since we refused to wait on her.

We're silent for a moment, then Jacob says, "I know she does really good work in the world, but I'm beginning to think she may be just a tiny bit spoiled."

"I'm proud of us for holding our ground."

"Yeah, we were magnificent." Another pause. He shoots me a sideways look. "So about that making-out idea..."

I grin. "What about it?"

He returns the grin. "Nothing. Just thought it was an interesting subject to explore."

"I'll bet you did." I shift toward him. "Did you know that Mom keeps making me go out with all these random guys? She says I have to make up for all the years of dating I missed."

"How's that working out?"

"Honestly? It's made me miss hanging out with you."

"Yeah?" Now it's his turn to move a little closer. "That's nice to hear. So why haven't you called me or anything?"

"Well, one, you basically threw me out last time I tried to talk to you—"

"I'm sorry. I was mad. But I got over it."

"But mostly I thought I should leave you alone because of Cathy."

"That's just—" He stops. "Actually, that was kind of decent of you."

"I know, right? You don't need to sound so surprised."

He laughs. "Well, Cathy's out of the picture now, and I'm not angry anymore. So do you think you'd be willing to have dinner with me sometime? Or is your schedule too full with the random guys your mother keeps fixing you up with?"

The relief is almost unbearable, almost like joy. "I think I could squeeze you in."

"Good," he says, and then we just sit there for a while, close to each other but not touching, listening to the sold house creak and Hopkins yelling for my mother to come help her with something and Milton's door closing shut below us, and it feels like everything is ending and starting all at the same time.

Reading Group Guide

Essay: The Only Normal One

It is a truth universally acknowledged that a young woman of independent means and moderate disposition will, upon returning to her ancestral home for a visit of any length, suddenly come face-to-face with the realization that her family is totally bat-shit crazy.

The working title for this novel, which always made me smile, even though I knew it would never make it onto the actual cover, was *Cousin Marilyn in Massachusetts*. It was partially a J. D. Salinger tribute—"Uncle Wiggily in Connecticut" being the greatest short story ever written—but I was also referencing an iconic female character from my childhood, Cousin Marilyn from the 1960s TV show *The Munsters*.

Cousin Marilyn was blond and beautiful and normal and lived happily with a family of monsters. Nice monsters. Loving monsters. Caring monsters. But still…monsters. Vampires, werewolves, dead body parts put together to make a man. Like that.

Being the only *non*monster made Marilyn the family freak, kind of like in that *Twilight Zone* episode where the beautiful blond is considered ugly because everyone else in the world looks like a deformed pig. (You know, it just occurred to me that all my references come from black-and-white TV shows—clearly I never went to school when I was a kid, just pretended to be sick and watched old reruns all day long while my mother made me Jell-O.) Poor normal Marilyn stood apart from the rest of her kin, accepted and loved by them, but always visibly different.

She never seemed to find any of this disturbing—up to and including the fact that Grandpa liked to suck blood and little Eddie slept in a coffin—but you've got to figure that once in a while she lay in bed at night thinking, *Why are all my relatives so . . . you know . . . monstrous? How come I'm the only normal one? Why couldn't I have had a human family like all my friends do?* And maybe even, *I wonder if I was switched at birth with a harpy, and my real home is a nice split-level in New Rochelle?*

Don't we all occasionally wonder why the other members of our families are so much crazier than we are? Certainly almost everyone *I* know does. Of course, it's like the statistic that eighty percent of adults over thirty think they look younger than their age. A certain percentage of us must be in denial. So while you may be the sane one from *your* perspective, odds are your sister Sue over there thinks you're totally cuckoo and can't wait to leave family dinner to go complain about you to her boyfriend.

Keats Sedlak, the protagonist of this book, starts off fairly certain that she's the only one who's escaped her family's particular brand of lunatic brilliance and that her only hope for continued sanity lies in making a life for herself that's as separate from theirs as possible. But as her family pulls her back in (families have a way of doing that, don't they?), she finds her place with them again and realizes that maybe she does belong there after all.

She might be more competent, more social, more self-aware

than anyone else in her family, but deep down she's still very much a Sedlak, just as Cousin Marilyn was, despite her blond beauty, a Munster to the bone. We can ponder the mysteries of our crazy (and sometimes monstrous) families all we want, but two facts remain: they are us and we are them.

~~~~~~~~

Reading Group Questions

1. Do you relate to being "the normal one" in a nutty family, or do you feel like an outlier or outsider in your more traditional family?

2. Were you rooting for Keats and Tom to stay together, or did their eventual breakup seem inevitable to you?

3. Have you ever known a couple like Larry and Eloise, who continue to live together after the decision to divorce is made? Is it possible to move on while you're still under the same roof as an ex?

4. Have you been in the position of seeing one of your parents back on the dating scene? Is it inspiring? Uncomfortable? A little of both?

5. Keats tries to get Milton out of the house throughout the book—what has changed by the time she's actually successful?

6. How does your impression of Hopkins throughout the book change when she shows up in the latter half?

7. Do you think that the Sedlaks are rude to or dismissive of Tom? Or is Keats projecting some of that attitude onto her family?

8. What do you think of the story of how Tom and Keats met? Do you think it's charming or creepy?

9. What do you see happening to the Sedlaks after the book ends?